An Empress
on the Throne Of Russia

Eva Martens

Copyright © 2015 M.M.Bruns
All Rights Reserved

Cover: Virgilius Erichsen, *Portrait of Catherine II in Front of a Mirror.* ca 1762-1764
The State Hermitage Museum, St Petersburg

Cover design: www.wifo-digital.de

By the same author

A Princess at the Court of Russia
Love and Other Affairs in the Empire of Russia

Do you know where there is earthly paradise? I know: it is everywhere that there is Catherine II. You are not the aurora borealis, you are the brightest star of the North, and there never has been any other luminary so beneficial.

Voltaire, December 1766

PART ONE
1762-1763

Chapter One

"You may remove all but the diamonds," Grigory Orlov said from the pile of silk cushions on the bed where he was lounging. Catherine could see him in the looking glass behind her own reflection but she could not make out his features. The candlelight was too dim and her eyesight, which had never been sharp, was deteriorating. Her mother had been right about too much reading, but at least the belladonna drops helped to clear her vision. She looked at the shape of Grigory's reflection fondly. He had the eyes of an eagle, which he had proved on their frequent hunting trips, but no patience for reading. On the few occasions when Catherine read aloud to him, he listened impatiently, declaring he was not a man of lifeless words but of ready action. And so he was, she thought with satisfaction. Her days were filled with words, too many of them. She wrote them for hours on end, listened to them, read them, used them to convince and cajole. With Grigory words were not needed.

Catherine fingered the diamonds at her neck. Diamonds were her favourite gem. They were pure and strong, their brilliance rarely dimmed.

"I already have," Catherine said, without turning. "I am never unprepared."

Orlov leapt to his feet to come and stand behind her. Catherine watched in the mirror as he slowly removed the robe from her shoulders, his fingers following as it slipped the length of her body to the floor. She turned to face him, naked except for the coils of diamonds at her neck. They caught the flickering lights from the candle.

"You are as magnificent as always, my Empress," he said, lifting the heavy necklace before bending to kiss her breasts.

"Shall you require more diamonds?" Catherine's voice was breathless.

"No," Grigory said as he knelt before her. "I know where to find your real jewels."

Later Catherine lay in Grigory's arms, sated. She savoured the feeling of relaxed contentment, knowing it would be fleeting. Her conscience would soon drive her to her writing desk. There was so much to do, so much chaos to bring to order, so many tasks that only she could tackle. She was Russia's sovereign and she must serve its people well. But for now she revelled in the smooth softness of the silk cushions, in her lover's strong muscular body sprawled beside her. Grigory's richly decorated chambers were her oasis, her escape from the onus of duty. Her own chambers, directly above and accessible by a private staircase, were sparsely furnished, books and papers scattered over several tables. There she was the Empress. Here she was a woman. Grigory's woman.

This was the only time she stole from the day for herself. She habitually rose at five o'clock in the morning, splashed herself with cold water, drank several cups of coffee which she prepared on a little burner in her room and worked through till dinner at two in the afternoon. After dinner, her court had strict instructions that she was not to be disturbed, indeed not to be found. Any enquiry as to her whereabouts was countered with officially shrugged shoulders. She knew the Court called this after-dinner hour with her personal adjutant the Time of Mystery. For her, it was indeed a mystery that she could be so happy with Grigory. He lightened the heavy burden of rule without participating in it.

The thought of duty disturbed her contentment and she stirred restlessly. She still had to check the Senate's last report. One could not trust such lazeabouts to do their duty. During the first months of her reign she had attended the Senate twice a week and was shocked at the empty rows of seats, at the snoozing and snoring figures on the benches, at their lack of knowledge. Why, they did not even have a map of the Empire. She had immediately ordered one from the Academy of Science. She had also ordered the senators to attend to their duties for four hours every morning and three afternoons a week. When she complained to Grigory about the time she had to spend making sure the senators did their duty, he had said, "Take my young brother Fyodor. He is more of a scholar than a soldier and will serve well and willingly as your watchdog at the Senate." Fyodor Orlov had indeed proved diligent in his reporting, freeing Catherine from hours of tedious sessions at the Senate.

Catherine looked fondly at the naked Grigory lying beside her. He was so handsome, she sighed. She moved to caress his long muscular legs but then remembered she had to be dressed for a ceremony at Moscow University. The Empress Elizabeth had founded the institution just ten years ago and although Catherine was its enthusiastic patron, she planned to elevate the St Petersburg Academy of Science to a university, one which would lead the way in all fields, not just philosophy, medicine and law, important as these subjects were. Agriculture, she was sure, was of great value to a country and she planned to pave the way with a Society of Improvement modelled on that in Scotland, where reports of systematic farming had impressed her. The landed dukes and earls of the Scottish Society knew how to benefit themselves and their country and Grigory could do the same. He would chair the Society, she decided. After all, thanks to her own generosity, he now owned much land with thousands of serfs.

She had asked Grigory to accompany her to the

University. He was not at ease with academics nor with politicians but he cut a very fine figure at her side. Men envied him his strong physique, his height and his easy charm. Women wished him in their beds. The ten days since the coronation had been full of celebrations, and Grigory had been with her constantly. They had attended operas and plays in her honour, banquets and balls and a magnificent firework display, which lit up the night sky.

Catherine fretted at the time these extravagant celebrations were taking from the endless list of state affairs, but the coronation festivities were needed to seal her image as Empress of Russia. Grigory had been right about the need for theatre. Words were of no consequence to those who could neither read nor write. The people must see and feel her as their rightful and benevolent sovereign, her and no other.

And there were other contenders. There was Ivan under close guard in prison, deposed by Empress Elizabeth when he was but a child. Her own son, the Grand Duke Paul, was seen by many as the legitimate heir. His father was Catherine's dead husband Peter, Elizabeth's named successor. Peter III had sat on the throne for no longer than half a year and had threatened to banish Catherine, making his uncouth mistress Empress in her stead.

But Catherine knew that reality could be created and so she had done just that. She had become Empress not by waiting for fate to intercede but by seizing the throne from her inept, unfaithful and pro-Prussian husband. She shivered. Orlov and his brothers had solved the problem of her deposed husband and he now lay in his grave. The reality she must now create was her divine right to sovereignty over Russia and the allegiance of its people. There must be no contenders.

As Catherine carefully unclasped the diamond collier which had left marks on her body and on Grigory's chest, she recognised the necklace as one that had belonged to her mother, Princess Johanna. Catherine had had it reset, as she often did with her diamond jewellery, always attracted by a new design. The original of this one had been among her mother's belongings rescued from auctioneers in Paris. Poor Johanna, Catherine thought. She had been banished from the court of Russia for allegedly spying for the Prussian King Frederick. And then Frederick had chased her from Prussia for allegedly spying against him. It was her mother's quest for excitement in love affairs that had led her to be caught in many webs of intrigue. Johanna's greatest wish had been to see her daughter become Empress of Russia, thereby securing a life of ease and luxury for herself, but she had died alone and impoverished in the French capital. Johanna had written to Catherine with desperate pleas for funds but Empress Elizabeth had kept the letters from her.

"Your mother died after several months confined to bed," the Empress had informed Catherine laconically at the time. "Severe dropsy. She apparently looked like a monster. Not a trace of her former beauty," she had added with some satisfaction.

"She has left debts of some 400,000 francs," Elizabeth continued coldly. "And her pearls and diamonds have been seized by her creditors. To be auctioned publicly."

Catherine had begged the Empress to save her mother's reputation from such shame.

The Empress had made Catherine wait several anxious day before she answered. "I have given it due thought. I do not care about your mother's shame but it is, alas, also our shame. It would taint a future Empress of Russia. Our court must not be associated with French debts or with French auctioneers who will scoff at the poverty of Princess Johanna's Russian relatives. Your mother, Catherine, always caused us trouble and she does not desist even now in death."

The Empress had settled all Johanna's debts in Paris and had her jewellery brought to St Petersburg.

Scarcely two years later, Empress Elizabeth herself was dead and Catherine was on the throne of Russia. This had been her mother's dream for her. A sparkling court, a weighty crown. The duties the crown brought were certainly weighty but Catherine had little time for the social sparkle her mother had so loved. Her mother would have been such a danger at court, Catherine thought. An Empress was safer with no ties, not even those of family. There was no-one she trusted, not even Count Panin, into whose care she had given her son. She had brought her old ally, the exiled ex-Chancellor Bestuzhev, back to court but his advanced years had clouded his mind. There was Count Betskoy, her mother's erstwhile lover, but he was less interested in consolidation of her political power than the practice of what he called "enlightened culture".

Grigory and his brothers were her closest allies but they were soldiers, not politicians or courtiers. They had put her on the throne and she had rewarded them amply but they expected her hand in marriage to Grigory. Their plan had always been for him to rule Russia by her side. But it had never been her plan.

She felt Grigory stir beside her. "Lost in which thoughts, my love? What, only your diamonds to play with?"

Grigory removed the necklace gently from her hands. "Come," he said. "Let me give you something better."

Chapter Two

Count Nikita Panin wiped the boy's fevered brow with a cool cloth. The Grand Duke Paul had been in Panin's charge for the last two years, a responsibility the Count exercised diligently while never heedless of the dangers it brought. The Grand Duke should have been Emperor, but his mother had claimed the throne for herself, blatantly going back on the understanding with Panin that she would rule as regent for her son until he came of age. He had only supported the coup to ensure the boy's place on the throne. In answer to his objections, Catherine had said with an assurance which surprised him,

"It is the people's will, dear Count. What am I to do? I cannot go against the will of the people."

Panin knew it was not the people's will which had prevailed but rather that of the Orlov brothers. Grigory Orlov had charmed his way into Catherine's bed in the hope of sharing the throne with her. Panin's vanity was piqued that Catherine would prefer a rough and uneducated guardsman instead of someone of refined manners and taste like himself. Panin's elegant advances to Catherine had been politely but firmly rejected. His own richly canopied bed was rarely empty of a willing companion but it riled him that the upstart Orlovs were treated better than he was.

Just recently Catherine had even tried to supplant Panin in his post of guardian to the Grand Duke Paul with one of the French *philosophes* she was so fond of quoting. She had offered Jean d'Alembert 100,000 roubles to come to Russia to be Paul's tutor. She had also promised him permission to freely publish his *Encyclopédie*, which was running into difficulties with the French censors. Both offers had been politely declined. Panin had heard of d'Alembert's quip, referring to the official version of how Catherine's husband had died, that he would not feel safe in a country where haemorrhoids were such a dangerous condition, especially since he suffered from them himself.

A feverish illness in the crown's heir was also a very dangerous condition. As he regarded his pale charge, Panin thought, not for the first time, that his younger brother, Pyotr Panin, a highly decorated general in the recent years of war, had chosen the less dangerous course in life. If the Grand Duke Paul were to die, Panin knew his own survival at court was at risk. As was the Empress's.

Panin was used to the illnesses of his frail charge but this time anxiety clouded his usual practical reasoning. He turned to the figure sitting in the dark beyond the light shed by the few candles.

"He burns, Dr Kruse," he said, trying to keep the panic from his voice.

Dr Kruse approached the bed. Taking his watch from his pocket, he lifted the boy's limp wrist.

"The Grand Duke is highly strung. He is prone to fever attacks, as you know. Any exertion or excitement strains his constitution," Dr Kruse said casually.

Dr Kruse, Panin thought, may have come recently from the University of Leiden in Holland, reputed to be the best centre of medical studies in Europe, but he was more used to sturdy men with syphilis and wounds and hangovers. He had been physician to the Guards until Orlov recommended him as a replacement for the royal physician, Dr Mounsey, whom Catherine had sent back to Scotland. Mounsey was a person of scientific repute who had experimented with many herbal cures, which he brought from China and Persia, but Catherine did not trust him because he had been close to her husband. Mounsey had said openly that Peter could not have died from a haemorrhoidal colic since not only did he not suffer from haemorrhoids but that there was no such thing as a haemorrhoidal colic. Contradicting the Empress was tantamount to treason and Mounsey had been lucky to be sent home rather than into the depths of cold Siberia, or worse. Thinking of Mounsey had given Panin an idea.

"Would a compote of rhubarb ease the fever?" he asked.

Mounsey had successfully grown this new plant from seeds brought from China. It was said to be a panacea, curing everything from dysentery to epilepsy, from scurvy to smallpox. There was a high demand for it despite its exorbitant price of nearly 1000 roubles a pound.

"It is certainly a cooling dish and may be, as Dr Mounsey has claimed, an effective febrifuge, but not to be recommended to our patient. He has too much acid in his stomach already. Better an infusion of cooled apple tea," Dr Kruse said.

The Grand Duke Paul suffered from frequent bouts of vomiting and loose bowels. Every remedy had been tried including regular doses of wormwood in brandy. But the child did not gain in strength. Panin looked at the boy's thin face. It was a face that rarely smiled. Rumour had it that Sergei Saltykov, reputed to be Catherine's first lover, was his natural father but there was little of *le beau Serge* in the boy and much of Peter III's ugliness.

"Yes, I am sure you are right, Dr Kruse," Panin said briskly, suppressing his anxiety. There must be no scope for rumours to swiftly take wing. "The Grand Duke has been overexerted. He was sickly on the journey from St Petersburg and had hardly recovered before he had to attend the coronation ceremony and all the celebrations in the days after."

The Empress required the Grand Duke to be constantly at her side in public. She paraded her pale son to the people, knowing he gave her legitimacy, as if she were merely keeping the throne warm for him.

Panin had let the Emperor Peter, Paul's official father, slip through his fingers. He would not be so careless with his son. He had vowed to see him on the throne of Russia.

He would bide his time. The child was but eight years old.

There was a sudden gust of cold air as Catherine swept into the room.

"How is he? Why was I not called earlier?" she hissed angrily at Panin as she approached the bed.

"But Your Majesty, I did inform you immediately of the Grand Duke's illness. After the fireworks. He has caught a chill. But now he has a fever." Panin did not meet the Empress's eye. "Which does not abate," he added.

Catherine knelt at the bedside and grasped her son's hand. Whereas the boy had lain still and pale till now, he was suddenly flushed and restless.

"Is it smallpox?" Catherine asked. "Where is Dr Kruse?"

From the shadows, the doctor appeared.

"Your Majesty, there are no signs of pustules. I think the Grand Duke suffers from over-exertion. And must rest." The doctor spoke calmly.

"You will not bleed him!" the Empress commanded. "I myself know what it means to be weakened by bleeding at a young age. His blood must be strengthened."

"No, he will not be bled," Dr Kruse agreed mildly. "There is no sign of infection. I recommend a well-aired chamber – "

The Empress interrupted. "But he must not be chilled. There must be no drafts."

The Empress's fear of drafts was well known. Many of the cracks in walls or warped window frames were beyond repair but the Empress never travelled without a large trunk of heavy tapestries. She had once told Panin, "I survived much danger in the Russian court but there was nothing to match the danger of icy drafts which almost took my life on more than one occasion."

"And cooling cloths and perhaps a valerian tincture," Dr Kruse continued smoothly. "But rest is what the Grand Duke needs most."

The Empress suddenly rose from her knees and faced Dr Kruse. "Could he have been poisoned?" she asked.

Kruse remained calm. "There are no symptoms to suggest such. And Count Panin gives me to understand that he follows the ... normal precautions."

When the Grand Duke first suffered his vomiting attacks, Panin thought of poison. There were enough enemies who would wrest the throne from what they perceived as German hands. The Grand Duke was not allowed to eat or drink of anything which had not been tasted in front of Panin by courtiers chosen randomly.

"Only you and Count Panin will attend him," the Empress said. "Let no other near his bed."

Both Panin and Kruse bowed their agreement.

"And I will remain by his side until he recovers," Catherine added.

Dr Kruse looked alarmed. As the Empress once more bent to her son, he turned to Panin, his eyebrows raised enquiringly.

"We would not deprive Your Majesty of a mother's right," Panin bowed to the Empress. "But nor would we deprive Russia of its sovereign at this time of great joy. The people would wish to see the Mother of all Russia."

"I will have my work brought to the ante-chamber. I will not neglect my duties but nor will I leave my beloved son." Catherine had now stood again. "And I will have my prie-dieu brought. God will hear my prayers."

Panin wondered about the use of 'beloved'. He was sure the Empress had little affection for the awkward, frail boy. He knew she cared for the son she bore Orlov while her husband Peter was still on the throne. That child was now scarcely half a year old and it was an open secret that the Empress slipped off in disguise to see him. Even old Count Bestuzhev, once Grand Chancellor of Russia, had been trying to persuade the Empress to send the child to be brought up some distance away. This was one of the few things Panin agreed with the ex-chancellor on. The child's presence brought uncertainty. The Orlov brothers had not given up their attempts to persuade Catherine to marry Grigory. If she succumbed to their pleas and the Grand Duke to his illness, it was not inconceivable that they would name this bastard child heir to the throne. Panin knew he was panicking but the Grand Duke was far from robust and Catherine was besotted with Orlov. Anything was possible.

Just then, as if Panin's thoughts had summoned him, Orlov himself burst into the chamber. Catherine had barely risen to her feet in surprise before Orlov had grabbed her arm pulling her to the door.

"You must come at once!" Panin heard Orlov hiss. We have uncovered a conspiracy to overthrow you!"

Chapter Three

Bestuzhev found Catherine at her desk in her chambers, as he knew he would. Her quill flew in and out of the well, scattering ink across the paper. She wore her usual loose silk dressing gown, covered in ink stains. Bestuzhev was one of the few allowed to disturb her during her morning work hours. He was not sure whether this underlined his importance but the fact that the Empress often called him Batiushka, Little Father, would argue more for personal affection than political weight.

He generally waited until after her sessions with her secretaries before visiting her. Today was Wednesday, which meant that Teplov, Catherine's chief executor of projects, would have reported at eight o'clock that morning. As head of the Commission on Church Lands, he was busy exploring ways of tapping into the considerable income the church enjoyed. Teplov also had more colourful interests. He thought himself something of a musician and not only translated Italian opera libretti into Russian but also wrote his own. He liked to feature prominently in court theatre, where he played roles much too young for him. This, Bestuzhev was sure, had to do with his predilection for young boys. Still, Teplov was affable and Catherine well disposed towards him. She would be even-tempered. Had it been Tuesday or Thursday, when Olsuyev reported, she would have been sharp-tongued. Olsuyev was in charge of the distribution of imperial funds, of which there was never a sufficiency for all Catherine's projects.

"I know why you have come," Catherine said without raising her head from her task. "Do not chastise me. They had to be tortured. They would not confess freely, they had to be made to see the error of their ways."

Bestuzhev knew how men could be broken by torture. As Elizabeth's Chancellor, he had often employed it to gain the truth he wanted. He had feared it when he himself was arrested under Empress Elizabeth's orders before being banished from the court. He had managed to save Catherine by burning all evidence that could be used against her, a measure he sometimes regretted. It was proving difficult to build up a new capital of information. Still, Catherine had brought him back to court. He had hoped to spend the rest of his days in comfortable retirement with the income from his nerve drops but a traitor of a chemist had run off when Bestuzhev was in prison and sold the recipe to a French general, who was making a fortune selling the drops as Elixir d'Or. Ridiculous, Bestuzhev thought. People paid good gold to buy false gold. Bestuzhev had now perfected a new recipe and hoped to sell it to the court chemist. He took a few drops surreptitiously now. Yes, the added quicksilver was definitely an improvement.

His musings were interrupted by the Empress rustling through papers. He must concentrate. Where were they? Ah, yes. Torture. He had been surprised that Catherine had ordered it. She had immersed herself in philosophers from every era, had professed herself enlightened by modern French thinkers, claimed that reason was all that was needed to prevail. Oh, but his brain was sluggish. What should he reply? He felt compelled to pursue the matter. Any over-reaction on Catherine's part, and surely torture was over-reacting, would fan the embers of discontent.

He coughed discreetly.

"Yes, Batiushka," Catherine said gently, "you may speak. While you were considering your response, I have gone through the commission's latest report on the matter. I was not satisfied with their first report. The proposed sentences were much too mild. Of the fifteen officers arrested, four were to be declared innocent while the remaining eleven were to be sent ... elsewhere." She waved the sheath of papers vaguely with one hand while continuing to write with the other. She wrote ceaselessly. Everything she read – books, reports, letters – were covered in her notes.

"But the accused, even under torture, did not confess to any crimes," Bestuzhev said carefully. The officers had been beaten by sticks, one of the milder methods, but often the torturers took it into their heads to compete with each other for who could make the most bruises or break the most bones or indeed set up a drum-like rhythm.

"I heard that the accused still maintained it was all just drunken banter in the barracks. Surely banishment is somewhat severe, Your Majesty?" Bestuzhev asked gently.

"Not severe enough, as I told the commission. And it was hardly the barracks, Bestuzhev. It was a gathering of officers." She still did not lay down her quill.

Once Catherine embarked on the road of torturing and banishing those suspected of being her enemies, there would be little manoeuvring space for turning back. Bestuzhev had to convince Catherine that the more enemies one punished, the more enemies one created.

"Do you remember when I was arrested, along with many others?" he asked. "You told me that you had asked Prince Trubetskoy, who was in charge of the investigation, if he had found more crimes than criminals or more criminals than crimes? Do you recall his answer?"

Catherine stopped writing and looked at Bestuzhev. "Of course I do! I have always had an excellent memory. Prince Trubetskoy said they would find the crimes to fit. That there was no prescribed order. Criminals or crimes. They could be made to match."

Catherine returned to her papers.

"With all due respect, Your Majesty, but is that not what you are doing now? Ascribing crimes not committed?" Bestuzhev knew he had gone too far. But he was too old for diplomatic patience. And in any case,

Catherine had so often reiterated, sometimes in a fury, that she wanted to be told nothing but the truth.

Catherine now gave Bestuzhev her full attention. "I cannot have seditious talk," she said in a reasonable tone. "Drunken or otherwise. As soon as the words are spoken, they become reality. I cannot have talk of change. I am ruler of this country and I have much to do. This is not a time for change. I cannot have treason spread among my Guards."

Bestuzhev was not so sure of the 'my'. While the Guards were loyal to Catherine, many thought that the Orlov brothers had been too well rewarded. The state coffers were empty when Catherine seized the throne but she had distributed more than a million roubles in money, land and serfs to those who had helped her, half of it to the Orlovs. Catherine did insist on keeping accounts and Bestuzhev had seen them. Future funds in the form of generous pensions to the principal leaders of the coup had been added to the lavish rewards. The Orlovs would live in luxury for the rest of their days. She had even given her old lover Sergei Saltykov 20,000 roubles and sent him as her ambassador to France. Admittedly, she had rewarded over three hundred Guardsmen with smaller sums but there were many more Guards who were resentful that they had received nothing. The Empress's insistence on open honesty had caused her to publish the rewards in the St Petersburg Gazette. For all to see. In Bestuzhev's opinion, this was bound to rouse jealousy and discontent. Bribes, for that is what they were, were only effective if kept secret.

Bestuzhev struggled to find the thread of their conversation. "And what does the commission now recommend?"

"Oh, they have come to their senses," Catherine answered, consulting her papers. "Five of the accused will be sentenced to death. The others to hard labour in Siberia." Catherine shuffled her papers together. "These are the punishments we need to deter others from daring to think of ... change."

Bestuzhev was taken by surprise. He could find no clear thought to formulate.

"But Your Majesty!" was all he could manage to splutter.

"Oh do not worry, Batiushka. I will leave the sentences long enough to instil fear. When I return, I will take care of the matter."

Bestuzhev clutched at the chance to leave the subject of executions. "Return, Your Majesty?"

"Yes, from my pilgrimage."

"Ah, there has been improvement in the Grand Duke?" The child had been ill for a week now. The Empress spent the afternoon hours at his bedside and would not leave the Kremlin. The coronation festivities had continued without her.

"His fever continues. But we are of good faith," Catherine said briskly. "I pray constantly for his restored health. I have promised to build a hospital in his name in Moscow. And I will go on pilgrimage to the Trinity Monastery. I am confident my prayers will be answered."

Bestuzhev hoped so. If the Grand Duke were to die, Catherine's hold on the throne would be precarious. There were still powerful factions who saw her as a German usurper. They would tolerate her until Paul, in their eyes the legitimate heir to the throne of Russia, came of age. If Paul were to die, his supporters might very well join those who favoured rescuing the deposed Ivan from prison and putting him on the throne. Although Bestuzhev's former flow of information had been reduced to a trickle, word had reached him that even Louis XV of France had expressed interest in Ivan. And then there was Catherine's bastard son with Grigory Orlov.

Bestuzhev could not deny Catherine's intelligence and zeal, but he was still of the opinion that women did not belong on the throne. The drunken conspirators were now facing the death penalty for expressing the same opinion. Bestuzhev had attended the first hearing of the investigating committee. The officers were accused of saying a man was needed on the throne, not a woman who was ruled by any man she took to her bed. They had also been heard to say that there were two rightful male heirs to the throne and one of them should be ruler of Russia. The talk had apparently become heated when the respective merits of Paul and Ivan were discussed. The accused would admit to nothing.

"We had all been drinking and revelling for ten days to celebrate our new Empress on the throne, God bless her and save her." One of the officers spoke for them all.

"Yes," another had added, "we were so drunk that we can't remember anything we or anyone else said."

Bestuzhev knew well that there were enough discontents, drunk and sober, who would prefer Paul or Ivan on the throne. What he did not know was if Catherine would dare to embark on the dangerous path of eliminating her enemies. Not even the Empress Elizabeth, a capricious tyrant with no respect for any laws, had sentenced anyone to death in the twenty years of her reign.

"I am sure God will have mercy on the Grand Duke as you have mercy on your subjects," Bestuzhev said as he took his leave.

The Empress looked at him sharply. Bestuzhev bowed quickly and headed for the door, fumbling for his nerve drops.

Chapter Four

The Earl of Buckingham's carriage made its way towards the Kremlin. As Britain's new ambassador, he was invited to join the Empress Catherine and her entourage for the evening. Since arriving in Moscow just a few weeks previously, he had attended such gatherings several times. Generally, there was a musical concert or performance and then cards were played.

Buckingham had been eager to meet the Empress. After all, his looks and charms had been important criteria in his being selected to persuade her into commercial friendship with England, a task which would be made easier if she were an attractive woman. His hopes were not disappointed. The Empress was not beautiful but she was striking in her looks, not charming but commanding. She preferred to talk rather than listen, her blue eyes shining when she warmed to her subject. During her monologues, Buckingham was content to watch her rather well-shaped lips which would lift in a smile at an apt compliment. All women, in the Earl's experience, were susceptible to flattery, and the Empress was no exception. He had noted, however, that Catherine was most pleased when her intellect or knowledge was praised. Yes, the Empress of Russia was definitely an interesting challenge and the Earl was sure he would make progress. For England, of course, rather than for himself, which did not prevent him from wondering what it would be like to bed her.

From what Buckingham could gather, she had few advisors, preferring to keep the reins of government in her own hands. Nikita Panin, a courtier of the old school with perfect court manners, seemed very able but his ideas of a constitution sat oddly with his huge wig of long powdered plaits. Panin favoured a northern alliance of England, Russia, Prussia and Holland and openly adulated Frederick of Prussia. He would do all in his power to prevent the rise of Austria or the House of Bourbon. The formidable Bestuzhev, on the other hand, of whom Buckingham had heard much in London, would support no alliance which did not include Austria. While age had reduced him to a tired and stubborn old man, Bestuzhev still retained Catherine's affection. Buckingham must tread a fine line to bring about George III's wish for peace in Europe to allow England to concentrate on consolidating its American colonies.

Buckingham's carriage crossed the Red Square in front of the colourful and onion-domed St Basil's Cathedral, which looked, he thought, as if an exuberant child had built it. Still, it would have formed a fitting background for the coronation festivities just a few weeks earlier, which Buckingham had missed. While his ship had docked at Kronstadt some days before the coronation, his luggage had not been off loaded with him. By the time it caught up with him, St Petersburg was empty and it was impossible to hire a horse and carriage for the journey to Moscow. The roads were reported impassable with carriages held fast in the churned up mud, blocking the way for the thousands trying to get to Moscow for the celebrations, where, it was rumoured, gold coins would be scattered to the crowds and the fountains would run with wine.

Buckingham set out after the coronation when a sudden snowfall promised a smoother journey, but it had taken nine miserable days of broken wheels and dirty hovels before he reached Moscow. The house he had been taken to was scarce in furnishings and abundant in rats.

Although he missed the coronation of the Empress, he had been witness to a much more sombre public spectacle. It had been announced that conspirators against the Empress were to be executed, and the Square had been thronged with crowds eager for excitement. Five officers of the Guards had been sentenced to beheading and were lined up in front of the blocks. At the last minute, the

Empress sent word of her clemency, commuting their sentences to permanent exile. As a sign of their political death, however, the accused had been required to lay their heads on the blocks. Buckingham shivered, expecting an executioner to appear suddenly, as he felt sure the accused did. But the officers held themselves well. Their wives and families sobbed as the men were herded into carriages to be taken under heavy guard to the coldest reaches of Siberia. A herald struggled to be heard above the disappointed clamour of the crowds.

Buckingham's companion, a young Russian of the landed gentry, whose father had married the daughter of a Scottish merchant, translated for him.

"They have to be kept separate from one another on the journey and allowed no converse with each other or any other person. They shall be allowed no fork or knife or any other instrument with which they could kill a person. They will be kept under strict guard until they reach their destination, where prison and hard labour await them."

The mock execution had dampened the festive coronation mood in the capital. Even Catherine was subdued.

"My mind is elsewhere," she had said to Buckingham as they played piquet one evening shortly after the mock executions. The Earl was not fond of the card game but, since it required only two players, Catherine chose it when she desired a tête-à-tête.

"But the Grand Duke has recovered well," Buckingham probed carefully.

"Yes, and I have already ordered plans for the hospital in his name to be built at once. I keep my promises." She lost the next trick.

"Unlike others," she continued, "who pledged their loyalty and then spoke against me. It is not easy to be sovereign. Do you know how many people rely on me?"

Buckingham thought the population of the Russian

Empire to be about fourteen million but deemed it wise not to answer.

"Eighteen million!" Catherine answered her own question. "I am mother to eighteen million subjects. And some of them seem to think I rule for my own pleasure, not aware that it is the hand of God which gave me the throne. It is my duty to bring Russia fame and good order and justice. It is my duty as long as I live on this earth." Catherine laid her cards with a slap on the table. "A sin against the sovereign is a sin against God and those who commit it are damned forever. But I must show mercy as well. Where does one find the balance?"

A hush had descended on the room as the Empress's voice rose.

"Perhaps Your Majesty does too much?" Buckingham said quietly, examining the cards on the table. "You must look to your own health. And use councillors and advisers to help you in your huge task."

"Ah yes, you English are fond of your Parliament," Catherine said less stridently. "But you are a small country. The extent of my Empire demands, if I may quote Montesquieu, absolute power vested in one person."

Buckingham felt that Montesquieu was being misquoted but moved on to safer terrain.

"With all due respect, Your Majesty, our Empire is a large one. We have our American colonies and our islands in the Caribbean. Why, we have now taken Havana – "

"Yes, yes," Catherine interrupted impatiently as she lost yet another trick, "but my Empire is all in one piece. Yours has bits scattered across oceans and seas. No, no, my dear Earl. My Empire is so vast that it can only be governed by one ruler. Every other form allows passions and differing opinions to dissipate its strength –"

She suddenly broke off, throwing down her cards.

"I have lost this round, Buckingham. I concede." She looked around impatiently. "Where is Count Orlov? Has he not yet arrived?"

This, rather than the onus of government, was often the root of her discontent, Buckingham thought. Orlov, as everyone knew, wandered far, on bear hunts and other escapades with his brothers. He was often gone for days and it was an open secret that the company he kept was not all male.

Buckingham's carriage had now crossed the Square and reached the palace in the Kremlin. As he descended, he straightened his wig. He hoped Count Orlov would be present this evening. The Empress would be in better mood and perhaps more open to English requests. He needed something to report back to London other than winning at piquet.

Chapter Five

Grigory Orlov sighed with quiet impatience. Catherine was always at her desk, constantly engaged in affairs of state, or writing letters to her French friends. She spent more time on Voltaire than she did on him.

"Come, lay down your pen," he said with feigned cheerfulness. "You are scattering ink over your dress. You have secretaries to write for you."

"Grigory, they are not scribes. They are state secretaries. I create more than enough work for them. They cannot keep up with me," she replied. Suddenly, she laid down her quill. "Nor, it seems, can you, Grigory."

"What do you mean?" Grigory's voice was wary.

"I rarely see you. Your other ... activities keep you so busy?"

"Come, Catherine. You know I can't be cooped up inside all day."

Grigory hated court life. It was full of people who spoke too much in order to hide the fact that they had nothing to say. Or those who idled the day away playing cards. They were all parasites. Catherine worked hard, he could not deny it, but she was the only one. In any case, reading and writing did not, in his opinion, constitute ruling. Commands did, just as in the army.

He softened his voice, as he added, "I need to be out, riding, hunting. Where I can breathe."

"Ah, I would love to ride out again," she said.

"But you can!" Grigory exclaimed. "You are the Empress. You can do as you wish."

Grigory missed the wilder side of Catherine, the one who rode astride better than most men. Before she had taken the throne, they had ridden out every day, hawking and hunting or just galloping for the exhilaration of the race against each other. Now Catherine scarcely managed a short ride once a week. Grigory had noticed a slackening of her once lithesome muscles. All this sitting around and writing would turn her into a mound of flesh. Grigory shuddered and thought of his recent companion on his bear hunt. She was but nineteen and had no interest in writing. She probably could not even read.

"Yes, Grigory, I am the Empress and therefore must rule rather than ride. I too would like nothing better than to ride out when I pleased. But you know that I am in the midst of serious attack. I would appreciate your support."

Grigory gave her his full attention. Any threats to her power were threats to him. He still hoped to persuade her into marriage. Russia needed a man.

"From what quarter does this threat come? Why do I not know of it?" he asked.

"Because you are out riding and hunting so much!" Her voice was querulous but she stilled it quickly. "The attack comes from the church," she added more calmly.

Grigory sighed his relief. There was not much danger from the clerics. They were too concerned with their own welfare, using the words of the gospels to their own advantage. Grigory had no time for their hypocrisy and had advised Catherine to secularise church property and wealth. The state coffers needed replenishment and the wealth of the church was a profitable source.

"But you have told them they should render to their sovereign the things that are his," he said reassuringly, "and to God the things that are God's. As it says in the Bible. The things which belong to God are their prayers and candles. All the rest belongs to the sovereign."

"Hers, Grigory," Catherine said.

"What?" Grigory was confused.

"Render to their sovereign the things that are hers. You said 'his'. I am a woman."

"Difficult to remember that these days," Grigory muttered. Aloud, he said, "I beg your pardon." He bent to kiss her hand. "You must arrest all those who speak against

25

your judgements. They will soon stop."

"Not if they are made martyrs of. We cannot have martyrs," Catherine replied.

"You have arrested the Metropolitan. Surely that will silence the Synod."

The Metropolitan of Rostov had openly voiced his opposition to state interference in Church matters. Rather than support him, the Synod had condemned his words as inflammatory and had delivered him to the Empress for judgement.

"Yes, but Bestuzhev warned me that it has caused talk among the people. Harmful talk."

"What? The old man dares to criticise his sovereign?" Grigory did not understand why Catherine still listened to Bestuzhev. Half the time he was asleep, whether in bed or on his feet, and the other half he was drunk.

"Well, he does have a point," Catherine continued. "The clergy argue that their lands belong to them. What was given to them was given to God. Hence, they say the lands belong to God. As Bestuzhev pointed out, I cannot fight God. And I will not fight Him. He is on my side and I will use Him to fight them."

"And fight them you must!" This was language Grigory understood. "The church and its clerics sit on riches which rightly belong to the state. They are richer than their sovereign."

"And yet, I did not remove their lands from them. I merely ordered that they keep accounts of their wealth, of what monies come in and what go out. I have forbidden them to spend on luxury. The money is only for the poor and sick. But the Metropolitan dares to remind me that the law of God is above my own law and that I am impoverishing His church. Oh, I have had enough of his lies and calumny!" Catherine threw down her pen.

"You have arrested him. Now you must silence him. That will be an end of the matter. The Synod will follow your will now. You must speak to them." Grigory spoke with military precision. Orders had to be clear.

"I will but Bestuzhev recommends clemency. I don't think there has been such a lèse-majesté as this under any ruler of Russia." Her voice rose in anger. "I don't know how one can doubt my compassion and mercy. In earlier times one would have had the cleric's head off for much less. I don't know how I can give my people peace and welfare if I leave upstarts unpunished!"

It was not like Catherine to be irritable, Grigory thought. It was a tedious subject but surely did not merit such loss of composure on her part. Not usually a man to consider nuances and shades of meaning, he suddenly felt that her anger was not so much directed at the renegade archbishop as at himself.

"Then punish him," Grigory said quietly, in the voice he used to calm unsettled horses. "You are the Empress. You decide. But now," he said as he lifted her hair to kiss her neck, "come with me. Leave your papers for a while."

"I cannot," she said, with a shake of her head. "I am writing my speech to the Synod."

Grigory moved his hands away abruptly. He did not understand Catherine's passion for justifying her every move. A few of his Guards would soon bring the Synod of fat clerics to heel. She must learn to lash out if she were to stay Empress. And he certainly did not understand why she did not accept his offer to share some hours of pleasure in his bed. It was normally he who received eager offers, from women of youth and beauty. He would go and find Alexey, down a few drinks with him and find some more entertaining company.

"Then I will leave you," he said as evenly as he could. "And return after dinner to my chambers. If you are not too busy."

She nodded her assent, her hand moving swiftly over the papers. She did not lift her eyes as he left.

Grigory knew he would not return that night. Let her miss him. Let her suffer a little. She would make up for it with some lavish gift. His last sulk had been rewarded with a very fine sword with a diamond-studded hilt. Eventually she would give him what he really wanted and what Russia needed. Her hand in marriage.

Chapter Six

"It has all gone wrong, this great scheme of yours, Batiushka!" Catherine had sent an urgent summons to Bestuzhev. Still drowsy from his afternoon sleep and the bottle of good red wine he had downed with his dinner, Bestuzhev struggled to concentrate.

Yes, his scheme had indeed gone very wrong. He had persuaded Catherine to consider marriage. To Orlov. Although the Grand Duke Paul had recovered from his latest illness, it only served to underline his frailty. Catherine needed a legitimate heir, alive and well, but all she had was one sickly heir and one in prison. And the vultures were already circling. Catherine knew this. Bestuzhev had found out that she had given instructions for Ivan to be killed by his own guards if there were any attempt to free him.

A healthy son was needed, one born of a legitimate Empress, as long as she was still accepted by the people as such, and fathered by a good Russian. Catherine had agreed to let Bestuzhev sound out higher court officials on how they would view a marriage between the Empress and Count Orlov. Bestuzhev had done so, discreetly as he thought, but rumours began seeping into every crevice in court and beyond. Bestuzhev had not even mentioned Orlov's name when seeking opinions, referring only to a husband of Russian birth who had proved his loyalty to his country.

"Let us remain calm and summarize what we know," Bestuzhev said, trying to marshal his own thoughts which were flitting about like moths looking for light. Catherine, who had been writing since he entered the room, now lifted the paper from her desk and waved it at him.

"The Guard Captain Khitrovo has been arrested for expressing opposition to my marrying? But could this not express affection?" she asked. "Many of my people see their sovereign as married to them and would not have her owned by one man."

"Your Majesty," Bestuzhev said quietly, "Khitrovo is not against you marrying but against you marrying Count Orlov. If you must marry, he says, then you should marry a brother of Ivan."

He did not tell her that some had voiced the opinion that she should marry Ivan, thus solving all problems of who had a right to sit on the throne. They could share it.

"No-one shall tell me whom to marry!" Catherine said sharply.

"Or not to, in this case, Your Majesty," Bestuzhev continued. "Captain Khitrovo was arrested for threatening the lives of Count Orlov and his brothers. He would kill them all, he said, to prevent the Empress marrying any one of them."

Catherine raised her head in alarm. "And does he act alone? Does he have co-conspirators? How many?"

"One cannot say. He says he acts alone." Bestuzhev paused, considering where the crux of the problem lay. Ah, yes, rumours! "Rumours are rife," he continued confidently. "But rumours cannot be fought. It is in their nature to be ... elusive."

"Then we will command silence on the matter!" Catherine spoke quietly but decisively. She resumed writing.

Bestuzhev remained silent. He had learned it was better not to contradict the Empress but rather leave her scope to find the best path herself. He suppressed a yawn.

"And what is his reasoning?" Catherine asked suddenly, startling him. "Is he a personal enemy of Count Orlov? Has the Count ever wronged him?"

Bestuzhev deemed this a more fruitful line of thought.

"Captain Khitrovo claims that someone in Panin's circle told him that Your Majesty had promised Panin on the eve of the ... on the day before you were declared

Empress that you would be regent to your son, the Grand Duke Paul, and that you would not take the throne for yourself. He claims Panin would never have given his consent otherwise." Bestuzhev kept his voice neutral, as a good courtier must. "So Captain Khitrovo sees it as a breach of promise," he added and then wished he had not.

"How dare he judge *me*, his sovereign! I am on this throne by God's blessing not by the hand of any man!"

Bestuzhev said carefully, "May I speak frankly, Your Majesty?"

"I have always ordered you to do so! Speak, Batiushka!" Catherine rose from her desk and began pacing the room. This was unusual and did not bode well, Bestuzhev was sure.

"Captain Khitrovo says that it was the Orlov brothers who forced you to take the throne not as regent for your son, as Count Panin wished, but for yourself as Empress. Because one of theirs would be Emperor. It is this which he wished to prevent."

Catherine marched silently back to her desk. Her quill scratched furiously across the paper.

Bestuzhev waited. Suddenly, the door flew open and Orlov strode into the room.

Without preamble, he said, "And what are you going to do about Khitrovo? Shall that little upstart dictate whom you shall marry? Are you not sovereign?"

Catherine swept her arm across her desk. Papers fluttered to the floor and the inkwell toppled over. Bestuzhev had rarely seen the Empress lose control, not even during her most difficult early years in Russia, when she was no more than a little homesick German princess. She had always shown discipline, and it was this which had secured her the throne in the end.

"Am I never to be free of this burden?" she shouted. "I give my life to my people and there are those who would still question me. It is only months since I dealt severely with the upstarts, who dared to throw the names of my son and the imprisoned Ivan in my face as being better occupants of this throne. My son is but eight years old and I will keep this throne for him and I will turn this empire into one where justice and wealth reign." She stared at the two men defiantly, her eyes flashing like the diamond earrings which trembled in her agitation. "And it seems I must do it alone," she added more calmly. "My people would not have me marry. So be it. I will not marry."

"Surely – " Orlov began.

"No, Grigory. It cannot be. I would not put your life in danger," Catherine said firmly. "But I would have you by my side, always," she added softly.

She bent to gather the papers from the floor. Orlov moved to help her but she waved him off.

"I shall rule alone," she said with emphasis. "Now leave me, if you would. I must consider how to deal with Captain Khitrovo."

"But there is surely nothing to consider?" Orlov protested. "Treason is a serious crime. He must lose his head for it! "

"No, Grigory. That will not be the way. We must not encourage further opposition. I will order silence on this subject. As if it never happened. We will seal all the papers of the case, confine Khitrovo to his estates, and I will forbid all talk which is considered unseemly or dangerous to our public peace. I will have the matter silenced. I will have a manifesto distributed throughout the whole of my empire."

"Very well, Your Majesty," Orlov said curtly turning on his heel. Bestuzhev knew he would drown his anger in drinking with his brothers and find softer solace in the arms of one of the very young ladies always ready to share the Orlovs. Together, he had heard. As Orlov passed him, Bestuzhev imagined he detected a strong whiff of stable. There was a rumour at court that Orlov had received an anonymous gift of a large cheese filled with horse dung.

Fortunately, he had not opened it in his palace chambers.

Bestuzhev turned his attention to the scribbling Empress.

"A manifesto on silence, Your Majesty?" he quietly asked.

Chapter Seven

Alexey Orlov regarded his brother with less of the envy he usually felt. Grigory, three years his senior, had always been better at everything. Alexey had spent his life trying to ride better, fight better, drink and whore better than his older brother. But Grigory remained the charmed one. Alexey had been as handsome as all the Orlov brothers until a deep slash in a duel left one side of his face disfigured. Grigory's good looks remained flawless. Alexey's loyalty, however, was stronger than his envy, even stronger than his conscience. He chose not to think too often about what he and his brothers had undertaken to put Grigory on the throne. He was not sure that brotherly love could justify regicide. Yet, despite all their best efforts, fate was not smiling on Grigory as she usually did. Nor, it would seem, was the Empress. Grigory was still not on the throne and probably never would be. All their efforts had been in vain.

"So she has decided she will never marry you?" Alexey asked curtly.

"She says it will endanger my life," Grigory said scornfully. "I would like to know who has been turning her against me. Count Panin for sure. He has never been on our side."

"She has been clever in her reasoning, you must admit," Alexey said. "You cannot argue against it unless you argue yourself into danger. And if it's not this plot, then it will be another. Our enemies will supply them, real or imagined, for as long as it takes to rid the court of our presence."

"That will never happen!" Grigory said quietly. "I do not intend to argue with her. And you know well enough I would never beg. We will find another way. She will marry me."

"But you are still sure of her ... affection?" Alexey asked carefully.

"What do you imply, Alexey? The Empress has eyes for no other!"

"But would you be so sure there are no other contenders, brother? After all, it is a coveted place, to be the Empress's favourite."

Grigory whirled round. "Be careful, Alexey! I will not have her slandered."

"I intend no slander. But look around you. There are so many ambitious young men at court who would further their careers by gaining the Empress's favours."

"Yes, yes. I see these puppy dogs every day. They throw themselves to their knees and declare their love for Her Majesty as if they were in some French play. Catherine is merely amused by it. It does no harm. Better than if she were to walk through court ignored."

"But some would seem to receive special attention?" Alexey persisted. He had to risk his brother's wrath if they were not to lose everything they had fought for, everything they had risked even their eternal souls for.

"Alexey, if you have something to say, say it plainly." Grigory's voice was resigned rather than impatient. "I am tired of your innuendos."

"Consider who stands behind her at table every day. Constantly in her presence, even when you are not. Very tall. Taller than you, Grigory, with a very fine mane of thick hair. Very sought after by women." Alexey gave his attention to a fine crystal decanter then added, "Must be the hair."

The look of puzzlement on Grigory's face cleared quickly.

"Oh, you mean, Grigory Potemkin? Well, that is no riddle. He proved himself useful when we needed loyal men. He was well rewarded by the Empress, as were many."

"And it was we who introduced him to court, you remember? We thought the Empress would be entertained by his power to mimic any person or voice. And she was."

"Yes," Grigory said, laughing out loud, "and the impudent young scoundrel impersonated the Empress's German accent perfectly, which delighted her. Yes, he could make her laugh, and us too."

"And you may remember she said at the time that we should never have introduced anyone to court whose hair was better than hers."

"Hair?" Grigory echoed.

"And that we would regret it."

"Regret what? His hair? I am lost, Alexey!"

"Regret bringing him to court. And I think we will."

"It was no more than a meaningless compliment, a turn of phrase. The court is full of such empty words," Grigory said impatiently.

"But Potemkin receives much attention from the Empress, which, if you were with her more often, you would see," Alexey remonstrated. "And if you were with her more often, she would not be so susceptible to his attentions, adolescent as they are."

Grigory swung round to face his brother. "What? You would chide me, Alexey? Do not presume to tell me how to keep the Empress happy!"

"I ask only that you listen to me. And then observe for yourself. Catherine calls Potemkin her student, she has arranged French lessons for him, she praises his mastery of Greek and his grasp of theology. She has appointed him assistant imperial commissioner at the Holy Synod –"

"It is but a church appointment!" Grigory said with a dismissive wave of his hand but Alexey detected with satisfaction the note of doubt in his voice.

"Perhaps the young Potemkin is one reason why she does not wish to marry?" Alexey persisted. "He is open in his adulation for her. She permits it. She encourages his silly attentions. A married Empress would not be able to."

"Ah, she treats him like one of her lapdogs, that is all!" Grigory said lightly. "I do not doubt the Empress's feelings for me, Alexey, but I will watch Potemkin. And if I see that he is overstepping his position, we will deal with him."

Grigory rose suddenly and slapped Alexey on the back. "Come, let us find some entertainment. Court life wearies me! And turns you into a nagging wife!"

Chapter Eight

Catherine threw down her quill and clenched her teeth together. She had one of her crippling headaches coming on. She read too much and the letters often danced before her eyes in the flicker of the candles, especially those written in a poor hand, which were most of them. But how could she stop the onslaught of work? There was so much to do and no-one but herself to rely on.

Orlov was the only one who could help her. He massaged her shoulders, his hands gradually circling down her body until tension melted into desire. But she had not seen Orlov since he left for yet another hunting trip five days ago. This time she had asked him not to go.

"Stay here at court. I like to have you by my side," she had said.

Orlov bowed to kiss her hand.

"Ah, but you spend all the time I am here with your papers and secretaries and commissions. That is the point - – I am not at your side as I would like to be. You could have had me as your husband but you choose to serve your people instead. Each to his way, my love."

Since the Khitrovo affair had rendered marriage to Orlov impossible, he had not been so attentive. His absences made her uneasy and she could not concentrate. He was still a very attractive man, coveted by many women. She had seen it in their eyes as they looked his strong figure up and down behind their fans, giggling. Surely he had not succumbed to any of them? She was tempted to join him on the hunt, tempted by hours of carefree riding followed by long nights together, but she knew in the end that she could not abandon her duties for personal pleasure.

A major task was to find money. And it was this thought which had brought her headache on. Elizabeth had left state debts of seventeen million roubles, a figure that was constantly rising. Catherine looked down at her list of projects. It was overwhelming. Obtaining external credit and issuing paper money were of immediate importance. These measures would ensure stability to tackle manufacturing and agriculture, town guilds and serfs, foreign trade and foreign threats, new territory to acquire and populate, universities and schools, the health of her citizens and the security of her empire. Why, she even had to see to the proper lighting of streets in the city. And every day brought new demands and new tasks. She straightened her back and dipped her pen into the inkwell. She would not be defeated. She would make Russia a nation to be proud of, a power to be reckoned with. Let the rest of Europe scoff arrogantly! She would prove herself an able sovereign, equal to Frederick of Prussia.

It had been a long hot summer and she had rarely left St Petersburg for the fresher air of the palace at Tsarskoye Selo, allowing herself leisure only in the evenings, which she spent listening to music or playing cards. She was too exhausted for balls or masquerades. She knew her Court was bored, and she also knew that a bored Court could be a dangerous one.

Late September had brought news which roused her from her lethargy. On reading it, she jumped from her desk in excitement. After several false alarms which had thrown Europe into diplomatic flurries, King August III of Poland had died at last. He had spent scarcely three years of his thirty-year reign in Poland, preferring to live in Dresden as Elector of Saxony in the Holy Roman Empire. He and his wife, Maria Josepha of Austria, had borne many children whom they scattered in marriage throughout Europe – in Spain and France, in Bavaria and Austria. While Augustus devoted himself to a life of hunting and pleasure, Poland was plundered by his greedy representatives, driving it to ruin.

With the death of Augustus, Catherine knew she must

move swiftly to acquire the weakened state before others did. She would not have the French or the Austrians ruling directly on her borders. And although Prussia's forces were weakened by the recent war, Frederick would not let Poland be snatched so easily from under his nose.

Catherine's plan had always been to make Stanislav Poniatovsky King of Poland. At the height of their love affair before she became Empress, they had dreamed of uniting Russia and Poland into one empire which they would rule over as enlightened sovereigns together. Or at least Poniatovsky had. She had never intended to allow the quarrelsome Poles with their ties to Saxony to gain any hold in Russia. But she did intend to keep Poland under Russian dominion, and Poniatovsky was the perfect way to achieve this. He wrote to her regularly, his letters full of declarations of love and impassioned pleas to marry him. He had no interest in being King of Poland, desiring only a place at her side.

Such a marriage had always been impossible, she knew, and now even more so. She would lose the throne of Russia and he the chance to rule Poland. And besides, while her thoughts lingered fondly on Poniatovsky's cultured mind and elegant grace, she was fonder still of Orlov's rough charms and strong body.

Her advisors were not in agreement on her plan to put Poniatovsky on the Polish throne. At the hastily called conference after the death of Augustus, Bestuzhev and Panin had faced each other with ill-concealed enmity.

"Russia, Your Majesty, has no choice but to favour a Saxon candidate for the Polish throne. This would secure the support of Austria and France." Bestuzhev spoke with a composure Catherine knew he struggled to maintain. He had expressed himself much more forthrightly in the privacy of her chambers.

"But do we want their support?" Panin asked. "Why should we rush into the arms of our enemies?"

"Is it better to antagonise them?" Bestuzhev retorted. "If we put a native Pole on the throne, France would feel justified in encouraging its ally the Ottoman Empire to attack us in the south. The Turks have already made gains against us there. We do not have the forces to counter more than their present skirmishes. We cannot have war."

"But we have another ally to support our choice of Stanislav Poniatovsky," Catherine said. "Frederick of Prussia is in agreement with us. He too does not wish a Saxon king in Poland." Catherine would rather have had the British on her side. The Earl of Buckingham had been charming and persistent in his attempts to renew a treaty of commerce and friendship between England and Russia but he had remained resistant to her own efforts to gain English support for Poniatovsky in Poland.

Count Chernyshev, head of the College of War, had recommended immediate annexation of Poland's northeastern region. "It is our duty," he argued," to free our Orthodox brothers from the yoke of Catholic repression."

There had been reports of violence against Orthodox churches and Catherine was happy to use this as justification for interference in Poland. But she would try other means before resorting to force. Through her minister in Warsaw, she had been funding the pro-Russian party in Poland. She had also ordered 30,000 troops stationed at the Polish border with another 50,000 in reserve. This was threat enough. The Poles would elect Count Poniatovsky. She would make him king.

Oh, but she was tired of it all! In exasperation, she threw her lists to the side. Did she not deserve some lightness in life? Where was Orlov? She should have gone with him on the hunting expedition but who would rule in her place for these few days of pleasure? Everyone seemed to have left the Court. Only dullards remained, and she among them. Perhaps she too had become a dullard. Where was the young Potemkin? He could make her laugh. She enjoyed his company, his lack of reverence, his thick waves of hair framing his open face. She would send for him and make up a card party this evening.

***

The invitation to join the Empress for cards that evening surprised Count Panin. He rarely joined in evening entertainment, citing his responsibility for the Grand Duke as an excuse. The Empress's soirées, however, were often frequented by ambassadors, wishing to avail themselves of the opportunity for informal influence which such an invitation provided. The British ambassador was bound to be there. The Empress was fond of the Earl of Buckingham.

Panin had barely entered the chamber when Catherine beckoned him to her. Without preamble, she asked him about the young Potemkin, whom, she said, she had not seen at Court for several days, or perhaps weeks, and nor had he answered her invitation for this evening. Panin felt dismay.

"I think he has left the Court, Your Majesty," he said carefully.

"What do you mean, he has left the Court?" Catherine asked abruptly. "Who gave him permission to do so?"

"Well, left is perhaps not the correct term. I think he has been unable to appear at Court."

"Unable? You must explain, Count Panin."

Panin could not explain. The Orlovs were no friends of his but neither was it in his interest to take the young Potemkin's part.

"He apparently hurt his eye," Panin said carefully. "It became infected and he has lost his sight."

Panin could not divulge to Catherine what he had heard. The luckless Potemkin had been invited to play billiards by Grigory and Alexey Orlov and had mysteriously lost his eye doing so. A physician had been called and told that Potemkin had struck himself in the eye with the long cue as he was lining up a shot. Those who had rushed to the scene reported finding a badly beaten Potemkin in a pool of blood. "This is how we deal with those who would oust the Orlovs," Alexey Orlov had been heard to boast.

"Billiards?" Catherine interrupted Panin's thoughts. "I did not think his taste ran to such games. With whom was he playing?"

"I am not sure," Panin faltered.

"I trust he has had the best physician. I cannot understand why he did not avail himself of the court physicians. When will he return?"

Panin knew the Orlovs would not permit his return to Court so easily. And perhaps they were right. The young Potemkin was open in his adulation of the Empress. He was intelligent and quixotic. Not only was he very handsome of feature possessing enviable waves of thick hair but his figure was a fine one ... and his legs were long and muscular, Panin thought despondently. Till now, the Empress had evidenced not much more than an interested fondness for the young man but it was a short way from protégé to lover, as Panin knew from his own experience with his protégées. The Orlovs had acted timely if rather violently. It was whispered that Potemkin's nickname at Court was now Cyclops.

"Count Panin?" The Empress's voice broke into his thoughts once more. He must keep his wits about him.

"Return, Your Majesty?" he said. "I am sure Count Orlov will be able to tell you all you need to know. Not only was he present at the ... accident, but he is apprised of the allocation of all Your Majesty's grooms and guardsmen."

The Empress looked startled.

"Yes, I will do that. I will have Count Orlov report on the matter to me," she said curtly. "But now I find I have lost my enthusiasm for cards this evening. I cannot think of that young man having lost an eye. Are you sure it is only one? Will he be able to read? He had been making such progress with his French lessons. And he is so interested in theology and philosophy. Will he be able to ride? What can a blind person do? His future is ruined before it has begun!"

Panin was alarmed. The Empress's voice was rising with a note of panic in it. Perhaps hysteria.

"I am assured it is only one eye, Your Majesty. And I have heard that Potemkin has retired to a monastery – I do not know which one – and is said to be devoting himself to prayer and study."

"I will retire now, Count Panin. Please take care of my guests."

Panin watched as Catherine swept from the room without making her farewells. Perhaps she never had a particular care for the young man but she may very well do so now, he thought.

Chapter Nine

Count Betskoy settled himself comfortably in the armchair he usually occupied while waiting for Catherine. He surveyed her room. Every surface was filled with papers. No matter how many extra desks she ordered to be brought to her chambers, there was never any space free of papers. He wished she would work less. She often looked tired but her blue eyes were always bright, almost feverish in their glitter.

Betskoy read aloud to her most afternoons so that, as she said, she could rest her eyes for an hour or two without wasting time. The room was gloomy and he had to use a magnifying glass. While he read, Catherine knotted silk threads. When Betskoy pointed out that this pastime might also strain her eyes, she said working with colours was easier than with ink and besides, she could not sit with idle hands. The work did seem to soothe her. She gave these ornamental braids, some of them very beautiful in pattern and colour, as little rewards to her ladies-in-waiting. But while she knotted, she listened attentively, often interrupting to ask a question or to instruct Betskoy to write a note in the margin for her to consider later.

Betskoy, now over sixty, thought back to Paris thirty-five years ago, when he had fallen under the spell of Catherine's mother, then a vivacious young princess, newly wed but still a virgin. Their passionate affair ended when Princess Johanna suddenly left in tears for home and husband. Betskoy missed her in his bed but was relieved to be able to return to Russia unencumbered with another man's wife. They had resumed their affair sporadically in the following years when they met in Hamburg or Berlin but it had taken some time for Betskoy to realise that he could be the father of Johanna's first child. It would explain her precipitous and unexplained flight from Paris back to her husband. And now that very child was Empress of

Russia.

Apart from her well-shaped mouth, Catherine had not inherited her mother's pretty looks. If there was anything of his own mother in her, Betskoy would not recognise it. He was the illegitimate but acknowledged son of Prince Trubetskoy, borne by his Swedish mistress while he was held prisoner in Stockholm during the Great Northern War. Illegitimate children in higher circles generally received their father's name with the first syllable removed. Betskoy was not sure what occurred when there were no more syllables to be chopped off a name. There was not much one could do with Betskoy. But parentage did not matter. Upbringing and education were paramount. It was Betskoy's opinion that any child could be taken from the streets and turned into a moral, upright, and useful citizen.

Betskoy, anxious to escape the dangerous and tiring intrigues of the Russian court, had spent many years in Paris, where he had mixed with the great French thinkers that Catherine had become so fond of, mainly through Betskoy's part in sending her volumes of their works. It was the works of the *philosophes* that Catherine choose to have Betskoy read aloud to her and they had just finished reading *Émile,* Jean-Jacques Rousseau's treatise on education. Rousseau, of course, was not French but Genevan and had only spent time in France because he had at some point converted to Catholicism and had thus been banned from his native city. But Catherine was not interested in personal details although she may have been had Betskoy told her just how handsome Rousseau was. But he would not add that he was slightly mad. Rousseau had refused a pension from Louis XV, lived with his illiterate seamstress mistress and, both Voltaire and Diderot claimed, stole ideas from other thinkers. Still, his ideas on raising children struck a chord with Betskoy. And seemingly with Catherine too. She was enthusiastic about opening a Foundling Home in Moscow which would offer shelter to babies left to die on the streets by mothers unable to feed them. Such mothers could come to the Home, ring a bell to have a basket lowered and leave their babies with no questions asked and no commitments demanded. Instead of being deprived of their first breath by mothers made desperate by despair, these destitute illegitimate children would be raised far from the evil influences of the society into which they had had the misfortune to be born. They would be formed into a new kind of people with a high moral sense of right and wrong as well as with a sense of duty to Russia, their true mother. They would not become drunkards and murderers but rather a new class of craftsmen. Rousseau, himself originally a watchmaker, had emphasised that artists lived lazily on the proceeds of the rich, while artisans pursued a worthy trade beneficial to the needs of society. Betskoy would not go quite so far as to condemn artists and he had carefully skipped over such diatribes when reading aloud to Catherine, who gladly spent the state's money on acquiring masterpieces of art for the edification of society. She was in the process of trying to acquire a collection of 225 paintings by Flemish and Dutch masters, which Frederick of Prussia had ordered a Berlin dealer to collect for him. The recent war had emptied his coffers and he could no longer afford to purchase them. Catherine would make sure she could, if only to snub the Prussian King.

Still, let her have her art, he thought, as long as she continued to fund the educational projects which he urged on her. She maintained the money was her own but where hers stopped and the state's began was not a line she ever strictly adhered to. Betskoy had convinced her that a nation's prosperity would increase with the formation of a solid third estate of loyal citizens. Manual skills would keep the mind and body occupied and would produce artefacts which would benefit society and allow the artisan to earn a living. There must be a middle ground between lord and peasant. Betskoy had given Grand Duke Paul a carpentry set for his birthday, perhaps a little early according to Rousseau's timetable of child development. But a prince must start young. Rousseau himself had cited the very example of Peter the Great having learned carpentry and other manual skills.

Betskoy stood up as Catherine entered the room and went to sit in her favourite upright chair near the window. Betskoy regarded her frowning face with fatherly concern. She was still an attractive woman in her mid-thirties, but her face had filled out and her lips, once softly shaped, had thinned in severity.

"Count Orlov is absent from court again," she said as she took up her silk threads.

"I am sure he has ... military duties to attend to," Betskoy said calmly. He must divert her from dark thoughts "But I have good news for you," he continued brightly. "Our Foundling Home is almost finished! We can mark your birthday with its official opening."

Catherine's interest was caught. "Are we so near completion?" she asked eagerly. "And how many children can we accommodate?"

"We can easily take five hundred to begin with although I am sure we must increase to double that as speedily as possible," Betskoy replied. "And we must open a similar institution here in St Petersburg."

"And we can also take in unmarried mothers whose children have yet to be born?" Catherine asked.

"We have made provision for such mothers also. They may bring their children into the world anonymously under our care and then leave them with us. But if they have a change of heart, they may leave with the child."

Ah, society was full of illegitimate children, Betskoy sighed. Why, alone in this room, there were a possible half dozen involved: himself, the Empress, Catherine's son Paul, if rumour served right, her daughter with Poniatovsky, the little Anna Petrovna, who had died in infancy, as well as Catherine's baby son with Orlov. Orlov alone had scattered his seed everywhere and was rumoured to have several children. Society, at least in aristocratic circles, coped politely with illegitimate children. Husbands, unwilling to be public cuckolds, accepted any children as their own. It was not gentlemanly to question one's wife as to the paternity of her child. Unmarried mothers relied on secrecy and the benevolence of the alleged father. Betskoy believed that all children, both legitimate an illegitimate, belonged to society. Rousseau had given his own children, borne by his seamstress mistress, to a Foundling Home in Paris.

"And have we made provision for the dairy?" Catherine asked. "Monsieur Rousseau emphasized the need for natural milk as nourishment for the mothers," Catherine asked. "We must have it fresh. No soured milk."

"The dairy is established, with some eighty cows."

"And the mothers will be encouraged to nurse their own children?"

This was a sensitive issue. Rousseau had indeed advocated natural nursing for mothers but he had ranted against wet nurses, chiding the natural mother for not caring for her own child as God had designed it, and berating the wet nurse who neglected her own child to nourish a stranger's for payment. He had painted bleak pictures of wet-nursed children hung in their tight swaddling clothes on pegs all day, to be taken down only for feeding. But Betskoy could not envisage aristocratic mothers baring their breasts to feed their offspring. It was a grotesque notion and, in his opinion, subtracted substantially from the erotic role of the female. He had therefore skipped much of the natural nursing paragraphs while reading Rousseau to Catherine. She may have taken a liking to the idea and ordered all the ladies at court to feed their own children. Betskoy shuddered. It would be like a cowshed.

"In this respect, all will be done to encourage the mothers to nourish their children. But for those children left on the doorstep without mothers, they will have to be wet-nursed until they can stomach cow's milk," he said smoothly.

Betskoy quickly decided it was time to change the subject. He had had enough of milk. In fact, he was beginning to feel quite nauseous.

"What about plans for the school for young ladies of noble birth?" he asked brightly. Yes, young girls were a much brighter topic.

"Ah yes. I have decided the Smolny Convent will be ideal for the purpose," Catherine said, looking up from her silk threads. "We must work on the curriculum. It must have psychological as well as practical aspects. The heart and personality must be educated. The girls will only shine in dance and singing if their manners are excellent and their minds pure. That is what nobility means. Not just status but demeanour."

Betskoy had already been working on the curriculum. He could envisage sleek young heads bowed over carefully selected French texts, or sorting silk threads, or delicate feet in satin-covered slippers dancing contredanses. He intended to oversee all aspects of their education and spend more time there than at the Foundling Home.

Betskoy had to concede that Johanna, despite her flightiness, had brought her daughter up with that nobility of spirit that Catherine wished to instil in others. As Empress, she had swept through the Court like a strict governess, disciplining her twenty ladies-in waiting, who were wont to spend their nights merry-making while they yawned through the day with idle hands. They now all slept in the chambers above the Empress, with two older ladies of court as chaperones while Catherine sought a proper governess for her charges. She had instructed

Betskoy to use their connections in Hamburg to find the ideal woman to fill this post, convinced no such person could be found in Russia. She should be "not young and not of the Catholic religion. She should be of good morals but not nit-picking, should know how to insist but also be gentle, should have wit, prudence and accomplishments and enjoy reading." Betskoy was still searching. Meanwhile, Catherine herself had taken over much of the guidance of her ladies. She prescribed reading, introduced strict timetables, told them how to dress, how to stand, how to sit. If any of them contravened her instructions, she would forfeit the diamond brooch shaped in the initial letter of the Empress's name, which she said was a "badge of honour and not to be sullied". The offending lady could redeem her brooch through exemplary behaviour.

Yes, Betskoy thought, Johanna would have been proud of her daughter although she would not have approved of her strictness. She had gained the throne of Russia, just as Johanna had dreamed and plotted for, forfeiting, in many ways, her own happiness in the attempt. The glittering world she had hoped for as mother of the Empress had eluded her. Her demise in Paris had been pitiful to watch and Betskoy had done all he could to ensure she was cared for but she had died alone and in debt before Catherine had become Empress.

On the other hand, Johanna may have been disappointed in her daughter. Catherine's court still looked opulent, with much shimmering gold and silver to impress. She herself was rarely without diamonds, but there was not much sparkle elsewhere. Frugality reigned. There were no more banquets served, and there was not much more than soured milk or weak beer to drink at masquerades and balls. Count Panin had even recommended giving up such public events since few of the nobility attended. They were popular only with the merchant class who would do anything to have a foot in the door of the court. Catherine was even considering a ban on card-playing although she herself enjoyed it. Betskoy had quickly reminded her that revenues of some 30,000 roubles would be lost from the tax on playing cards alone. To salve her conscience, he had suggested she donate these revenues to the Foundling Home.

Betskoy turned his thoughts back to the Smolny project. "I have been working on the curriculum. I shall bring it tomorrow for your approval."

"I think," said Catherine, "I shall even take up a little teaching there. Some guidance on history or philosophy."

Betskoy looked up in alarm. It would be very inconvenient and not at all fitting for the Empress to be teaching young girls. But history and philosophy? Betskoy's vision was a lighter one of his young charges being prepared for the salons of Europe's high society. They would float as effortlessly and as aesthetically as butterflies in summer meadows.

"Count Betskoy?" The Empress's voice shook him from his reverie.

"Your Majesty?" Betskoy looked up to find the Empress scrabbling among papers on the writing desk nearest her.

"I was saying I will devise a history curriculum now!" The Empress's voice was excited. Betskoy recognised the fire of enthusiasm for a new project, which would take her attention away from other projects. "You may leave, dear Count, while I make a full reading list. I will give it to you tomorrow."

Betskoy muttered, "Excellent, Your Majesty, excellent." He bowed his exit, thinking forlornly of his lost butterflies.

Chapter Ten

Once the wine had been poured, the Earl of Buckingham coughed politely for the attention of his guests. Baron de Breteuil, the French ambassador, was in full monologue flow, as usual, in his nasal and pompous French. He had been in Russia since 1760 and felt superior in having served under, as he always emphasized, three rulers of Russia. He had little time for Buckingham, nor for England. Buckingham noted with satisfaction that the Baron's wig was slightly askew.

Buckingham coughed again. Breteuil turned from Count Mercy, the Austrian ambassador.

"My dear Earl! Have you caught a cold? Ah, it is this climate. One must get used to it."

This was a ludicrous comment to make in the middle of a hot summer. Even in winter, one could not blame the cold but rather the shoddiness of the buildings, which all seemed to have chinks and cracks designed to conduct icy drafts. In summer, as now, they acted as efficient channels for odours and mosquitoes from the river. Only this morning, Buckingham had spotted three swollen animal carcasses floating by as well as something he hoped was not a human corpse.

Ignoring Bretueil's comment but seizing the gap in conversation, Buckingham said quickly,

"Gentlemen, I have invited you here this evening to share our information. We are all unsure of the situation but are agreed we must be prepared for any event. It is better that we are prepared together rather than work against each other to the possible detriment of each. And all." Buckingham was not sure he had expressed his view as succinctly as he had perceived it in his mind.

Breteuil drew breath to speak but Mercy was faster. "You have heard about the desecration of the Empress's portrait on the triumphal arch. This speaks of dangerous discontent."

Count Solms, the Prussian ambassador, had been engrossed in moving his glass to and fro on the table. The settings were luxurious, silver and gold gleaming in the candlelight, the porcelain of the finest. Buckingham, however, would exchange it all for a decent water closet without cockroaches.

"The Empress has been overhasty in certain matters," Solms intoned in his ponderous manner. "She has alienated the church. She has dared to take from them what they see as theirs."

"Yes, she even dared to preach to the Synod," Breteuil said. "Told them men of God did not need riches. Quoted the Bible at them. Accused them of stealing from the state. Give back to the state what belongs to the state, she said. Dangerous stuff, don't you think?"

"Yes, not to mention what she did to the Metropolitan.That is bound to get people upset," Mercy agreed.

Buckingham had also been taken aback by Catherine's punishment of the cleric. The old man had been stripped of his bishop's robe and staff in front of the Synod. The Empress had allowed him to continue being a monk, a sign of her gracious mercy she said, but had banished him to a remote monastery in Archangel. He was to be kept isolated in a cell under guard and denied visitors, books, paper and ink. It was of little wonder that no other voice in the Synod had been raised to protest the state's appropriation of church property.

"Well, it has relieved her financial problems somewhat," said Solms. "By all accounts, she has gained one million serfs from the church, and that's only counting the males. That's a considerable amount of tax-payers. Not to mention the gold and silver from the church coffers. And lands."

Buckingham thought he detected a note of envy in the

Prussian ambassador's voice.

"But you would know all about that, my dear Earl," Solms continued. "Didn't your Henry of the many wives do the exact same thing and get away with it?"

"Well, there were consequences. For England. And for Europe," Buckingham said lightly. "But let us return to the subject in hand. What are the consequences here?"

Count Mercy filled his glass and said, "No matter how many monasteries have to close, the monks will not launch any attack on their sovereign. They are not ... worldly enough."

"Besides which," Breteuil interjected, "the people see her as devout in her faith. She never misses an opportunity to display her devotions in public. No, I think the Church is not the danger. The danger comes from another quarter."

The other three men looked at him expectantly, just as he wanted them to, Buckingham thought. Breteuil took his time, pouring himself another glass of wine before he resumed.

"Her choice of favourite has not endeared her to the Guards. Orlov has been heaped with wealth and honours – count, chamberlain, lieutenant-general, aide-de-camp, Knight of the Order of St Andrew, countless roubles, jewels, estates and serfs. And he remains what he was – a gambler and a philanderer. He makes a laughing stock of the Empress. He and his brothers live lavishly at the court's expense."

"Will she marry him, do you think?" Buckingham asked. England could send as many handsome envoys as they liked to further their commercial interests with Russia but to no avail if Count Orlov became Catherine's legal husband.

"It has been said that the last conspiracy put paid to that plan," Count Mercy said. "She issued a manifesto of silence but rumours are still rife. How ridiculous. A manifesto ordering silence. How can this be enforced?"

Buckingham decided it was time to find out who among them was favourable to the Empress. "The Empress," he said, "does involve herself seriously with the affairs of state. She works hard. Surely that must count?"

Count Mercy said, "Yes, but she has no system. She thinks she has but she has too many projects, simultaneously, and can finish none. Her plans are not mature. They are precipitous."

Buckingham tried again. "She has much knowledge and reading. She shines in any conversation. Her intellect is far above those that surround her."

"Yes, yes," Solms agreed. "She is very vain in that respect."

Buckingham thought back to a conversation where the Empress had claimed knowledge about man o' war tactics when she had never seen a ship of war at sea.

"Yes, she will admit to no superior knowledge in another," Buckingham said before he could stop himself. "Understanding clearly what she has learnt, she sometimes thinks she is mistress of what she has not."

Breteuil chuckled. "You have a pretty turn of phrase, Buckingham. I'll give you that."

"The Empress makes her first move on foreign soil, in Poland," Solms said. "As we all know, gentlemen, it is foreign policy that makes a great ruler. But one must know which pieces to move on the chessboard of power and I am not sure that she does. At least making a former lover king does not reflect political wisdom."

"In this case, she may not have heeded us ambassadors sufficiently but what about her advisors?" Mercy asked. "She ignores the Senate but surely she has advisors she listens to?"

"I can tell you that Count Panin is disenchanted," Solms said. "She will not hear of any reform which diminishes her power. His constitutional project, for which she showed so much enthusiasm when she was still Grand Duchess, has been consigned to some dark cupboard, useful only to the mice."

Or rats more likely, Buckingham thought.

"No," Solms continued, "Panin will bide his time and support the Grand Duke Paul as Emperor. Therein lies his loyalty, not with the Empress."

"And Bestuzhev?" Mercy asked.

"He suffers from old age and even the Empress does not take him seriously, fond of him as she is," Solms said. "He cannot reach the end of a sentence without forgetting how he started. And he drowns any little sense that remains in wine and brandy."

Breteuil fidgeted in his seat. "Any other so-called advisors are not worth mentioning.," he said impatiently. "They are either men like her secretary Teplov with principles and no abilities or like Suvorov with abilities but no principles."

"That is also a neat turn of phrase, Baron," Buckingham said.

Breteuil bowed in acknowledgement.

"She is indecisive," he continued. "She dissipates time and energy and power on her commissions. There is a commission for everything. Ask a question, you get a commission."

"And then there is the question of the state coffers," Solms said. "They are empty despite new income from church property. The country lurches on from one crisis to the next. The army has not been paid in months. How much loyalty can one expect from unpaid soldiers? And her ban on the export of wheat has solved the bread problem but only temporarily. What cannot be produced cannot be eaten. A hungry nation is not a loyal nation."

"And what money there is is being spent too lavishly," Mercy added. "Look at the coronation celebrations. Why the carnival procession at the beginning of the year was at least two kilometres long!"

"Yes, did you decipher all the allegories?" Breteuil asked. "They all seemed to portray drunkenness."

"A Russian trait, perhaps," Mercy said.

"And then there was that poem," Breteuil said, warming to the subject. "Forty carriages, one for each verse with music. And a moral at the end. Most didactic."

The conversation threatened to disintegrate. Buckingham noted that the wine was being drunk quickly.

"Gentlemen," he called, "let us return to our topic. On what are we in agreement?"

"That the Empress is beset on all sides by potential enemies who would wish to restore Ivan or her son to the throne," Solms said.

"She may be well-intentioned but she is no statesman," Mercy said. "And certainly not on an international parquet."

"She will wrought her own demise. Her ambition and her ... desires know no bounds," Breteuil said.

The three men turned expectantly to the Earl. "And you, Buckingham? What do you think?" Breteuil asked.

"I think she does not sit a throne as well as she does a horse."

Breteuil laughed appreciatively. "Well said, Buckingham! Well said! The English may not have much but they do have wit."

"If an opinion can acquire authority by unanimous consent," Count Solms said dryly, "then it is certain that the reign of the Empress Catherine II, like that of the Emperor her husband, will make only a brief appearance in the history of the world."

PART TWO
1764 -1767

Chapter Eleven

General Pyotr Panin watched as his older brother approached. Nikita Panin walked, as always, with small steps, as if to the music of a minuet. A slow minuet. He would never have made a soldier and was certainly more suited to the soft life of a courtier. The General squared his shoulders and marched towards his brother.

"Nikita! Good to see you!" he said, briskly shaking his hand. "But to what do I owe the pleasure of your invitation? Or is it more in the nature of a summons?"

"It is indeed state business. But you will stay for dinner afterwards, I hope." Nikita said motioning his brother to take a seat.

The General was immediately mollified. His brother employed the best chef in St Petersburg and dinner would be a culinary experience with excellent wine from French vineyards. And there would be good company too. Nikita always had an eye for beautiful women.

"Well, best to proceed then," the General began. "Outline the problem and we will consider the best means of attack."

"It is not so much a problem as a potential problem," Nikita began in his slow drawl.

"Ah, pre-emptive action called for then?"

"Yes, that might be what is needed," Nikita conceded. "We have a ... person, a danger to the security of the state."

"Well, arrest him and lock him up! Try him for treason and have him sent off to Siberia!" The General had no patience for so-called diplomatic approaches to problems. Nikita would beat about the bush so long that the birds escaped for others to bag.

"Yes, well he has been locked up most of his life. Every

precaution has been taken to keep his identity a secret but it seems there are enough who know," Nikita said gloomily. "And would have him free," he added, looking directly at his brother.

The General suddenly understood what his brother was referring to. The unfortunate Ivan VI, baby Emperor, had been snatched from his cradle over twenty years ago and locked up in isolation in a fortress on the cold White Sea. As a prisoner, he was given no name but the secret leaked out through the massive walls of the bastion. Some years ago, Empress Elizabeth, failing in health and beset by fears, ordered him removed in the greatest secrecy to the mighty fortress on Lake Ladoga, some fifty versts along the River Neva from St Petersburg. Some said the Empress wished him near at hand since she intended to make him her heir instead of her drunken nephew Peter. But Peter had assumed the throne on her death, only to have his wife take it from him and banish *him* to Ladoga. He had died before he even got there, which was just as well, the General thought. A depot of deposed tsars would have been an embarrassment.

He turned to his brother. "You talk of – "

"We need no names," Nikita Panin interrupted quickly. "We talk of the Nameless Prisoner."

"What is the problem?" the General asked impatiently. "He is well guarded. No-one has access to him but two officers of the guard and they may not tell him where he is, or indeed who he is, under penalty of death. And the Empress's orders have been carried out."

Catherine had made a secret visit to the Nameless Prisoner shortly before her coronation. She had complained to the Panin brothers that the Prisoner had been filthy and underfed. "Just because he is witless and stutters incomprehensibly does not mean he has to be treated worse than a dog on the street," Catherine had said. But while she had written careful instructions on what the Nameless Prisoner was to be fed, she had also ordered that in any attempt to free him his guards should kill him instantly rather than try to fight off the attackers.

The General knew that conditions in the prison were disastrous. The Prisoner was often chained to the wall and baited by his two guards, Captain Vlassiev and Lieutenant Chekin, who were mostly drunk from boredom. They had submitted requests to be re-assigned, complaining that they had had no time off in six years and that they were not even allowed to communicate with their own families. "We are as much prisoners, as he whom we guard," they had complained in a poorly written letter, "but have done nothing to deserve it."

"The conditions of his imprisonment cannot be so harsh," Nikita Panin said. "He lives. And according to all reports, he is healthy enough. And may indeed live for another two decades. But is this in Russia's interests?"

"What do you imply?" The General preferred plain speaking. "Would you have his life shortened?"

After Catherine's coronation, new instructions had reached Ladoga. The Prisoner was to be allowed no medical help of any kind, no matter how serious his symptoms. If he fell mortally ill, he was to be allowed a priest but not a doctor.

"You know well, brother," Nikita said, "that my loyalty lies with the Empress and after that her son Paul, my charge, who will be Emperor one day. That is, if Catherine does not name someone else her successor, like one of Orlov's brats. That would definitely open the way for those who support the Prisoner. There are many at court who have become more ... Russian. I will not have the throne stolen from the Grand Duke Paul!"

"Calm yourself, Nikita. Let us move to action. What would you have done?"

"The Prisoner has unfortunately not fallen ill. A natural death would have been the most politic solution," Nikita said. "All else is fraught with danger. Only his guards have licence to kill him."

The General considered. The officers may be drunk and uneducated but they followed commands to the letter. They could have secured their own freedom by poisoning the prisoner, or by staging an attack and killing the hapless captive. But they were stubborn in their duty.

"The guards will do nothing that they are not commanded to," the General said.

"Precisely," his brother answered. "But it *is* their command to kill the Prisoner *if* there is an attempt to free him."

"Yes, we know that – "

"We must engineer that attempt," Nikita said quietly.

The General had to admire his brother's astuteness. Perhaps there were skills to being a courtier. It was a simple plan and therein lay its strength. All that was needed was good military planning.

"Go on," the General said.

"You have in your staff a young sub-lieutenant of Ukrainian origin," Nikita continued. "His name is Vasily Mirovich. A discontent and a wastrel. He has petitioned the Senate and the Empress several times to have his family's lands restored to him. I had thought him one of those willing to stir discontent in Little Russia, which they still insist on calling Ukraine, so I have had him watched. And listened to. He has been heard to praise the 'old order' where he is convinced his own glory lies."

The General was puzzled. This did not seem to have anything to do with a simple plan. "I am impressed with the information you glean in your capacity as head of the Secret Chancery," he said, "but what has the drunken talk of a lowly officer to do with the matter?"

"I wish you to plant in him the seeds of a bright future, a future which can only come about with the restoration of the rightful Emperor. You will choose intelligent staff to influence him. It should not be too difficult. He already sees himself as belonging to the higher nobility, as his family did at one time. He will do anything for gold, for land, for a name. Let him be told what to dream. Let him be told how to realise his dream. Have him transferred to Ladoga. Give him a few supporters."

The General was surprised at his brother's sudden burst of commands. He had rarely heard him speak so fast or so determinedly. And the plan was beginning to make sense.

"Ah, Nikita, you are clever! Mirovich, like many young guardsmen, does indeed mutter of how the Empress showers gold on the Orlovs. He too can have gold showered on him from a grateful Emperor, freed from captivity. Your time at court has not been wasted. You have learned how to write a good drama. I will find the actors and direct the whole to its ... tragic end."

"Let it be speedy. The Empress will travel to the Baltic provinces in summer. It would be better if ... events happened when she is not in the capital. No suspicion must fall on her. I will have some anonymous threats against her written and distributed just as she is leaving. That way, the end of the story will be made believable. The audience will be expecting it."

"Perhaps you would have made a good military strategist after all, Nikita! It is a good plan. I will take care of the details. But come, I am of a mind to eat and drink well while I am here in the capital and I know you keep an excellent table. Who will be joining us?"

Chapter Twelve

Catherine was pleased with her journey through the Baltic provinces. She had been welcomed with due ceremony wherever she went: with cannon volleys and fireworks, masquerades and balls, odes and eulogies. The women had strewn flower petals in her path. She had been lodged in comfortable castles with no drafts. The German knights of Livonia, Estonia and Courland had proved to her that they ran their provinces efficiently. Well, *her* provinces. She must not let them think that they were in any way independent of the empire. She had even refused to speak publicly in German, ordering that all speeches be translated into Russian. She had promised to ratify the rights and privileges the German barons claimed had been given to them 200 hundred years ago although she had little idea, nor did anyone, of what these rights were. But peace in the provinces was more important than long drawn out wrangles over the crumbling old tomes which the barons proudly displayed. Any dispute could be settled quickly with armed force if necessary. For now, these German knights were of use to her. Russia could learn from them. She would keep them pliant. Prussia and Poland and even Sweden coveted Russia's strategic hold on the Baltic, with its valuable ports along the coastlines of the provinces. Catherine had been very impressed by the hydraulic dock at the mouth of the River Dvina. This would open up more lucrative trade routes to the West.

But a shadow of worry had been her constant companion during the three weeks of her visit. Count Panin had warned her not to be alarmed by any events she might hear of during her absence from St Petersburg. He had everything in control, he said, and it would all be to her benefit in the end. Catherine had to trust Panin but she could not forget that he had once been a supporter of her husband and was now her son's champion. Was he aiming to put Paul on the throne? And what about the imprisoned Ivan? Did he have supporters?

Anonymous letters had been found shortly before her departure for the Baltic and she had almost called off the journey. "The rightful heir will be restored to the throne. The German usurper will be overthrown. Long live Emperor Ivan!" Orlov had brought them to her and she had felt a shiver of fear.

"We will have them hunted down!" Orlov said. "I will go to Ladoga this very day and find out who has been there."

Count Panin said calmly, "It is best if we proceed as planned, as normally as possible. It will not do to show fear. There is no cause for alarm. It is as I have planned."

"What do you mean, Panin?" Orlov was indignant. "How can treason such as this be planned? Not only is there danger to the Empress's person but to all of Russia."

Panin turned to Catherine. "You are not in danger but you will be if the plan is not allowed to unfold. Go to the provinces. When you return, you will be more secure on your throne."

Talk of the throne made Catherine uneasy. "But I must know what is afoot! I must be informed."

"It is better that you are not," Panin said firmly. "My brother will be in your staff and will impart to you any news which I shall send to him."

Orlov paced up and down, not convinced. "I do not like it, Panin. The Empress is accused of being a German usurper and you are sending her to pay court to the German barons? This surely gives credence to the lies!"

"I do not go to pay court, Grigory," Catherine snapped. "I go to remind them that they are part of our empire and, as such, Russian subjects."

She had left St Petersburg with serious misgivings and only after Panin had whispered to her, "There will be no more anonymous letters because there will be no more pretender to the throne. You must not be here in the capital. You must be seen to be far removed from events which it is too late to stop now."

She accepted the ceremonial obeisance of the German barons and was gratified by their generous show of loyalty. The Duke of Courland, whom Catherine had brought back from his twenty-year banishment in Siberia, had coins struck in her image and thrown to the cheering crowds. But she was desperate to return to St Petersburg. She fretted at what could be happening in her absence. Never had she let the reins of power leave her hands. Why had Panin insisted on her trip to the Baltic? Why had she let herself be persuaded? Were there factions plotting to take the throne in her absence? She herself knew how easy it was to effect a coup, as long as one had the Guards on one's side. Was Orlov loyal to her? She knew now that he was not faithful but would he betray her? Where was he? He had not accompanied her to the Baltic provinces. He and Panin had deemed it wiser to have him in St Petersburg to keep the Guards under control. And it would not have done to flaunt her lover officially in front of the German barons, so conservative in their Protestantism.

In the third week of her stay, on reaching Riga, she sent a letter by courier to Panin. "I will return to my capital as soon as possible. I am made uneasy by my absence and your silence. I cannot be 600 versts away from my duties."

Panin's reply came speedily. "It is of the utmost importance that you do not return to the capital at this point. All is going according to plan. It is a critical time. I will send a full report. Your Majesty must stay in Riga until further notice."

Catherine, shocked by the peremptory tone and mention of a plan she was not apprised of, was caught in indecision, a state she was not accustomed to. Whom should she trust? What was going on? How could she be sure it was to her advantage when she did not know what it was?

Chapter Thirteen

Lieutenant Mirovich paced restlessly in the darkening courtyard, drawing nervously on his pipe, its bowl lighting up like a small warning beacon. The summer evenings were long and night never really came, sunset melting into sunrise. It was not a good time to execute the plan but Lieutenant Ushakov said they must take their chance while the false Empress was absent from the capital. And now Ushakov was not here to advise him. Had he not been detailed by his superior officers to accompany a money transport to Smolensk, the matter would already have been resolved and he, Mirovich, would be basking in the favour, gratitude and wealth of the new and rightful Emperor Ivan VI.

Lieutenant Ushakov had been a godsend. He had befriended Mirovich after his transfer to Lake Ladoga, confirmed Mirovich's suspicions that the Emperor was being held prisoner in the fortress which they were guarding and shared Mirovich's horror at the fate of the poor Nameless Prisoner. They had both gone to the Church of the Mother of God in the nearby town and had sworn their loyalty to one another and to the rightful Emperor. They took an oath never to divulge their plan to any other, to carry it out two to three days after the Empress's departure for the Baltic and no longer than eight days after. This was Ushakov's idea. "We can get the Emperor to the throne more easily if the German usurper is not there." Ushakov was good at planning and Mirovich was glad to have him. The plan was that when Mirovich was on guard duty, Ushakov would arrive by boat and call out that he was a courier from the Empress. Mirovich would take the order, read it out to his unit, and then order his men to arrest the commander and chain him up. The unit would then free the Nameless Prisoner, bring him to the boat and they would sail to St Petersburg to proclaim

Ivan Emperor of all Russia. It was a simple plan. Mirovich had worked long on the manifesto which Ivan would read out in the capital. It was persuasive, convincing, patriotic. The people would bow in obeisance to their new and rightful Emperor. The days of the German usurper were numbered.

Ushakov had promised to return swiftly from Smolensk, and Mirovich waited impatiently. The time for the Empress's departure for the Baltic provinces was fast approaching and there was still no sign of Ushakov. There would not be another opportunity of the throne being left vacant in the foreseeable future. Mirovich was fraught with anxiety by the time the Smolensk contingent returned – without Ushakov. In his panic, Mirovich could barely take in what the soldiers of the transport guard, related. Ushakov had taken very ill on the way and had collapsed in a fevered state. He ordered the transport to continue without him and pick him up on the way back, but on the return journey from Smolensk, the soldiers could not find Lieutenant Ushakov. They asked at every village. "Even those not directly on our route," they assured Mirovich. There were reports at some villages that Ushakov had returned to St Petersburg. Eventually, at the village where Ushakov had first taken ill, they were told that a carriage had been found floating in the river and soon after a body had been washed ashore, which the villagers had buried. The soldiers recognised the hat and dagger they were shown as those of Lieutenant Ushakov.

Mirovich lamented the fate of the good Lieutenant but more his own plight of having to undertake the attack alone. He had sworn an oath to the Virgin Mother to involve no-one else in the plot. Now that Ushakov was dead, he could not break his oath. They had sworn it together. No-one but Ushakov could release him from it.

And so here he was in the courtyard, some two weeks after the Empress had left the capital for the Baltic provinces. Mirovich had already broken part of the oath, which stipulated action no later than eight days after the false Empress's departure. But he had waited for Ushakov and then it had taken him some time to arrange a change of guard duty. Now that he was the officer in charge, he had to seize the chance. That evening he had spoken to each of his soldiers individually.

"The Emperor Ivan is imprisoned here. He is innocent and suffers. It is our duty to help him. Will you help?"

The soldiers had muttered in response, "We don't do anything but follow orders."

Mirovich finished his pipe and emptied the ashes. Despite the season, he felt cold in the evening air. He would have a brazier lit in the officers' room and rest for a few hours. Nothing could be done until the fortress was asleep.

He only realised he must have fallen asleep himself when he was suddenly wakened by one of the guards. "Reporting, sir. The commandant ordered the gate to be raised to allow a boat in and again some ten minutes later to let the boat out."

Ah, Mirovich thought, his heart beating loudly, the commandant has sent a courier to St Petersburg. He suspects something. I must act. In panic, Mirovich grabbed his coat and sword and rushed to the guardroom. "Get your weapons!" he said. "Load them. At the ready!"

He then ordered a detachment of men to guard the gates. No-one was to enter or leave the castle without his express command.

The commandant rushed out in his nightshirt. "What is going on here? Who has given the command to load weapons?"

Mirovich turned to face him in the flickering light of the torches "I, Captain Vasily Mirovich, have," he said. "You are keeping an innocent Emperor prisoner. This is treason." Before the commandant had time to answer,

Mirovich rushed at him and struck him a heavy blow on the head with the butt of his musket, blood spurting as the commandant fell to the ground. Mirovich pointed to two soldiers. "Lock him in the officers' room!" He then ran towards the garrison tower ordering his soldiers to follow him but a salvo of shots from the tower embrasures suddenly stopped them. Several of the soldiers retreated some fifty paces.

"Who goes there?" a voice rang out.

"We are the Emperor's loyal subjects!" Mirovich shouted back. "We would have you hand him over."

His words were greeted by another burst of shots.

"Fire!" Mirovich commanded his remaining men but they also retreated, muttering. "Show us the command which requires us to shoot on our fellow soldiers. We would see it in writing."

Mirovich had no choice but to follow them. He could not storm the tower alone. Ushakov would have known what to do. He, Mirovich, was not a worthy saviour of an Emperor. A sudden mist began rolling in from the river, turning the men into ghostly figures. Mirovich took the manifesto from his pocket and, holding the paper close to his face, began reading, trying to keep his voice and hands steady.

"Peter III had scarcely taken the throne when he was poisoned by his scheming ambitious spendthrift of a spouse. The German usurper is at this moment selling as much of Russia as she can to her accomplices the German Knights in the Baltic provinces. She does not intend to return to Russia but I, Ivan, the rightful Emperor of Russia, will save my land and its people. God will serve the false Empress the punishment she deserves at the Last Judgement. I, your rightful ruler – "

But the soldiers interrupted him with more muttering. "We understand nothing of that," they said. "Show us the written orders."

Meanwhile, the garrison command had opened fire again. Mirovich was enraged that his plan was falling apart. If only he had Ushakov to help.

"Stop!" he shouted at the garrison tower, "Or we will fire with cannon!"

His words were answered by another volley of shots. When the noise had subsided, the voice rang out once more in the night air. "Retreat or we will continue to fire. We will only stop when we see the commandant."

Mirovich ordered the cannons to be filled with powder. There was confusion in the mist. The key to the powder room could not be found until Mirovich remembered it must be on the ring of keys in his keeping as officer of the guard. While the soldiers were filling the cannon, Mirovich ordered one of his men to approach the tower with a white flag. "Tell the garrison officer that if he shoots once more, I will order the heavy cannon to be fired," Mirovich said.

The officer came back quickly. "There will be no more firing," he said.

"Ah," Mirovich sighed with relief, "they have seen reason. They too are loyal to the rightful Emperor."

Mirovich, followed by a few soldiers, rushed to the garrison tower and met no resistance at the gate. A lieutenant whom he did not recognise stood waiting for them.

"Take me to the Emperor at once!" Mirovich shouted.

"We have no Emperor, only an Empress!" the lieutenant answered sullenly.

Mirovich grabbed him by the collar and pushed him with his musket butt. "I will run you through if you do not take me to him!"

After only a few steps, the lieutenant stopped in front of a stout wooden door. The bars hung loose, unlocked.

"Open it!" Mirovich said as he pushed the lieutenant forward.

They stumbled into darkness. Mirovich sniffed at the

mustiness, like stale straw in a stable. But there was a sharper tang he could not identify. "Bring torches!" Mirovich called.

As soon as light was brought, Mirovich recoiled at the scene before him. A body, gashed horribly in several places, lay in a pool of blood. A young pale face gazed unseeing into the room. Mirovich sank to his knees beside the body, heedless of the blood which soaked through his breeches.

"You have killed the Emperor?" he cried. "What monsters are you?"

Mirovich lifted one of the hands, still warm he noticed, from the pool of blood and kissed it reverently. "My Emperor," he said. "I came too late. Forgive me."

The lieutenant, freed from Mirovich's grasp, straightened himself and said, "I, Lieutenant Chekin, and my fellow officer Captain Vlassiev here, have done our duty as commanded. We know of no Emperor. Our orders were to kill the Nameless Prisoner in the event of an attack. Any attack. This we have done, with a clear conscience."

Mirovich ignored him. He bent over the body. "They killed him as he slept," he muttered. "He has many wounds. His hands are run through. He must have tried to protect himself. He was slaughtered like a wild beast. What a miserable life he had and what a miserable end! My poor Emperor! And poor me! I am finished."

Mirovich quietly ordered his soldiers to take the body to the courtyard, the fortress wakened and a general march-by with full honours organised.

When everything was arranged to his satisfaction, Mirovich addressed the orderly lines of soldiers. Streaks of dawn light only served to make the mist more opaque. "Brothers," he said, "look on our Emperor Ivan. Now he is dead and we, his unfortunate subjects, remain. You are innocent. I take full responsibility. You knew not what I did. I will be the one to suffer."

He then went through the rows of soldiers, kissing each in turn. He had reached the fourth row when the commandant appeared, fastening his uniform buttons with one hand and holding a cloth to his bleeding head with the other. "Seize that man! Arrest him!"

Mirovich offered no resistance as a guard of confused soldiers led him away.

Chapter Fourteen

General Panin had received instructions from his brother to keep a close watch on the Empress. On no condition was she to rush back to the capital. He, Nikita, would send word when the time was right for Her Majesty's return.

When word did come, it was not to recall the Empress but to deliver the dramatic news of Ivan's death. Nikita had deemed it wiser to send a courier to his brother rather than directly to the Empress. "You can then inform Her Majesty and ensure that she acts as we would wish. She must do nothing untoward," he had written.

General Panin was not sure what behaviour he was meant to encourage or discourage, but he approached the Empress with military efficiency.

She had listened to him carefully, her features composed but her forehead lined with a frown, as he delivered the news briefly and concisely.

When he had finished, the Empress sank into an armchair. "Oh, I have been in constant fear of something dreadful," she sighed, "but this is indeed news for which I am grateful."

This was not the reaction General Panin had expected and so he was at a loss for words.

But the Empress was not. Her face brightened as she said, "God's ways are indeed wondrous. Providence has shown me her mercy and brought light to this dark and dangerous corner of my life!" She rose to her feet, startling the General. "I must return to St Petersburg at once!"

The General was back on safe ground. He knew his brother did not want the Empress to return to St Petersburg – although he did not know why.

"Your Majesty, my brother recommends prudence. No haste must be shown. He advises you to continue as planned, to finish your visit here in the provinces. Haste might show fear, or indeed too much joy, or – "

"But those who have failed to put the usurper Ivan on my throne may now turn to even more desperate measures! I must be there! My son may be in danger!" The General noted with concern that the relief Catherine had shown on hearing the news of Ivan's death had now turned to agitation. "I cannot linger here in Riga," she continued, "while St Petersburg is in danger. Indeed while my whole Empire is in danger!"

"There are no conspirators, Your Majesty," the General said calmly. "The Captain said he acted alone. His was the work of a deranged mind and the officers followed instructions to the letter. Their loyalty was to you."

They did no more than seize the chance to gain their own freedom, he thought. And they were thorough, fortunately.

"The danger, indeed if there had been any, is past, Your Majesty," the General added soothingly.

But he wondered if that were true. What was his brother's part in the whole plot? The ruse of Lieutenant Ushakov had worked well, the gullible Mirovich easy to convince. It was unfortunate that Ushakov had fallen ill and in his delirium driven himself into the river. Or had he? Perhaps that had all been a ruse too – assigning him to the Smolensk transport, effecting his illness, drowning him in the river – to eliminate Ushakov. General Panin felt uneasy. Why should his brother go to such lengths? Did he intend to put the child Paul on the throne? Was this why he was eager to keep Catherine in the provinces? The General looked around. Did he intend the Empress harm? Or even himself, his own brother, as complicit in the plot?

"The danger is from what has been left behind," the Empress interrupted his thoughts. "These papers, which you say were found on the traitor's person, are full of lies and calumny. Were they to reach the streets of St Petersburg, they may find willing ears."

The General was of the same opinion. Mirovich's so-called manifesto accused the Empress of being an ambitious and ruthless schemer, who had poisoned her innocent husband, the rightful Emperor. It accused her of shipping 25 million roubles worth of gold and silver of the state's money to her relatives in Germany to safekeep for her. It accused her of using her trip to the Baltic provinces as a ruse to marry Poniatovsky and hand him Russia on a plate. It accused her of many absurd things, but all of them containing a grain of truth.

"You must not fear, Your Majesty," Panin said. "My brother will manage what has to be managed in your absence."

"I am not afraid," Catherine continued, her sudden agitation replaced with calm composure, "and I will not exercise undue haste but I will return to St Petersburg five days hence, not a day later. Thus we lend the matter attention but not excited attention, which can indeed be a sign of weakness."

"That is well thought, Your Majesty. I am sure my brother will keep you informed of all developments in close detail." The General had tried to deliver his words with a conviction he did not feel. He was more at home on a battlefield. "But you will attend the soirée this evening in your honour?"

"Yes, I will not disappoint the Governor. He has done so much for us."

General Panin did not like the Governor mainly because he was not Russian. He was an Irishman who had started out as a soldier of fortune and now lorded it over the provinces as Catherine's Governor General. Well, at least there was no danger of him wheedling himself into her bed. He was in his sixties. Thoughts of bed reminded Panin of another guest. There was more danger for the Empress from that quarter especially as Orlov remained in the capital.

"Have you met the Italian, Your Majesty? Giacomo Casanova?"

"Yes, and I do not know why ladies are said to fight to share his bed. He is heavy of feature and although his manners may be light, they are false. And he wears too much powder." Catherine rose. General Panin was about to bow his leave when she added,

"You know, he was trying to persuade me to start a state lottery. Apparently, the French have adopted his scheme but the sensible English will not. I told him I was contemplating a ban on gambling not a way of encouraging it. Please ask theGovernor to prevent him from joining any card table I may be engaged in tonight."

General Panin bowed his leave, satisfied that the Empress would not act in panic. In fact, he was puzzled by her composure. Could she have been complicit with his brother Count Panin in the elimination of Ivan? Was her Baltic tour part of yet another ruse? The General shook himself impatiently. The longer one stayed at Court, the more ruses one saw lurking at every turn. It was time he returned to his troops.

Chapter Fifteen

Although she did not allow herself to show it, the Mirovich affair had shaken Catherine. Even before she left Riga, she had ordered the body of the Nameless Prisoner – she had forbidden the name Ivan to be used – to be buried at the Ladoga fortress, without ceremony but with Christian rites. His former guards, Chekin and Vlassiev, were to carry him to his final resting place. No-one else, apart from the priest, was to attend. His grave was to be left unmarked.

Catherine's relief at the removal of a pretender to the throne – and one with a rightful claim – was quickly dispelled by what the aftermath brought. Following Mirovich's interrogation, the members of the investigation committee declared themselves satisfied that he had acted alone and out of misguided idealism. This should have been welcome news but Catherine still suspected a plot and felt that not enough had been done to uncover it. Mirovich was to be judged by the Upper Court, which duly sat in session for almost a week, and then, astonishingly in Catherine's eyes, had requested her permission to decide Mirovich's fate by majority vote rather than the unanimous vote stipulated. Catherine was alarmed. There were obviously members of the Upper Court who did not find Mirovich guilty of a treasonous plot to take her throne from her. They were probably supporters of Ivan. But, she reminded herself, he was dead and she was alive and as such, she had the definite advantage.

Catherine had personally selected the Upper Court members, all forty-eight of them, both dignitaries and clerics, and had included Prince Vyazemsky. He would be her eyes and ears, reporting Court proceedings to her and, through him, she would instruct the Court.

"It is not the question of guilt which divides the Senate," the Prince explained, "but rather the sentence."

Catherine had instructed the Prince to let the Court know that there was only one sentence possible for a traitor. No mercy could be shown to enemies of the Empire. "Mirovich comports himself well and takes full responsibility for endeavouring to restore the 'rightful' Emperor to the throne – I only quote his words, Your Majesty – but some members of the Court argue that he has not killed anyone, nor indeed harmed Your Majesty, and therefore does not deserve the death penalty."

Catherine was furious. "Are intentions only criminal if they succeed? Are traitors who fail in their attempts innocent?" She knew, however, that she would have to acquiesce openly to the Court's requests on the voting issue. She could not enter into open conflict with them. Not yet. She needed justification, and she would find it. Meanwhile, she would continue to let her wishes be known through Prince Vyazemsky.

"Remind the esteemed members of the Upper Court," she told him, "that I hold each of them personally responsible for the safety of the Empire."

However, the Upper Court sessions dragged on despite Catherine's discreet but clear instructions. Two months after the death of the Nameless Prisoner, Mirovich had still not been sentenced. The Court sent back more questions than answers. Catherine's nights were made restless by anxiety, her days blurred by lack of concentration.

"Perhaps the only way to expedite the matter," Prince Vyazemsky said, "is to use more persuasive measures. Mirovich's composure cannot be shaken and he has added nothing to his statements. He gains in sympathy."

"Torture will only prolong the matter even more," Catherine answered impatiently. "If pain forces him to name accomplices, fictional or otherwise, we will be bound to find them and try them also. I wish the matter resolved as soon as possible. It already awakens too much interest."

"What do you suggest, Your Majesty?" The Prince's

tone was a little too sharp, Catherine thought. She feared that the Upper Court now viewed her compliance as weakness. There may be plots and conspiracies hatching in their midst. She must put an end to it.

"Let it be known," she instructed Prince Vyazemsky firmly, "that if the members of the Court do not overcome their differences and reach a decision forthwith, I will disband the Court. Let them know that their Empress and her people have waited too long. They know what justice, and the Empress of Russia, demands."

At last, more than two months after the assassination of the imprisoned Ivan, the sentence was delivered. Mirovich was to be beheaded and his body left on display until the evening when it was to be burned along with the gallows. Catherine sighed her relief. She skimmed over the list of punishments – the corporals who had obeyed Mirovich's order to fire on the garrison were sentenced to run the gauntlet of a 1000 soldiers ten times each and then to be imprisoned for life, if they survived. The other thirty or so soldiers under Mirovich's command at the time were also sentenced to various gauntlets, banishments or de-ranking. Catherine did not concern herself with the details. She was only interested in Mirovich.

She signed his death sentence firmly with a flourish, spattering the ink.

A few days after Mirovich had been beheaded – and she had heard that he had faced his fate calmly and with dignity and fortitude – the dreams began. Mostly, he appeared benevolently in a white robe and asked her in a quiet and terribly sad voice, why she had not allowed him to live. With Ivan gone, the apparition said, it would have been his duty to serve her loyally. Sometimes he appeared without his head and Catherine would wake gasping for air.

The matter of the Nameless Prisoner's two guards also caused her sleepless nights. What if they talked?

"And what would they say?" Count Panin asked. "Only that they followed orders."

"Yes, but that is the point. Whose orders? They could say that I ordered the attack on the prisoner!" Catherine said.

"The two guards were made to witness Mirovich's end at close quarters. They will not talk. They have each been given 10,000 roubles and promotion. They know they are fortunate to keep their lives. And we must allow that." Count Panin was uncharacteristically firm. "We cannot afford any more imprisonments or executions. There have already been critical voices raised. This was the first execution in Russia in twenty-two years. We must not make a habit of it."

"But – " Catherine began.

"With respect, Your Majesty, it must be forgotten. Let us move on to other matters, matters which will benefit you and your empire."

Catherine thought about Panin's words. Yes, it was her calling to look after her empire and this she had done by dealing severely with traitors. But now she must once more create reality. She would create the Empire she had always envisaged, an Empire whose subjects would not wish to replace their benevolent ruler, an Empire ruled by reason and just laws.

She would start with the laws, for therein lay the basis of all politically healthy states. It had been one of Peter the Great's ambitious projects to codify Russian law. Under Elizabeth there had been chaotic attempts to restore Petrine law to Russia – whatever that was. No-one seemed to know. She was brought ancient manuscripts, parchments and disintegrating tomes. When she asked to see the current laws, they brought her the same.

In a flash of inspiration, she realised what her task would be. It would be a worthy endeavour which would assure her name in history. She would create a new code of laws, one which would not only benefit her own Empire but serve as an example for others to follow. Frederick of Prussia had published his political maxims. She would do better. Diderot had written in his *Encyclopédie* that a sovereign must listen to the people through their representatives. Frederick had not done this but she, Catherine of Russia, would call the people's representatives to her, to St Petersburg, and she would listen to them and together they would create a great code of laws by which Russia would be governed. It would be a document to dazzle Europe.

Fired by an enthusiasm she had long been lacking, she compiled a list of possible deputies and was struck by its diversity. It was like weaving the colours of her silk knots. There would be deputies from the nobility, the church, the towns, the peasants, from the Cossacks and the Tartars, from the Kalmucks, Kazakhs, Bashkirs, Mordvins, even from the Chuvash, Cheremis, Votyaks and the distant Yakuts. As she read her list, which she did often and could now recite like one of the litanies she murmured in church, she was seized by a longing to see these peoples of whom she knew nothing but whom she ruled and was responsible for. She had another inspiration for her Great Project. She would not only call the deputies to her but before doing so, she herself would visit the far reaches of her Empire. She would see her Empire, and her Empire would see her.

Meanwhile, she would prepare instructions for them, a document of guidance for what she now thought of as the Great Assembly. This would be the basis on which they would all work together, subjects and sovereign alike. It would be *the* Legislative Commission, the greatest of all her commissions.

She began rising an hour earlier at 4.am. and, fortified with her usual black coffee, she set to work. She would use Montesquieu's *L'Esprit des Lois*, which, published in 1748, was most modern and would provide the foundation for her own work for the Commission. She wrote till her hands ached and the letters blurred before her eyes and her throat was dry from the candles. She was constantly running out of ink and her quills blunted. Her work also provided escape from her troubled sleep, from her dreadful nightmares, from the absence of Orlov's limbs around her own.

Mindful once more of the need for theatre in the presentation of her sovereignty, she turned her attention to opulent robes, ordered new diamonds and commissioned an opera from Baldassare Galuppi, recently poached from Venice at great cost, for her name day in November. His *Dido Abandoned* had premiered in Modena some two decades previously. The drama of the Carthaginian queen being left abandoned by her lovers might shock her subjects, and particularly Count Orlov, into understanding their own sovereign's loneliness. As it was, Galuppi, who had arrived in St Petersburg in September, was unable to stage the opera by November. While he praised the high standard of the court choir, he declared the orchestra not up to his standards and the hundreds of extras he required demanded elaborate staging. Instead, on Catherine's name day, a cantata entitled *Virtue Emancipated* was performed and received three encores. Catherine, grateful for the allegory, presented Galuppi with a diamond encrusted snuff box. Music, which she could neither play nor sing, soothed her and she had Galuppi arrange chamber concerts in her own ante-chamber every Wednesday afternoon.

Gradually, the horrors of the Mirovich affair began to fade and she looked forward to the new year. She would travel through her Empire and show her subjects that she cared for them. She must allow herself no idle moment for if she did, she would wonder who cared for her, or rather why Grigory Orlov no longer did.

Chapter Sixteen

"But where are you week after week, Grigory? You leave me alone even in times of trouble? Have I not shown you great favour? I, Your Empress, have raised you to the highest rank in the empire!"

Count Orlov had come to Court that evening with every intention of staying in his chambers for Catherine to visit him. He knew he had neglected her. But she had shown him little attention at supper and had made him wait a long hour before she appeared from the secret staircase. Noting that she had changed into her night robes, he rose to his feet with a heavy heart. How could he make her feel desired when he no longer desired her? Respected her, yes. Loyal to her, yes. But desire? When had it fled? It was normal for a man to wish to enjoy varied fare. The same dish day after day blunted the appetite. But it was more than that. Or less. He just did not desire her body anymore. The lithesome Catherine, who loved to ride out with the wind in her hair, was gone. Her body had become heavy and although her eyes could shine and her smile still charm, her face was lined with worry. Her hair, once glossy chestnut, was dull and grey with too much powder. And the longer she was Empress, the less of a woman she became. What woman would order the execution of a Captain of the Guard? She had not even consulted Grigory, which was an insult to his rank as a Guard officer and to his position as the man at her side. Women should be ... womanly and allow a man to be a man.

Grigory made an effort. He came to her and lifted one of her hands in both of his. He kissed it, noticing the ink stains.

"I am your grateful and loyal servant, Catherine, and always will be." He was pleased that these were honest words he offered her.

"But you are with me so seldom," she said.

"But you have so many affairs of state to attend to. You are forever busy." He wanted to add, "And life is dull with you. There is no light-heartedness any more." Instead, he said cheerfully, "But I like your plan to travel your Empire. I will come with you. Where shall we go first?"

"I have thought of the Volga," she said, her voice brighter. "It is a great waterway and leads to the far reaches of my Empire. There are many great cities on its banks: Yaroslavl, Kostroma, Nizhny Novgorod. I will visit Kazan and Simbirsk and assure the Tatars and other peoples of my loyalty to them."

Grigory Orlov indeed thought a boat trip along the Volga would be a fine adventure. He had never been to Kazan although his brother Ivan had lands there, by all accounts fertile and rich. Ivan also reported on the exotic beauty of the local women, especially those, he said, kept under strict guard by their Muslim fathers and brothers. Grigory relished the thought of such a challenge. His life had become too easy. Women threw themselves at him, desperate to sleep with the Empress's lover. He had riches and estates in abundance, power and influence to do as he pleased. What he needed was a war. He longed to be out on a battlefield again, chaotic, dangerous, full of blood and bravery. But Catherine was intent on peace. Until the Turks tried her patience too much, a trip along the Volga would be a distraction.

"I will oversee the planning," he said eagerly. "We shall need galleys. New ones must be built. I will go to Tver at once to consult with the shipbuilders. I am pleased you can be torn away from your papers and projects."

"I have much to do and would gladly not have to do it," Catherine sighed. "But it is my duty."

"It is also your duty to please your subjects," Grigory said quickly. "And to bestow on them the great privilege of seeing you. This is important. You have, if I may say so, neglected the spectacle of your sovereignty. You cannot hide in your writing room. You must blind the people with your splendour. You must make them happy. You must dispel the dark clouds of rumour and uncertainty." Grigory was surprised by his own enthusiasm. Catherine as Empress was still a worthy task, one which he enjoyed shaping.

"Yes, perhaps I have been too much engaged in my writing," Catherine said thoughtfully. "My people have not seen me. What spectacle do you suggest?"

It took Orlov a moment before he realised she was talking of something in addition to the Volga trip. He thought swiftly. They needed something light but spectacular, something that would entertain rather than edify like the operas and plays he had to endure, or rather escaped from enduring.

"What about a carousel like Empress Elizabeth once had. You remember?"

Orlov had taken part in these trials of horsemanship and fighting skills with great enthusiasm. A huge oval had been constructed in front of the palace with tiered seating for the spectators. There were four quadrilles, each consisting of four knights and two ladies. Each quadrille represented a nation – Slavonian, Indian, Turkish and Roman, as Orlov recalled. Everyone was dressed most colourfully in the costumes of their quadrille and the teams had been led into the arena by musicians playing the relevant music. It was a joyful cacophony. Catherine had not been in Orlov's quadrille but with the Indian team, which had been equipped with bows and arrows. Orlov remembered how well she had acquitted herself, rarely missing a target from her galloping horse. Orlov himself had won the prize for the best horsemanship, a diamond-encrusted sword.

"A tournament? What a good idea, Grigory!" Catherine's face brightened. "We shall indeed have a

Grand Carousel. The Court must have something to look forward to over the long winter and the people must see that all is well. There must still be costumes in the palace. And we will have Rinaldi design a new oval. We can rehearse while the weather still holds so that all will be ready for summer."

As she turned to Orlov, he read open desire in her face. "And you shall have a new costume with as many diamonds as you wish. Your quadrille should be Persia and you should dress as a sheikh."

And the ladies as harem girls, Orlov thought. How exciting. If he closed his eyes and concentrated on Persian costumes for some of the ladies of the court, he might be able to satisfy Catherine's desire convincingly. Slowly he reached for her robe.

Chapter Seventeen

Catherine knew Nikita Panin was right. It could not go on like this.

"You are the Empress. You are a beautiful woman. You may choose any man you wish to bestow your favours on. Perhaps Count Orlov is, shall we say, less than grateful for your benevolence?"

Yes, but it was Grigory she wanted even if he did not want her. Or perhaps she wanted him because he did not grovel at her feet. Or because he was sought after by so many others and had the bravado to take them. She now knew of the mistresses he kept in St Petersburg and in Moscow and at every palace and estate she had bestowed on him. And she had given him many. His appetites were huge. No one woman would be sufficient for him, especially one who had to run an Empire.

Orlov had been caught in bed with his most recent conquest by her husband. Senator Muraviev was now intent on divorcing his wife. To avoid a very public scandal or indeed the risk of Madame Muraviev gaining a permanent place in Orlov's retinue, Catherine had invited the Senator to a discreet supper to persuade him that divorce should be avoided at all costs. He had been intractable.

"I will not be made a laughing stock of," he said. "And I do not wish an adulterous wife. She shall be left without a penny. And must find other beds to lie in. But it won't be mine."

Catherine had praised him, soothed him, flattered him, appealed to his Christian forgiveness but to no avail.

"Your wife undoubtedly loves you. It was but a moment of distraction, with no meaning." Catherine indeed hoped this was the case.

"Perhaps you need to leave the capital for a few months?" she suggested.

"Why? Where should I go? She should leave, not I," the senator retorted.

"The crown has some beautiful estates in Livonia," Catherine said gently. "Large estates. Some ten thousand serfs. With good hunting. And woodland walks for your wife. A married couple could find happiness there."

The senator had eventually succumbed to the bribe, agreeing to take both his unfaithful wife and the deeds for an even larger estate in Livonia.

"But Count Orlov's loyalty to me and that of his brothers is unswerving," Catherine now reminded Panin.

"I do not talk of politics, Your Majesty, but of matters human. In these you are – " Panin paused.

"Yes?" Catherine said impatiently.

"Neglected," Panin said quietly.

There had been a time when Nikita Panin had courted Catherine and occasionally desire for her flared up again. But Catherine knew he was now passionately in love with Countess Stroganova, the daughter of Vorontsov, the ex-chancellor and once Catherine's enemy. The Countess was indeed a beauty, with accomplished manners and lively wit but she was married, unhappily. Catherine was very fond of her husband, Count Stroganov, not least because of his fine library of some ten thousand volumes. He had broached the idea of an Imperial Lending Library and was willing for his collections to provide the basis for it. While he offered books, Count Stroganov also asked Catherine to grant him a divorce from his wife as he wished to marry the formidable Princess Trubetskaya. Catherine refused to become involved, pointing out to all parties, including the lovesick Panin, that divorce was a purely ecclesiastical matter.

Catherine was indignant at Panin's remark on her being neglected. Was he trying to take his revenge because she would not grant the Stroganovs a divorce? But in her heart she knew Panin was right. Orlov did neglect her. They had not shared a bed for several weeks. She missed his strong body. She often lay in bed stroking the cushions. She left her diamonds on at night in case he came. He loved diamonds as much as she did and she had given him many. She kept gifts for him at the ready to show her gratitude when he came to her. But the gifts mounted as her disappointment grew.

"Sometimes," Panin was saying carefully, "men can take for granted what they know they have. Men like Count Orlov enjoy the hunt. They enjoy conquest. If there is no fight, they lose interest."

"You think the Count has lost interest?" Catherine asked sharply.

"No, of course not," Panin assured her hastily, "but perhaps his appetite must be whetted."

Although Catherine thought the conversation was encroaching on the intimate, she needed to know. She could handle state affairs better than any man but she had to learn how to handle a man, her man.

"Continue," she said to Panin while turning to pick up a book on the desk behind her.

"Men desire what other men have. Just as women desire what other women have. As is the case with Count Orlov." Panin's voice was as neutral as if he had been talking about accounts.

Catherine waited for him to continue but he remained silent. Without turning to face him, she asked,

"Are you saying I should be more like a man and take lovers?"

"Well, perhaps only one to start with," Panin's tone was now encouraging. "It would comfort Your Majesty and make Count Orlov take notice. He would be afraid of being replaced as your ... personal chamberlain. You would regain his ... attention."

Catherine thought, "Why, yes that is exactly right. Why did I not think of it? Why should I pine in lonely fidelity while he roams as he will?" Aloud she said briefly to Panin, "Continue. I am listening."

"There are many young officers of good physique and manner at court," Panin said smoothly. "Is there none who has caught your eye?" He could have been talking about new desserts, Catherine thought. Something to tempt my appetite.

Perhaps there was something to her taste, she considered carefully. She watched the young people in her retinue dance almost every evening. She herself joined in less and less although as a young princess she was a graceful and tireless dancer, spending hours practising her steps for the frequent balls the Empress Elizabeth held. Some of the young officers now reminded her of those carefree days on the dance floor, when she was not weighed down by the burden of state. She longed for that lightness again. One officer had indeed caught her attention. He was graceful in dance but strong in leg muscle. He reminded her rather of Poniatovsky but with a touch more Orlov. She knew his name. She had asked.

"The officer Visotzky? What do we know of him?"

"Oh, an excellent choice, Your Majesty," Panin said. "Shall I have him brought to the Chamberlain's rooms or your own?"

Catherine thought swiftly. She wished only to rekindle Orlov's interest not drive him away. Using the Chamberlain's rooms, his rooms, would make her dalliance too public. And too dangerous. Orlov might appear at any time and draw his sword at any man he found in his bed. With or without the Empress.

"If all is well, offer him hospitality in chambers nearby every night this week. If I have need of his ... services, I will have him summoned."

"He will consider it a great honour to serve Your Majesty in any way he can," Panin said as he bowed and bustled out of the room.

Catherine sat down at her desk. What have I done? she thought. Or what am I about to do? She glared at the heap of papers. Her preparations for the Legal Commission were proving more than she had anticipated. She was tired, tired of work, tired of responsibility. Too tired to frolic in bed with a man ten years her junior. But she was also tired of being what Panin rightly observed as "neglected". Perhaps she could have the young Visotzky soothe her into sleep with caresses as Orlov used to do. The young man danced well. Perhaps his hands would move as elegantly as his fine legs did.

Chapter Eighteen

After dinner the Earl of Buckingham had dismissed the servants so that he and his guest could talk freely. There was much to cover. Buckingham would be leaving Russia in a few days, handing over to his successor, George Macartney, a man some fifteen years his junior. Macartney was a lawyer from Ireland but had not practised much, preferring to spend time in Europe as a prelude to a public career in England and a seat in the House of Commons. During his travels he had befriended several sons of noble houses, connections which opened many doors for him, including the one that brought him to St Petersburg to replace Buckingham as ambassador.

Buckingham knew that his failure to secure a treaty of alliance with Great Britain had not sat well in London. England needed Russia as an ally against France and to protect its European interests, particularly its own king's Hanover, from territorial predators. More pressingly, Buckingham had also failed to wrest any trading concessions for British merchants who complained bitterly about the loss of revenues caused by Russian trade restrictions. Foreigners were forbidden to trade with anyone but Russians and could not transport their goods where they willed. At the allotted ports, heavy import duties awaited them. Trade through Russia with Persia, once allowed, was now prohibited. Foreign merchants were denied the right to purchase a house or shop, or even to take their meals in their own houses. They were obliged to lodge *en pension* with Russian citizens. Russian merchants were subjected to no such restrictions in England, being free to trade where and with whom they chose.

He doubted Macartney would succeed where he had failed. The age difference between them gave Macartney the physical advantage of youth, and Buckingham had to concede he cut a fine figure. Despite his youth and lack of noble pedigree, Macartney was suave in manners, confident in opinion and politely articulate in speech. There was a note of foreign-ness about him, Buckingham thought. Was it the narrower cut of his coat or the shorter cuffs? Had fashion in England changed so much in the two years that Buckingham had been away? Buckingham pulled his own coat closer, stretched his cuffs and concentrated on what Macartney was saying.

"Such a mind. Such admiration of our English institutions," Macartney was concluding. He had been talking with enthusiasm of his visits to the philosopher Voltaire. Absurd name. It was said to be an anagram of his real name. In Buckingham's opinion, one who could not publish under his own name should not be published at all. In any country.

"And yet even the Swiss have banned his works," Buckingham said, knowing he was being petty. "And refused him."

And they did have a point, he felt. It did not do to upset the established order of society by sending treatises out into the world. There were political channels, at least in Great Britain, to achieve change legitimately. Voltaire's pages and pamphlets fluttered around unrestrained, landing dangerously on unprepared soil.

"Your acquaintance with him will put you in good standing with the Empress," Buckingham said grudgingly. "She is forever quoting her philosopher of Ferney, as she calls him."

"I think the Empress and I will have many points of common interest, which I will turn to the advantage of our own nation's interests," Macartney commented.

Buckingham said rather coolly, "Despite my unflagging and persistent attempts, the affairs of England do not enjoy an elevated position on the Empress's list of priorities."

"Of course, you have done what you could, Lord Buckingham, but now you may safely pass the baton to me." Macartney smiled.

"Oh, I think you have taken over admirably, Mr Macartney," Buckingham said, trying to keep the bitterness he felt out of his voice. Macartney had not waited for the baton to be passed – he had seized it. His first audience with the Empress that morning had gone well. Macartney had dressed himself most ceremoniously and Buckingham could not help notice his muscular calves in their silk stockings. No doubt the Empress did too. She was known to have a weakness for a well-shaped leg. Buckingham's own legs were long and slim enough but lacked rounding.

After an eloquent speech on the respectful and amicable intentions of their sovereign George III, Macartney had added, "And please allow me to express my own particular satisfaction in having been chosen for so pleasing, so important an employment. By this means I shall have the happiness of proximate contemplation of those extraordinary accomplishments, those heroic virtues, which make you the delight of half the globe over which you reign and which render you the admiration of the other half."

Buckingham found Macartney's words too flowery and was surprised they had gone down so well with the bookish Empress, who had, contrary to her usual custom, asked the Chancellor to translate her reply into Russian immediately. Vorontsov, fragile in age at the best of times, was taken by surprise and it was left to Count Panin to deliver the Empress's words. "We value the sentiments of your sovereign and your own personal thoughts. We welcome you to our court." The alarming addition was "personal thoughts".

Macartney was definitely a diplomat for a lady's court and no doubt he had been instructed to use his charms to seduce the Empress into political compliance with England's aims. That had been Buckingham's brief too and he had offered the Empress an abundance of flattering compliments, for which she seemed to have a hungry appetite.

"The crux of the matter," Macartney was saying eagerly when Buckingham's attention caught up with him, "is that Russia can no longer be gazed at as a distant glimmering star, but as a great planet which has obtruded itself into our system, its place as yet undetermined, but whose motions affect those of every other orb."

Buckingham all but spluttered into his wine.

Oblivious to his companion's reaction, Macartney continued, "And thus it is of paramount importance that we, and no other nation, must affect an alliance and thus determine the path this new planet takes. It must not cross ours but rather be in our orbit."

For years the English had been trying to revive the commercial treaty with Russia which had expired in 1734. Sir Charles Williams had not succeeded under the Empress Elizabeth; Mr Keith had enjoyed the favour of Peter III but he had also failed. And now he, Buckingham, had failed with Catherine. She was obdurate, obstinate, obsessive in her refusal to enter into any exclusive agreement with any one power. Why, she had even said to him over a game of piquet, "Freedom from alliances will give me the freedom to be the arbitrator of Europe." Much as he admired her intelligence and her commitment to her sovereign duties, Buckingham perceived her ambition as somewhat arrogant in light of the fact that Russia had scarcely been five decades out of its barbaric state. In fact, just fifty years ago, Peter the Great had banned his courtiers from wearing kaftans and had personally cut off their flowing beards.

"It is a difficult task, Macartney," Buckingham said, "and I do not envy you, but your best hope lies in Count Panin. He would wish a northern alliance with England and Denmark, maybe Poland too. And he would have Prussia on his side. But he would wish England to finance the anti-French party in Sweden, a costly venture. And then there is the question of Turkey."

Buckingham suddenly felt tired. Let Macartney find out for himself the stumbling blocks to a treaty with Russia. For his part, he had had enough of all-powerful sovereigns and looked forward to a return to a sovereignty limited by a parliamentary system, which gave more weight to sound arguments than to well-shaped calves or skill at card games.

"But can one not approach the Empress directly? Would that not be more efficacious? I have found that most women are susceptible to ... masculine influence?" Macartney asked as he filled his wine glass.

"You will find the Empress stubborn in her own ideas," Buckingham answered. "She will not yield. And she is very capable in matters of government, without doubt the most capable at court, more so than Panin even, who is the most capable of those who serve her. But the other problem is that she is always occupied, too busy to see anyone. Panin has access to her, and our interests are best represented by him."

In Buckingham's opinion, Catherine had too many projects and plans. She was hampered by her own ambition. One moment her attention was given to tobacco planting, the next to more ships for the navy, then developing trade with Spain and Portugal, then she concerned herself with the quality of silk and lace production and then with porcelain, and at the same time she was rewriting all the laws of the country. And planning a Grand Tour to all her subjects.

"You will find," Buckingham continued, "that she enjoys company in her leisure hours and this may be the best time to gain her attention. She is an enthusiastic card-player and you will no doubt receive invitations to opera and theatre performances." Buckingham had been impressed by the court theatre in the Winter Palace, which seated some 600 spectators, but found the Russian taste in word and music ponderous. Perhaps the new Italian composer would liven the stage. "But do not expect banquets. No business can be done there. She keeps a frugal table even if there is an abundance of gold and silver plates. No-one of importance comes. But if you can dance well, you will catch her attention."

Buckingham had heard at court that Catherine had once been a most elegant dancer. She moved well, he noted, when she did dance which was not often unless Orlov pulled her unceremoniously from her chair, but she lacked the lightness of the younger ladies. In her rich brocades and sparkling diamonds, she was like a magnificent ship whose abundant sails failed to catch the wind.

"And she is very fond of fireworks," Buckingham added, desperate to avoid any indiscretion of opinion which Macartney might include in his dispatches to London. "The spectacles often have themes and are most impressive. Allegory is combined with pyrotechnics to great effect. In one I remember well a goddess fired thunderbolts while in her other hand snakes of white flames squirmed on Medusa's head. Then as the figures burned, others appeared, pulled by some invisible mechanical traction and the next scene began. It was most remarkable." Buckingham thought he had perhaps had too much wine. "But you will experience everything for yourself," he added lamely.

"The Empress seems a paragon of ... activity. Does she ever sleep?" Macartney enquired, his eyebrows raised.

Buckingham understood the question. Macartney was less interested in how long the Empress slept than with whom.

"Grigory Orlov is still her Chamberlain. And favourite. But he appears less and less frequently at court."

"Then she must be lonely, at times?" Macartney asked,

twirling his wine glass nonchalantly in his hand.

"The Empress's fondness for Count Orlov is very strong. She would have him with her at all times." He would not be the one to tell Macartney that the Empress was assuaging her loneliness with a young and handsome officer. Buckingham himself had once found the Empress attractive but was relieved that neither he nor his calves had caught her eye. It was not virtue or fidelity to his wife and baby daughter in London; he had in fact indulged in a few dalliances with willing ladies of the court especially during the long winter. The more he got to know the Empress, the more he felt it would be like bedding a strict governess, who might give grades for performance. Let Macartney try.

Buckingham made an effort to gather his thoughts. He must leave Macartney with an accurate assessment of the Empress, a difficult task. Her intense application to the duties of ruling was combined with a passion for trivial amusements and, in Buckingham's opinion, childish games. Her favourite was Blind Man's Buff.

"But you would do well, Macartney, to remember always that she is first Empress and then woman. She may wear fine French silk but she has broken off diplomatic relations with the French because of their refusal to address her as imperial majesty, a partnering of words the French claim is an impossibility in their language. The Empress may show a soft heart when it comes to showering her favourite with riches and pining after him like a lovesick girl but she also signed the warrant of execution that led to the public execution of a Guardsman. The Empress Catherine is not to be underestimated. And as long as she has Orlov and her brothers on her side, and all those others she has rewarded in plenty, and continues to reward, she will do as she pleases. Not as England pleases."

"Yes, there has been a touch of, let us say, the medieval in recent events, has there not? Lots of blood shed.

Innocent princes killed. Rather Borgia-like, perhaps? Any truth in it all?" Macartney drawled.

Buckingham had read the pamphlets circulating in Europe condemning events in Russia and questioning the Empress 's role in both murder and execution. The latest which had come into his hands was entitled ""Scenes of Horror in Russia" and condemned the shedding of innocent royal blood. In fact, it claimed stridently that the throne of Russia was *awash* in the blood of its own princes. The exaggeration, Buckingham reflected gloomily, was based on a certain amount of truth. The image of Catherine as shining star of the North, much promoted by Voltaire, had been badly tarnished.

"In trying to secure her power, she has perhaps forfeited moral respect. And I am not convinced that she is more secure on the throne. A weakening in the people's trust is always dangerous. The last year has been one great mass of combustibles with incendiaries placed at every corner." Why was he thinking of fireworks again? "She will have little time for the wishes of Great Britain – unless one of them is to support her against the Turks. That is the only way forward for a treaty with Russia."

"Well, we both know that our government will not support Russian expansion. It will be left for me to find another way." Macartney stood and walked towards the large looking glass on the wall. "You say she prefers younger men and since I am about a decade younger than she is, perhaps I will have some sway, don't you think?"

"You must exercise your office as you see fit," Buckingham said rather stiffly. "But for now you must permit me to retire. I have many preparations to complete before I leave."

Buckingham was glad to be going home. The Russian court may glitter with gold and silks but it was a hollow luxury. Its new role on the European political stage was backed by no more than pettiness and caprice. There was no system, no hierarchy, no morals, no code of behaviour. And much as he acknowledged Catherine's attempts to enlighten, educate and organise, it was a mammoth task, which no one person could achieve, let alone a woman. And that was part of her problem, he thought. Trusting no-one, she shared none of her duties or responsibilities.

But she was Macartney's problem now, if she lasted on the throne, which Buckingham doubted. His thoughts turned to his journey home. It would be swift, January being the best time to travel when the snow was deep and firm and smooth, the air fresh and cold. More than half of it, all the way to the port of Danzig, could be done by sleigh. And then he would soon be in London, where political decisions were not based on whims and where the water closets at home were free of cockroaches.

Chapter Nineteen

Grigory Orlov strode enthusiastically into Catherine's chambers. She was already dressed, or rather undressed, for bed. A new diamond necklace sparkled in the dusky light of the few candles she had lit. The room smelled warmly of beeswax and oil of amber, Catherine's preferred scent. Catherine smiled and extended her hand.

"You came," she said simply.

Catherine looked better than she had done in months, maybe even years, Grigory thought. Her eyes, usually brightened by belladonna drops, had a more natural light in them this evening. While her visage was not the fresh face of youth– and Grigory was very familiar with the soft peach skin of much younger women – she certainly looked younger than her three and a half decades. He knew women of that age whose bodies slumped in folds and whose faces creased in wrinkles beneath too much powder.

Catherine's body had regained some of its firmness. That summer she had ridden out hawking twice a week and Grigory had often accompanied her. These outings brought not only colour to Catherine's cheeks but also vitality to her physical desires. This was especially so, Grigory recalled with a smile, after a visit to the imperial stud farms at Pakhrino, where some 500 stallions were stabled. Catherine revelled in the muscular beauty of the magnificent animals.

"They have the advantage," she said, "of physical strength without the weakness of spirit that often afflicts men."

The Grand Carousel had been a great success. While Catherine did not participate, she was an enthusiastic spectator, sitting beside her son the Grand Duke Paul. She distributed generous prizes of gold and diamonds to the members of court, both men and women, who had participated in tests of riding and shooting skills. Grigory had once again won the prize for horsemanship, much to his brother Alexey's chagrin.

"I am the better rider, Grigory, and you know it. It is only because you are the Empress's favourite that you have won," he said as he swept his horse off the field.

Yes, there were certainly advantages to being the favourite. He had riches in abundance and the freedom to do as he wished. He did not mind Catherine's dalliances with young Guards. He sometimes picked one out himself and manoeuvred matters so that the young officer would catch the Empress's attention. He knew her taste. But these young men, while adding a *frisson* to her desire, and even his, were no threat. Orlov knew the young officers who found the way to Catherine's bed were no more than playthings. They did not satisfy her but rather whetted her appetite for Orlov. He did not even mind the handsome English envoy Macartney. Catherine might toy with him but she was too astute to enter into a serious *liaison* with a political personage.

In any case, Catherine did not love easily. She had learned to hide her affections, she had told him in a rare moment of confidence, during the long years when Empress Elizabeth forbade her any close relationships with men or women. Those for whom she showed any fondness or preference were immediately banished from court, if not to the cold wastes of Siberia. It had become a habit to hide her heart. But not her body. Catherine had lovers instead of friends – although love had little to do with it, Grigory thought with some pity.

Still, Grigory knew women well and he knew that they needed each other's company. But Catherine had no *confidantes*. Some of her ladies had been with her since her days as a princess but, with few exceptions, she kept herself distant from them. The younger ones she treated more as a class of unruly schoolgirls.

Catherine's voice broke into his thoughts.

"Grigory, what occupies you? Come, your Empress is waiting!" she said as she threw back the covers.

Grigory hesitated only briefly before throwing off his jacket and sword belt. He was the only one allowed in the Empress's presence armed. He had told Catherine it was for her protection but it was also for his own. He did not wish to be caught unawares.

"Catherine," he said as she untied his shirt laces, "do you not wish for some female company? I mean a friend, an intimate friend?"

"Grigory! Ah, is this what happens in the next chapter?" Catherine asked playfully.

Grigory had become a connoisseur of sensuality precisely because there were so many women available to him. How to make rare what was in abundance? He sought out those who would not succumb. Seduction was what gave him most pleasure. Although he had no need to seduce Catherine, who was always avid for his body, he enjoyed controlling her desire.

He had surprised her with a copy of *Thérèse Philosophe*, the French novel which had been burning its way through Europe for the past decade.

"I know how fond you are of books," he had said the first time he brought it, "so I shall read to you of a young *philosophe*, just as you like to be, in Paris."

Catherine had expressed surprise but had lain acquiescently beside him. "Read if you must," she had said indulgently.

As the tale of the young Thérèse unfolded, as her innocence was tainted through priests and nuns, Catherine soon forced Grigory to stop reading. "Let us continue the next time," she said, her lips hot on his.

Grigory did continue with Thérèse's carnal education next time and Catherine was once more rendered breathless with excitement. But he would not leave the book with her despite her entreaties. "It will keep me company when you do not," Catherine had begged. Grigory was preparing Catherine for the last chapter. To withstand the Count who would make her his mistress, Thérèse must last for two weeks in a room full of erotic books, paintings and objects and emerge with her virtue unsullied. If she succeeds, the Count will no longer importune her. Thérèse of course fails and becomes the Count's mistress.

Orlov had been making gifts of sensual objects to Catherine for the trial he planned for her. He would insist that she foreswear all lovers in that time. Catherine loved a challenge and hated to lose. But Orlov was sure she would lose after no more than a day.

"Read to me then," Catherine said. "We must know what happens to our little Thérèse. We have left her languishing in a convent suffering from lack of ... gratification. Your talk of intimate friends makes me think that a fellow sister ... ?"

"She will be rescued, never fear, but first you must open your next present." Orlov handed her a small parcel wrapped in silk. Catherine's eyes opened wide in surprise as the tiny, exquisitely carved object was revealed.

"It warms as you hold it in your hand," Orlov said closing his hand over hers. "Or put it elsewhere," he added. "And now I shall continue reading to you," he whispered in her ear. "But you must not distract me."

PART THREE 1768 - 1771

Chapter Twenty

Count Betskoy arrived at the usual afternoon hour with the *Meditations* of the great Roman emperor Marcus Aurelius under his arm. Catherine, of course, had read the work of the great Stoic philosopher king and one could not doubt her adherence to the principles of service and duty, which Marcus Aurelius had advocated in a ruler. But, in Betskoy's opinion, she was being too easily swayed by the philosophising French. It was he who had introduced her to their ideas but it had not been his intention for them to meddle in Russian affairs. Yet another Frenchman had arrived at the Russian court and was sowing discontent with his ideas for Catherine's new project, which Betskoy was determined to wrest back into Russian, or at least classical, hands – with the help of Marcus Aurelius.

Betskoy had no great hope of being allowed to read to Catherine from the *Meditations*. She had found new energy in the past few months and was now wont to read aloud to him, usually Voltaire's letters. Betskoy fidgeted with anticipated impatience. Did she not detect the sycophantic tone in the philosopher's correspondence? These so-called men of letters all wanted something from her, usually money. Denis Diderot had certainly benefited from her generosity. When Catherine heard that Diderot was in financial straits and looking for someone to buy his library for the sum of 15000 livres, she immediately ordered its purchase and bestowed an annual pension of 1000 livres on Diderot to be his own librarian. Betskoy knew from his contacts in Paris that Diderot was not so much in financial straits as desirous of a generous dowry for his daughter. Catherine's generosity, however, had done much to remove the tarnish on her image, as Voltaire once more sang, or wrote, her praises throughout Europe, which,

Betskoy had to admit, was good for Russia's reputation in the so-called civilised world.

Catherine sat at her writing desk, almost hidden by heaps of paper. She greeted Betskoy enthusiastically.

"I have just received a new letter from my dear philosopher of Ferney," she said. "He calls me the northern Star, the benefactress of Europe! Who would have thought that the simple purchase of a library would earn so many compliments! And listen to this! 'You have acquired more subjects through the greatness of soul than others could conquer by force of arms,' he writes. You see, dear Count, Russia has gained a foremost place in Europe without one battle fought!"

Count Betskoy wanted to remind Catherine that it was she herself who had once said that words were not always mightier than swords. Words could be fickle. They could be forgotten, rewritten, misinterpreted, manipulated. He also wanted to remind her that grand philosophy did not translate into a political programme. Even with the best will in the world, including his own. The Foundling Home in Moscow had opened with more than 500 children. In one year 400 had died, earning it the nickname of Angel Factory. The Smolny Institute for Young Women was more successful, Betskoy comforted himself.

With his attention more on the young Smolny ladies than on the French philosopher, he murmured, "How gratifying, Your Majesty."

"Oh, come now, dear Count," Catherine said, "I work as hard inside our empire as outside."

It was true. The Empress was tireless in her plans and projects. She was fired by new energy and had never looked healthier. She sat firmly on the throne.

"Your Majesty could never be accused of dereliction of duty. Russia owes you much," Betskoy said sincerely.

"The elections for the Legislative Commission commence this month," Catherine said. "No other country has undertaken what I have, not even the parliament-obsessed British. Why, they only listen to aristocrats and landowners. Our deputies will be elected not only from the nobles but also from the merchants, the townsmen and even the state peasants. And I will listen to them all in six months when they gather in Moscow. I will find out what my country needs and make laws accordingly." Catherine's face was flushed as the words ran away from her. She paused for breath, then added, "It is a magnificent plan, one that other nations will emulate."

"They will, Your Majesty," Betskoy murmured again. "If they can." But Catherine paid him no heed.

"I will not rely on the deputies alone. I will use my own eyes and judgement. In a few months, when the spring thaw sets in, I will undertake my voyage along the Volga. The preparations are all but complete."

"And has the Academy delivered the new maps? How far will you venture?" Betskoy found geography less strenuous than politics.

"Why, to the limit of my Empire if we can, where we meet Asia. I should like to see Saratov. Count Orlov tells me we will soon have the area productively settled."

Count Betskoy admired Catherine's settlement drive. Russia, she said, may be vast but land was of little use if it was not cultivated and settled. She had audaciously sent out manifestos to every country she could name, luring settlers with the promise of land. Many countries, including France, Prussia, Austria and Spain, had forbidden emigration to Russia while others like Britain and Holland had their own colonies to settle. But several of the smaller German states, impoverished by long years of war, provided fertile ground for Catherine's recruiters, and settlers came in their thousands.

Catherine rustled through the papers on her desk. "Here is Orlov's latest report."

Catherine had made Grigory Orlov president of the

Chancellery of the Guardianship of Foreigners. It was unusual for Orlov to be doing something useful when there were no battles to fight, Betskoy thought.

"17,866 colonists have been dispatched to Russia through the port of Lübeck this year alone. My empire will be strengthened. Orlov says the settlers will provide a bulwark in the unstable Tatar territories in the south. In Saratov."

"Your Majesty must look to her safety," Count Betskoy said softly. He did not hold with this grand adventure. An Empress should not be sailing to barbaric parts. She had officers and armies to do that for her. But of all her projects, this was the one which set her cheeks aflame with excitement.

"Oh, we will be a fleet, dear Count, do not concern yourself," Catherine said. "There will be 25 vessels and hundreds of sailors, not to mention over three hundred guards. Count Orlov tells me we shall be a party of two thousand! Imagine, a small town on the move! Think what sights we shall see! What wonders await us!"

"Indeed, Your Majesty, your Empire is vast and diverse and you are its anchor," Betskoy said evenly. A vision of an anchor as a monument flashed through his mind. No, no, that would not do but he must broach the subject.

"And has Your Majesty given further thought to casting her greatness in stone? Or indeed in any other lasting material?" he asked with pretended nonchalance.

"Ah yes, I am glad you raise the subject," Catherine answered. "I have had fruitful meetings with Monsieur Falconet. Our project makes progress."

Count Betskoy kept his countenance. Like many others, he was convinced that Falconet was the wrong choice to execute a monumental sculpture to Russia's greatness. But Diderot had highly recommended him, supported by Voltaire, and Catherine thought more of their French opinion than that of her own advisors. And so Falconet had been brought to St Petersburg. And was sowing discontent with his French ideas.

"We will keep it simple," Catherine continued. "Monsieur Falconet says the simple is more effective than the complicated."

Count Betskoy refrained from remarking that the work that Falconet was known for was so embellished as to be almost fantastical. He had made table sculptures for Sèvres, to accompany their dinner services, of elegantly erotic figures surrounded by plump little cherubs. Where was the greatness in that? They pleased certainly, that was their aim, but it was no more than a prettified charm. He could not imagine Catherine coyly naked with a cherub kissing one of her hands.

"Our aim, your aim, is no doubt to impress, rather than to please?" he asked hurriedly, indicating the book in his hand. "I have brought Marcus Aurelius's writings. You much admired him. A great emperor, military commander and philosopher. The bronze statue of him in Rome is deservedly praised."

"Monsieur Falconet says we must not look to antiquity for inspiration," Catherine said firmly. "And I agree. I have seen the drawings of the statue you refer to. I find it lacks greatness. The horse, despite being a poor specimen of its species, seems to be in control of the emperor. But I do think a horse. Such great creatures. The rider, however, must be one with him. One great sculpture of movement and energy. Cast in bronze."

"But Monsieur Falconet has never executed a horse nor worked in bronze!" Betskoy protested.

"He has shown me a drawing of a bronze sculpture of Philip IV in Madrid. The horse rears. It is magnificent. But Russia's will be more magnificent."

"Philip IV?" Betskoy stuttered.

"I will erect this monument to Peter the Great."

Betskoy's composure was finally shaken. "I thought it

was to be a monument to your own reign? Something to stand immutable against men's vacillations, you said."

"And it will," Catherine assured him. "I will not be accused of turning myself into an idol. I will give the people an idol, a hero, a Russian! It will be my gift to them, the source of their Empire's greatness. I will write on it, to Peter the Great from Catherine the Second. Thus will our names be linked in greatness."

Once more, Catherine had surprised Betskoy with her astuteness. It was a clever and bold plan, unassailable.

"Your Majesty's wisdom humbles me," Betskoy said.

"Yes, but I have to humble our sculptor without offending his artistic sensibilities. I have not yet completely won him to my vision. But we are agreed on a pedestal of great natural proportion, rough and awesome, like Russia herself. Falconet may organise the finding of it. And he will see my vision of Russia's monument in the end. Have no fear, dear Count. We will have no coy table ornaments. Nor drooping Roman emperors."

Catherine smiled at him warmly. Betskoy was struck again by how charming she could be. How intelligently charming. At moments like these, he knew her to be his daughter.

"Now let me show you some of the entries I have received for our competition," she continued. "We have already had many replies, in German and French, even one from Sweden. And Voltaire has promised to submit."

Count Betskoy's good spirits were suddenly dampened. Catherine had ordered the newly founded Free Economic Society to organise an open competition on the question as to what was more useful to society: that the peasants own land or only moveable property. It was an audacious question and completely in opposition to the essence of Russian society. The nobles owned the land and the serfs were attached to the land. If the serfs were to own land, where would it come from? Would it be taken from the nobles?

"Your Majesty does well to consider the welfare of all her people, including the serfs, but you may remember that freedom can bring chaos to those unprepared for it," Betskoy said carefully.

Catherine had been on the throne but a few weeks when she issued a manifesto forbidding mine owners to buy serfs as their workforce, obliging them to use hired labour. The serfs, desperate to escape the miserable conditions they were kept in, immediately left their masters in droves, inciting more to join them, burning houses of masters and serfs alike, rampaging through the provinces with no aim other than venting their rage at a life of servitude and violence, and no means of sustaining themselves. The less they had, the more they needed. There was talk of them marching on St Petersburg. Alarmed, Catherine had authorised the use of cannons to quell the peasants and order them back to work.

"My dear Count, do not lecture me," Catherine said gently, "My aim is freedom for all my people but I am not so naive as to think that it can come without education. I merely gather ideas in order to prepare the way."

"You would not take the land from the nobles, Your Majesty?" Betskoy dared to ask.

"I do not intend to take anything from anyone. I seek to find the most advantageous system for the welfare of our empire. This is why we have a Free Economic Society. To explore such ideas. Besides, to whom does the land really belong? Surely, it belongs to Russia. It cannot be parcelled up into lots of little kingdoms."

This was dangerous thinking, Betskoy thought. It could only have come from her French friends. They sat safely at their desks spreading trouble with their pens to countries they knew little of.

"The peasant would say that while he belongs to his lord and master, the land belongs to him," Betskoy said, daring to add, "That cannot be right either."

"Ah, but it is perhaps more right. The peasant senses instinctively that he and the soil of Russian are one. The one cannot exist without the other."

And the Crown cannot exist without the support of the landowning nobility, Count Betskoy thought. Aloud he said, "I am sure the essays for the competition will yield some useful perspectives. Meanwhile, did you say whether the new maps of the Volga had been delivered by the Academy yet?"

"Oh yes," Catherine said enthusiastically, rustling through her papers, causing parchments to fall to the floor. Betskoy stooped with difficulty to catch them.

"Look," Catherine said, pointing at what looked like a large annotated illustration. "Here they have divided the river into sections with a map of each section and columns of texts showing distances, economic activity, towns, villages, landmarks! Just as I requested. And churches. Did you know that Nizhny Novgorod has thirty-nine churches, four cathedrals, three monasteries and two convents?" Catherine paused to turn some pages. "While Kokshaysk," Catherine raised her eyes to Betskoy, "which is near Kazan, dear Count, has but a single church."

The Count sighed his relief. Yes, geography was definitely a safer topic.

Chapter Twenty-One

Catherine viewed the deputies of the Legislative Commission with barely concealed impatience. 460 had arrived in Moscow from all over the Empire. She had ordered an investigation into what had detained the missing 100 from obeying an imperial summons. Despite her detailed instructions on how the assembled deputies were to conduct themselves at the plenary sessions of the Commission, many were talking amongst themselves, still others seemed to be nodding off to sleep and she was sure several were smoking for she could detect a strong whiff of tobacco.

It had taken five full sessions of the Commission to read aloud the 526 paragraphs of her Great Instructions to the deputies, which was little in comparison to the two years it had taken her to compose them. She did not pretend they were all her own thoughts. As she had written to Frederick of Prussia before he could fire criticisms of plagiarism at her, she was like the crow in the fable who made itself a garment of peacock feathers. But still, it was an *hommage* to the great enlightened thinkers whose works she had plundered. And the peacocks should be pleased. She was the one who dared to put their ideas into practice. What use were they on a library shelf?

The present reader, with clear but slow delivery, was now nearing the end of the Instructions. He had reached the section on how laws should be written. Catherine nodded her head in agreement. Laws should be written clearly and precisely, in language that everyone understood instead of in a web of deliberate incomprehensibility. Just as she had written her Instructions.

The deputies were showing little interest, not even attempting to stifle or hide their yawns. Catherine had to clench her teeth to stop herself following suit. The earlier sections of the Instructions dealing with abolishing torture and the death sentence had roused more attention but perhaps it was because the deputy she had appointed as second reader read very well. The honour of the first reader had gone to Grigory Orlov. His were the most rousing, most fundamental paragraphs. Russia is a European state with an Absolute Sovereign. The Sovereign is the Source of all Power. No other form of Rule is suitable to such a Vast Empire. Its Rule is a Christian one. All Subjects must seek the Mutual Good of each other. Therein lay the Summit of Happiness, Glory, Safety, and Tranquillity.

But Orlov had failed to do justice to her words. Catherine had been painstaking in the composition of the 526 paragraphs which constituted the Instructions, seeking not only to distil the content to its pure essence but to lend the language a rhythm pleasing to the ear. Many of the deputies, she knew, would not be literate, or not literate enough for such intellectual material no matter how distilled. She had therefore edited the Instructions by reading them aloud to test the flow of words. But Orlov had disappointed her. His delivery had been laconic, at times even staccato as if he were delivering military commands. She should have read it aloud herself.

Catherine closed her ears to the monotony of the slow enunciation and began composing in her head her next letter to Voltaire. As she surveyed the deputies in their different dress, some with colourful costumes, some in turbans and some long-haired, some bearded, many not, she would tell him how Orthodox, heretics and Muslims sat together, how they listened politely to each other's opinions – she had forbidden the wearing of swords and daggers, which had upset the deputies from far-flung parts of the empire who claimed they were being deprived of their manhood. She would point out that rather than rushing to burn each other at the stake as had been their wont, they were now learning the power of words and respect for others. Russia would flourish because its subjects were prepared to do each other good instead of harm. Could France boast such tolerance? Or even Britain with its vast empire?

The Volga trip had shown her the richness of her lands and people. In the stuffy heat of the Assembly Chamber, she now thought longingly of the days on the river. The beginning of the journey had been cool and windy and the river swelled in deep waves but she had not felt unwell as many of her ladies had. She had visited the textile mills at Yaroslav, gratified to learn that 65,000 yards of silk had been exported to England in the previous year. She had prayed at the picturesque Ipatiev Monastery at Kostroma and had spent a week in magnificent Kazan, at the end of which a sumptuous ball had been given in her honour. The local peoples – the Mordvins, the Chuvash, the Cheremis and Tatar – all in their colourful native costumes had danced their intricate but rhythmic dances in the grounds of the governor's palace. Inside, a ball of local dignitaries followed in a swirl of silk and jewels. She had visited the famous ruins of Bolghar, ancient city of the Volga Bulgars and a Muslim holy place rebuilt by Tamerlane. She had marvelled at the richness of the soil. There was plentiful grain everywhere, flowers and fruit in abundance, forests of oak and linden, fish from the rivers. But it had not all been pleasure or edification. Catherine had not stopped ruling for one minute of the journey. She replaced the provincial governor of Yaroslavl and cautioned the restive merchants to restore peace and harmony; in Nizhny Novgorod she had ordered crumbling government buildings and warehouses to be rebuilt in brick and had set up a trading company open to anyone with 25 roubles to invest; she scolded the Orthodox clergy for continued persecution against both Old Believers and Muslims; she ordered the governor's arrogant wife in Kazan to be more polite to the people.

Her two-week trip to the outer regions of her realm had shown her that such a diversity of subjects needed a firm hand to guide them. There must be laws to unify them, laws which would supplant local customs and which all subjects of her Empire would follow. This was the task of the Legislative Commission – to create a new code of laws for a new Russia. It was a mammoth task, she knew. And one fraught with the dangers of divided opinions. She would be the unifying force. She would stay in Moscow, a city she did not trust, to guide her deputies. She would be patient, she vowed, as she cast an irritated glance over the chamber.

Flies suddenly buzzed around her and she swatted at them with her fan. The summer heat was oppressive, especially under the heavy brocade of her dress. Her crown dug into her scalp. The odour of sweating male bodies overpowered the scent from the herb pastille burners she had ordered placed near her dais. Since the windows did not let in enough light to read by, deputies in the darker parts of the hall had lit candles, obviously of an inferior quality since they spluttered smokingly.

She signed to the Marshall of the Commission to approach.

"When the reader has finished," she whispered, "please dismiss the deputies and have them reconvene tomorrow morning at eight o'clock sharp. We may avail ourselves of the cool of the morning hours."

She had no wish to rush back to the Golovin Palace where she had chosen to stay instead of at the nearby Kremlin Palace. In spring the Construction Chancellery had asked for over 60,000 roubles to repair and clean both palaces in preparation for the imperial visit. Catherine had refused, rather loftily saying she was coming to the old capital for the good of the state and not to enjoy luxury. She regretted her decision. The two-storeyed wooden Golovin Palace offered no more than basic comfort while the Kremlin was in such a crumbling state that she immediately called for the city architects to offer solutions on how to save the buildings, particularly the Archangel Cathedral, which seemed in danger of collapse. How she longed for St Petersburg!

But meanwhile she would visit Alexey Orlov, who was in very bad health, unable to move due to some unknown injury to his back. Too many jolts from horse-riding, the doctors opined. His bones have rubbed against each other too long and are now disintegrating, they said. Now he had excruciating stomach pains and his skin had taken on a very pronounced yellow pallor. Gallstones, said the doctors. He must eat less and take the waters. But he was unable to travel and had not been well enough to join the Volga tour. His brother Grigory, on the other hand, was in excellent health and spirits but Catherine rarely saw him. There had been no more intimate reading in her chamber.

After the first two sessions of the Commission, he had sent her a note begging her to forgive his absence but that Alexey needed him. She would have her carriage take her directly to Alexey's and perhaps surprise Grigory there. She told herself she was checking on Alexey – not Grigory.

Chapter Twenty-Two

The heat of the summer had given way to the icy breath of winter without any autumnal transition. Moscow oppressed Catherine more and more. Its buildings, rather like its inhabitants, were old-fashioned and of no discernible style. The proliferation of bulbous domes was reminiscent of Mongols and Tatars, not modern Russia. Muddy roads meandered everywhere with no clear destination. When she spoke Russian, which she did often and fluently, she felt that the court dignitaries were smirking and pressing their lips together to avoid correcting her pronunciation. And if she spoke French, as was natural at any court, her Moscow courtiers replied with clumsy accents and ineloquent phrasing. She refused to speak her own native language. She, the Empress of All Russia, did not want to be known as "the German". It bore the taint of the usurper.

How she longed for the fresh air and clear architecture of St Petersburg, for civilisation. But the Legislative Commission dragged on. After the opening instructional sessions, she had taken to observing the assembly secretly from a covered gallery. Her rules of conduct were ignored: deputies interrupted one another, or talked amongst themselves instead of addressing the whole gathering, or lost themselves and their listeners (although Catherine doubted that anyone could assume that role in the cacophony of confusion) in long speeches of no substance or relevance. Where was the clarity? Where was the civilised exchange of opinion? Where was the concise condensation into precise laws? She had created a Directing Committee to organise disciplined procedures and there were nineteen sub-committees to prepare separate topics for the consideration of the plenary sessions. By November, there were no tangible results, not one law formulated let alone agreed upon.

Catherine's mood of optimism following the Volga tour and the opening of the Commission was dissipating. Her headaches had returned and she felt sluggish, like the Moskva River which flowed through the city. She longed for the waters of the Neva which brought the freshness of the north to St Petersburg.

Rumours were creeping out of crevices like rats on the hunt for food. Another alleged plot against Grigory Orlov had been uncovered. The suspects, mostly ex-guardsmen known as drunkards, spendthrifts and gamblers, accused Orlov of having strangled eight people. There was talk of the dead Ivan VI's brother and sister planning to take over the throne. Dark and threatening as the rumours were, they could not be substantiated – at least not without torture, which she refused to authorise. In her Instructions she had recommended the abolition of both torture and the death penalty, tying her own hands in dealing with those who threatened the peace and stability of her realm. In the end, she had the ringleaders of the plot against Orlov confined to their estates for life. No sooner had this been dealt with than word reached her that the youngest son of her old chaperone, Madame Choglokova, angered at not being promoted in the Guards, had slandered the Empress's name, swearing he would shoot or stab her. He was but fourteen years old. Catherine decided to have him treated like an unruly child and ordered a beating with rods. She then had him posted to a Siberian garrison.

One of the deputies in the hall below was reading out his province's submission in a low monotone. Catherine had ordered all deputies to bring before the Commission any proposals or petitions they considered essential to their region or advantageous to Russia. These would all be reduced to a common denominator and incorporated into the new code. Some deputies had brought endless lists. The six state peasant deputies from the Archangel Province had brought over seven hundred petitions. On her Volga tour,

Catherine had been presented with so many petitions from serfs that she had eventually refused to accept them.

Now she sighed in exasperation. All men should live in freedom but how could the nobles be persuaded that the land did not belong to them but to Russia and therefore to everyone, including the peasants? Many noble estates had tens of thousands of serfs. How could they become free? It was a question of great complexity and the serfs must learn to be patient until it had been solved. They must not present petitions against their lords and masters. They must not cause unrest through their disobedience. They must trust the Empress, who would care for them as a mother would. As soon as she could. Meanwhile, they must be brought to compliance, just as fractious children must.

At the end of summer, Catherine had issued an edict limiting the rights of the serf to denounce their masters. A wrongful petition would be punished by a month's hard labour in Siberian mines, a year for a second offence, and public whipping and permanent exile for a third. Just laws could not be made if there was unrest in the country. She must first create peace.

The thought of unrest brought Poland to mind. Latest reports were not encouraging. Catherine had made her former lover Stanislav Poniatovsky King in Poland out of affection but also to bind Poland to Russia. Instead, Poniatovsky had embarked on a series of reforms – "such as you and I dreamed of in our youth" he had written to her – and had stirred hornet nests of discontent among the conservatives, unwittingly strengthening those who wanted a strong Poland independent of Russia.

"I hope to impress you," Poniatovsky admitted. "You do remember the dreams of our youth, when we were excited not only by love but by ideals. I have not given up hope of a future with Your Majesty." Catherine had assured Poniatovsky of her continued affection but begged him to follow the counsel of her Russian advisers. "In this way," she wrote, "you will be assured of my continued high regard for you."

But reports of uprisings showered onto her writing desk and the latest news of an organised confederation against Russia angered her. Its leader was purported to be a young military officer with, reports said, "unfortunately all the makings of a national hero: noble of birth, tall of stature, handsome in looks, skilled in horsemanship, cultured in manners and speech." It was more a recommendation for a candidate for her bedchamber than a description of a revolutionary, Catherine thought.

But she did not want to think of her bedchamber. And certainly not with a Pole in it. She shivered despite the fur rug covering her lap. She felt ill. Perhaps she was ill. Her mind returned again and again to the young guardsman she had taken into her bed a few nights ago. As he dropped his breeches, she had stolen a covert look. And was grateful she had. His member was speckled with black pimples, not many but enough to make her sure. This was the disease she had warned about in her Great Instruction. It had been brought from America two hundred years ago and if unhalted would cause the destruction of the human race.

"It would therefore be highly prudent," she had written in her Instruction, "to stop the progress of this disease by law."

There had been no need to name it. Everyone knew what was referred to. In any case, it had many names. In Italy, Germany and Poland it was called the French disease while in France and Holland it was called the Spanish disease. The Turks called it the Christian disease. And here in Russia, it was called the Polish disease. Its medical name, syphilis, sounded much too gentle for the agonising scourges it caused. Those who had the great pox were shunned until they died. Its ravages could not be hidden no matter how clever the masks or the false noses were.

On seeing the spots on the young guardsman, Catherine had leapt from her bed and dismissed the confused boy, for he was not much more than that, with an admonition to see the court physician the next day. Perhaps it was not too late for an elixir of mercury to help him. She had called for hot water and herbs and had scrubbed ever part of her body although it had not come into contact with the young officer. She was furious that the boy had not been checked properly. She was also furious with Orlov. It was only because he stayed away from her bed that she was forced to seek company elsewhere to give her the attention she needed - and to attract his attention.

She would seek and install a new favourite, one who would share her bed alone. She could not subject herself to such dangers. She could not subject herself to the dangers of Orlov either. He slept with too many women, married women whose husbands were perhaps infected or they themselves, if they were willing to stray from the marital bed. He liked to seduce virgins. While they may not have the disease, could he not give it to them? Did he have the disease? Oh, her head was going round and round. From now on no-one would be allowed to enter her bedchamber unless he had been checked not only by the physician but also by a woman she could trust. Doctors limited themselves to a cursory examination. What could be discerned in a limp member? A woman could bring everything to light. Perhaps she could entrust the task to Praskovya Rumyantseva. She had been in Catherine's entourage for many years and was the same age as Catherine, attractive, perhaps too attractive, which made Catherine wary. She had married Count James Bruce, a Scot serving as a general in the Russian army. Countess Bruce, as Praskovya was then known, had a roving eye while her husband was absent for many months at a time.

Catherine did not approve of her dalliances but she was experienced in ... the nature of men. As long as Bruce's eye did not linger too long over her own choices, Catherine thought.

Catherine shivered and drew the fur rug more tightly round her. She felt ill. She was tired of Moscow, of the Commission, of plots and rumours, of fumbling boys and no Orlov, of attending to everything herself, the responsibilities of this great Empire and of keeping up its reputation in Europe, tired of Polish quarrels and Turkish threats, of the devious diplomacy of France and Austria.

Suddenly, she made up her mind. She was the Empress and could do as she wished. Surely her role brought privilege as well as duty. She would halt the Commission. She would leave Moscow. The Commission could continue its work in St Petersburg, reconvening in February or March. She would leave for St Petersburg, for the fresh air of Tsarskoye Selo. Elated with relief, she threw off the rug covering her stiff knees and rushed along the gallery heedless of the noise she caused on the wooden floors. Let the deputies know their Empress would not tolerate their ineptitude one minute longer.

Chapter Twenty-Three

Lord Charles Cathcart laid down his quill with a sigh. He checked his fob watch, a gift from the Duke of Cumberland to commemorate the English victory over the Scots at the Battle of Culloden over two decades ago. He wished he was preparing for battle again instead of yet another court appearance. He had led armies on many of Europe's battlefields, but he was not as sure-footed on the slippery parquet of court diplomacy. Russia had emerged from barbaric darkness to take a major role on the European stage. Every power, including Britain, sought an alliance to reduce the threat of Russian dominance but the Empress's terms were unconditional, arrogantly so in Cathcart's opinion. It was Cathcart's task to change that in Britain's favour.

Young Macartney, although he had performed his duties well, had not succeeded in securing Russia as an ally for Britain. He had, however, achieved a commercial treaty which put British merchants on an even footing with their Russian counterparts so that British ships could once more trade freely through Russia. London's shabby treatment of Macartney had not reflected any gratitude. The unofficial version had been that Macartney had acted too independently, was too much under Count Panin's influence and was too intimate with the Empress. Officially, Macartney had requested a return to England on the grounds of ill health. A few months after his return, a bride of influence and repute, the daughter of the Earl of Bute, had been found for him. The best thing for him, Cathcart thought. Young men needed to be anchored. Start a family. That was one advantage Cathcart had over his predecessors, and one which had obviously been taken into consideration. Cathcart was not only married but happily married. He was firmly anchored and would not fall prey to any Russian charms, imperial or otherwise. In any case, the Empress was not to his taste. She was possessed of regal posture which made her – already a head taller than most men – seem taller than she was. Her figure was very gracefully formed, as most men liked, but tending to corpulence, which her upright carriage could still compensate for. Comely was perhaps how Cathcart would describe her, but her appearance lacked that something which made a woman desirable. Perhaps it was her direct look, her eyes full of questioning observation. It would be doing her an injustice to say she was masculine, yet it would not be accurate to say she was entirely feminine.

Just then there was a light tap at the door and his wife Jane entered.

"Charles," she said, "you will be late, dearest."

Cathcart looked at his wife fondly. There was no doubting *her* femininity. They had been married some fifteen years and Jane had borne him six children, three of them sons. She was still a beautiful woman, with a refinement none of the Russian women at court seemed to have.

"Will you wear your patch? Shall I fix it for you?" she asked as she gently kissed his cheek.

Cathcart had been wounded deeply in the face by a vicious Scottish sword at Culloden. He had soon dispatched its owner to a bloody grave but had refused to leave the battlefield until victory was won. By the time he saw a surgeon, infection had set in. The damage left was not so much a scar as an angry scarlet gash which occasionally leaked a yellowish pus. Rather than inflict this on others, Cathcart covered it with black silk. He knew it earned him the soubriquet Patch Cathcart, which he rather liked. It lent him a touch of the daredevil pirate, which was very far from his character.

"Yes, would you, dearest?" he said, holding out the little ivory box which held his patches.

Cathcart relished his wife's nearness, her fingers light on his skin as she affixed the black silk.

"Do you think she will mention the book?" Jane asked.

"I doubt it," he answered." She is taken with her new hermitages. Count Orlov's pavilion is completed and is very grand."

On his arrival in St Petersburg just a few months earlier, Cathcart had been surprised by the grandeur of the Winter Palace, reminiscent, he thought, of London's Whitehall Palace. Cathcart was too young to have seen Whitehall before it burned to the ground but his grandfather described it with enthusiasm. "The most magnificent palace in all Europe," the old man had said. "Larger than Versailles or the Vatican. Over 1500 rooms." Which was more than the Winter Palace with its 1000 rooms, his grandfather would have been pleased to know. Shortly after their arrival in St Petersburg, Cathcart had taken his family to view the Winter Palace from the opposite side of the River Neva. The winter sun shone on the water and lit up the light yellow facade of the Palace, its myriads of window panes twinkling like jewels. Like a fairy tale, his daughter Mary had whispered in wonder. The older children had amused themselves counting the windows but had given up after several hundred. The Palace, Cathcart had been told it, had nearly two thousand windows. Such an expanse and expense of glass!

For all its magnitude, the Palace was obviously not large enough for the Empress Catherine. Or too large. She had ordered smaller adjoining palaces built, one especially for her favourite Orlov. Cathcart was uncertain of the role Orlov played in the Empress's decisions. He had assiduously read all of Macartney's reports but there was little to be gleaned.

"Oh, there was no point in including bedchamber squabbles in my reports," Macartney had explained before Cathcart left London.

"So the Empress and her favourite do quarrel?" Cathcart had asked.

"Yes, yes. Constantly. Sullen quarrels and sharp repartees rising from the Empress's excess of sensitivity or Orlov's excess of presumption. But they are never of great violence or duration. They resemble summer clouds which obscure the sun for a moment, then disperse to leave the sky bright and serene."

Cathcart knew of Macartney's penchant for flowery speech. It was a weakness which may have impeded negotiation, he thought.

Macartney surprised him by adding, "The history of today's dispute would vanish before the account of tomorrow's reconciliation."

"Then how should one incorporate Count Orlov into any ... equation?" Cathcart asked.

"Count Panin holds any strings not firmly in the Empress's own hands. Orlov's favour with Panin is undiminished even though Panin does not like him. For Panin would be sorry to see a minion of genius or even ability in Orlov's place. Orlov is affable, even biddable at times. He causes no trouble as long as he has his freedom and his riches." Cathcart thought he detected a note of bitterness in Macartney's answer.

Jane now laid the patch box gently on his desk and Cathcart, mindful of his wife's interest in details other than architectural, said, "Yes, Orlov's palace is very fine. It has hanging gardens. And a flying bridge to the Empress's chambers."

"How ... Russian," Jane said. "I mean, would a tunnel not have been more discreet?"

"There is nothing discreet about this Court," Cathcart said with a sigh. "And I am weary of ceremony and celebration. I know the Empress works hard but she plays hard too."

"I wonder that she does not tire," Jane remarked gently.

"She has not the advantage of youth."

The Empress was indeed not young. Cathcart and his wife had been invited, along with the other diplomats, to an opera to celebrate the Empress's thirty-ninth birthday in April. Baldassare Galuppi was to return to Venice having completed the three years of his agreed contract and had composed an opera as his farewell to the Empress. It was overly dramatic – and long – for Cathcart's taste but one could not dispute the wonder of the choruses sung by the chapel choir, their voices weaving in an out of one another, sweeping high and low. Jane declared the fashions worn by the women to be very French, whatever that meant, but the ostentation of jewels, especially the Empress's diamonds, to be on the vulgar side. "Still," Jane said, "I envy her her white teeth." Cathcart had not noticed the Empress's teeth but did notice that the women all painted their faces very white with spots of bright rouge on the cheeks and a proliferation of black beauty spots in many different shapes. "All very French, " Jane declared scathingly. "Their hair too. Too many curls and ornaments. Some even had feathers!"

"You are right, my dear. One would expect more dignified decorum from a woman of her age, more wisdom than wit. But her leisure hours are filled with light entertainment," Cathcart said. Sometimes boisterous, he did not add. "Those who form her society," he continued with a wry smile, "are either young people who are extremely gay, or those who possess the vivacity of disposition to keep pace with those who are younger than themselves."

"And such is not your disposition," Jane said with a laugh. "But would you mention the book if you have a chance? It would mean so much to my brother. And must be of interest to Britain. Mr Wedgwood could export his beautiful wares here to Russia. After all, our own Queen Charlotte and many of the European royal houses commission his work to grace their tables."

Jane's brother, Sir William Hamilton, was British special envoy to Naples and a renowned archaeologist. He had amassed a collection of antique Etruscan, Greek and Roman vases – his rivals accused him of even plundering tombs - and had published a catalogue of meticulous engravings. Josiah Wedgwood, the famous English potter, was said to be designing unusual jasper tableware mirroring the flowing figures on the antique vases. Jane had hired a German craftsman to paint the walls of their St Petersburg dining room with life-sized Etruscan figures based on her brother's engravings. Words of praise had quickly spread and the Empress had questioned Cathcart about the figures, asking to borrow the book of engravings.

"Besides which, " Jane added, "it is our only copy."

"I will do what I can, my love, but the Empress is not wont to allow one to choose the subject of discourse."

And what would his subject be if he did have a choice, Cathcart wondered as his carriage bore him towards the Winter Palace. The Empress Catherine had always insisted that any ally of Russia must promise unconditional support in case of war with the Ottoman Empire. In this point, she was, as Macartney had aptly reported when they met in London, "inflexible even beyond a woman's obstinacy". And Britain was equally adamant in its refusal to accept the "Turkish clause". Checkmate. It was of little wonder that Macartney had asked to return to London. He had done all he could, confessing to Cathcart that he had spent one thousand pounds of his own funds on spies, not to mention considerable other expenses incurred by the life of extravagant generosity encouraged in the Russian court. "I did my duty and more, and no man ever served his country with greater zeal but I dragged out a miserable existence," Macartney had said. "It is a court where the etiquette of diplomacy does not apply, where there are no common rules of negotiation as we know them."

"Then you think my task a hopeless one?" Cathcart had asked.

"I should think a treaty of alliance with the Empress of Russia is as unlikely to be brought about as a league with the King of Bantam!" Macartney had retorted scornfully.

Cathcart thought morosely of the welcome given to those who brought trinkets and curiosities to the Empress instead of diplomatic overtures. Catherine had shown him with childlike enthusiasm a clock in the form of a small egg which, as it struck the hours with Easter hymns, opened to reveal silver and golden figures enacting the Resurrection. Such bad taste, Cathcart thought, and perhaps blasphemous to reduce the crux of Christianity to a toy? Well, it was debatable if the Orthodox were really Christians after all.

The tolling of the noon bells broke into his thoughts, once more reminding him of the toy clock. Its inventor had apparently been rewarded with 1000 roubles. Perhaps a gift of Mr Wedgwood's porcelain would find favour with the Empress. If he could not make headway on the Turkish clause, he could, as his wife suggested, seek Britain's advantage in trade at least.

Chapter Twenty-Four

Catherine went to the window and held the looking glass up to her face. She was sure there was a pustule under her eye and there were definitely a few on her neck. She felt an itch under her bodice. She was suddenly flooded by alarm. What if she had made the wrong decision? If she had indeed contracted the disease, she would die, or if she survived, she would be blind or, perhaps worst of all, disfigured by scars. She had seen many beautiful young women lose their beauty and their futures to pock marks. An Empress with a scarred face? Was there such a thing as blemished dignity? The people would be quick to see the whole as flawed.

Catherine paced up and down trying to calm her thoughts. She must remain scientific. Dr Dimsdale had said only two to three people in a hundred died from the new smallpox variolation. In his opinion, these deaths were not due to the vaccination itself but to other factors. The health of the patient was important. A sickly constitution would not survive variolation. But Dr Dimsdale declared Catherine to be in robust health.

"Another major cause of failure," the doctor had gone on to explain through an interpreter, for the doctor's French was minimal as was the Empress's English, "lies with inexperienced practitioners who often confuse symptoms and use matter from persons infected with a different disease. This is especially the case with the great pox. Any patient inoculated with such pus is ensured a certain and slow death, lasting years. One must be able to distinguish the two poxes."

Catherine made a quick note to discuss measures against syphilis with Dr Dimsdale once the smallpox project was completed.

"Others use the pus of cowpox sores," Dimsdale continued, "A grave mistake. But Your Majesty need not fear. An eight-year old boy has been found. Healthy before the disease struck him. It is his pus I shall use in your inoculation."

The procedure itself had not been painful. She had been bled so many times as a young girl that her arms bore many scars caused by knives and scalpels not always competently used. Dr Dimsdale had tutted as he made two neat incisions before drawing the thread of pus under the skin.

He had instructed Catherine to wash her hands often, not to touch any pustules and to keep her hands away from her mouth and eyes. "The scourge, " he said, "of modern medicine is the lack of hygiene." She must rest to allow her body to fight the disease. She should go to Tsarskoye Selo in the country for fresh air.

She had felt well for the first day or two and had resolved to return to St Petersburg to deal with the Legislative Commission when she began to feel unwell. Her temperature rose and she had dizzy spells. The pustules had begun to appear about a week after the inoculation and the incision on her arm was inflamed and painful. She felt weak. But she ordered Count Panin to report that she was well and working as always. But she did not feel well.

Oh, but why had she done it? Of course, she wanted to impress the rest of Europe with her progressive practices. England's royal family had been inoculated. She would not trail behind in the advance of knowledge and science. Voltaire complained bitterly about the French King's refusal to support inoculation. The Sorbonne had even banned it as being against Divine Will. The great philosopher had cited examples of non-civilised peoples practising the method successfully, from the Chinese to the Circassians, whose beautiful unscarred daughters filled the seraglios of Turkey. The Ottoman Empire had even adopted the Circassian practice of the transfer of pus to infants. While Voltaire estimated that smallpox killed a fifth of mankind, the Ottoman Empire and England suffered few epidemics. In Siberia, a region settled at great effort, Catherine had lost 20,000 subjects in a recent outbreak. Eradication of the disease, Voltaire argued and Catherine believed, would add to a state's wealth: its princes would be saved, its peasants would cease to be decimated, its armed forces would not be defeated from within.

She, Catherine, Empress of Russia, would fight every enemy which threatened her Empire, and smallpox was an insidious enemy. She would not stand by while her Empire was weakened and others thrived. Her example would lead her subjects to be inoculated. Her people would be healthy and her Empire would flourish. Voltaire would admire her. No, she refused to be ill.

She suddenly felt another itch on her face. Mindful of Dr Dimsdale's warning not to explore with her fingers, she rushed back to the looking glass. It was of best Venetian glass but still she saw little. Her eyes did not deal well with near objects. She would order more belladonna drops. Was that spot on the glass or her face? And the itch under her arm? Was she going to break out in pox pustules? She thought of Maria Theresa of Austria, who less than a year ago had contracted smallpox from her daughter-in-law. She had survived, by all reports badly disfigured, but her daughter-in-law had died, followed closely by one of Maria Theresa's daughters, who, it was rumoured, had been forced by her mother to keep vigil at her dead sister-in-law's open coffin in the crypt. She, Catherine, had no intention of dying or becoming disfigured. She would take a walk in the fresh air.

Grigory Orlov had tried to dissuade her from the inoculation. "Inviting your enemy into your camp does not turn him into your friend," he had said.

"By my own example, Grigory," she had gently said, "I

can save from death countless of my loyal subjects, who will only follow this method if I show them the way. "

"But it is not without danger. You may contract the disease. You take it deliberately into your body. I would not do this."

"Your concern pleases me, Grigory, but I will fulfil the duty of my calling. According to the Gospel, the good shepherd lays down his life for his sheep."

"Sheep are worse off with no shepherd," Grigory said lazily as he poured more wine.

Catherine's mind wandered briefly. She made a note to have the Free Economic Society look into sheep breeding – wool, meat, milk, cheese. This may be a worthwhile agricultural project. She turned once more to Orlov.

"I had hoped you would be with me in setting an example," Catherine said more sharply than she intended. "But if you are afraid, then I would not oblige you. You are after all not beholden to our people."

Grigory guffawed. "Afraid? I have probably had smallpox ten times over and never noticed! There is hardly a guardsman without pockmarks in my regiment! If you wish me to be inoculated, I will let your doctor do his magic."

Catherine had indeed wished Orlov to be inoculated. Not only did she need an example for the troops to follow but she also had to calm her own fears. If her experiment failed and she was left disfigured, Orlov would forsake her bed completely. After the flush of interest following her *aventures* with young officers, he was once more a rare visitor in her chambers. He must be made to run the same risk as she did. She could not bear to have other women kiss his handsome face while her pock-marked one remained untouched by any lips. She had not seen Orlov since his inoculation but had heard that he had gone hunting in deep snow the next day. What if he takes ill and dies through my fault? Catherine shook herself. No, she would not deviate from her course. She would order Dr Dimsdale to start inoculations in three orphanages and a hospital and to coordinate with General Panin on a programme for the army.

But first she took up her pen. She owed Voltaire a letter. She would thank him for the books and a marble bust of himself which he had sent some six months ago. She had been much too busy to read the books, and without having done so she could not answer. Still, Europe must know of her example and Voltaire, as usual, could be relied upon to spread the word with appropriate praise. She dipped her quill in the inkpot.

My dear friend,

In May of this year I received the long awaited parcel of books penned by you, my preferred author above all others, along with the marble bust of yourself, the most famous man of our times. Both grace my chambers and have been the focus of my attention for the last six months. But such greatness has inhibited and delayed my response. What words in poor French would be worthy of such a great man? I have deliberated long in search of a worthy response.

My conclusion was that I must offer something that would benefit mankind. But what? Then I knew. I wrote to England and was able to procure the services of the famous Dr Dimsdale, who came to Russia and inoculated me with the smallpox. I am well and did not need to take to my bed, not even for one day, and have carried on my business as usual. I have ordered my only son to be inoculated. Many people will follow my example, from my own court circles to the peasants toiling in the fields. Russia will be a healthy empire and will light the way for other more cautious empires and kingdoms to follow, including, we hope, your own Louis XV.

Ah, I must not forget to mention the excellent remedies which I added to those of the good Doctor Dimsdale. Any patient with some intelligence will benefit greatly and cannot but feel well. The cure is in reading your Candide. How I laughed through his impossible adventures! How fast I turned the pages! But this did not blind me to the deeper meaning –

Catherine raised her head at a loud knock at her door.

"Yes?" she called out impatiently.

Count Panin entered, his wig slightly askew and out of breath.

"I came as soon as I could, Your Majesty!"

"I did not summon you. Have you ridden from St Petersburg?" Catherine asked.

"Yes, by horse," Panin said. "It was quicker than by carriage."

"Well, I am well as you see and there is no need for alarm," Catherine said with some irritation. This is how rumours start, she thought. Soon it will be reported that I am on my deathbed.

"The Ottoman Empire has declared war, Your Majesty! On us. On Russia. They have imprisoned our ambassador in Constantinople."

Catherine put down her quill carefully.

Chapter Twenty-Five

Lord Cathcart followed Count Solms along several passages and staircases till they came to a long corridor. The Prussian ambassador was one of the few members of the Russian court that Cathcart respected. He worked assiduously for his King and country and was unfailingly correct if a little stilted. In other circumstances, Cathcart might have enjoyed a game of billiards together. But did the Prussians play billiards? Cathcart missed his own table and vowed to have one made in St Petersburg. He had heard that the Russian nobility were partial to the game and that the Empress was said to be fond of it.

His dealings with Count Solms, however, must remain politically diplomatic. Frederick of Prussia was said to have entered into secret agreements with Catherine the Great, pushed into her arms, so to speak, by England's reluctance to enter into any meaningful alliance with him. The old diplomat Bestuzhev had been strongly opposed to Prussia but his death the previous year had left Count Solms a free hand.

"Is it usual to waylay rather than to make an appointment?" Cathcart asked Solms. The ways of the Russian court continued to surprise him.

"My dear Lord Cathcart, it is the only way to ensure a word with him," Solms said slowly and very clearly. "We must wait till he moves along the corridor from the Grand Duke's chambers to the Empress's. It is a long corridor and therefore gives us the opportunity for the words we seek to deliver."

"Is the Grand Duke ill again?" Cathcart asked. "Is that why the Count rarely leaves his chambers?"

"Ah, he is always ill." This was an unusually short answer for the Count, Cathcart thought.

"But the Grand Duke survived the smallpox inoculation. Dr Dimsdale said he was hale and hearty for his fourteen years." Cathcart felt it appropriate to remind the Prussian ambassador of Britain's achievements. He envied Dr Dimsdale. Rather like a soldier, he had an enemy to deal with and could conduct campaigns and chalk up successes. The Empress had bestowed on him the hereditary title of baron, and an award amounting to 10,000 pounds as well as a pension of 500 pounds a year. Who would have thought there were riches to be gained in the practice of medicine? Why, even the young boy whose pus had been used had survived and been raised to the ranks of nobility. He would be marked for life, however, for Catherine had given him the name of Ospenny, which, Cathcart had been reliably informed, meant smallpox in Russian.

"The Grand Duke's mother, the illustrious Empress, would prefer to have her son fragile rather than strong," Solms said. "She will brook no contender to her power. The Duke is kept closeted and cosseted. He is an heir that no-one wants. Except Count Panin. He hovers over him like a mother hen. Or so I hazard. His own power lies in his power over the Grand Duke. His future too."

The Count began striding up and down the corridor impatiently, consulting his fob watch. "I hope he makes an appearance soon. I have further appointments – not that this can be called an appointment! It is no use trying to run a country without a foreign minister. Especially now they are at war."

"But Count Panin is chief member of the Foreign Affairs Council, and therefore de facto –"

"Oh, he is only a front, not even de facto," Solms said scornfully. "The Empress decides everything. There is not a paper that does not pass through her hands. Panin is knowledgeable but he has no power, only influence. And he has not cared to use it this past year. He succumbed to the passion of love and now he succumbs to the passion of mourning. He neglects his duties."

At about the time Cathcart arrived in St Petersburg, Count Panin had become betrothed to the eldest daughter of the wealthy Grand Chamberlain Count Sheremetev. Unlike Countess Stroganova, Panin's most recent passion, she was not married. The divorce proceeedings initiated by Count Stroganov were reported to be acrimoniously complicated and had quickly extinguished, it seemed, Panin's love for the Countess. Anna Sheremeteva was not only unencumbered by a husband but was young, beautiful and immensely rich.

"Why," Cathcart had asked his wife, "would a man of fifty wish to marry one so young?"

"Ah," Jane had replied, "why he wishes to marry her is plain for all to see. 40,000 roubles a year, houses full of servants and jewels, and one of the best families in Russia."

How did his wife acquire all this information, Cathcart wondered.

"The question, my love, is more why does she wish to marry him?" Jane continued. "And there I find no answer for although the Count is well mannered and cultured, he is when all is said and done, an old man. Now if I were to replace you, dearest," Jane said in a teasing tone as she twitched his collar straight, "I would look for a younger man."

"Jane!" Cathcart was shocked. "But I am yet a few years off 50!"

He had felt obliged that night to prove his youthful ardour. His wife had seemed pleased.

Count Panin had not had time to please a wife, for his young betrothed took ill with smallpox and died as the winter thaws set in. Since then he had rarely been seen in public, keeping to the chambers of the Grand Duke. It was true that he neglected his duties. The Ottoman Empire was at war with Russia and the diplomats were given only crumbs of information and had to rely on their ambassadors in Constantinople for more.

"Do you have news of the war?" Cathcart asked without much hope of receiving a useful answer. It was Britain's suspicion – and fear – that part of the secret treaty with Prussia had included support of Russia in any war with Turkey.

"The Russians apparently go from victory to victory," Solms answered. "The Empress is giddy with delight."

Cathcart tried to imagine a giddy Catherine but failed.

In April, just in time for the Empress's fortieth birthday, news of the first major victory over the Turks had reached St Petersburg. Cathcart had attended the thanksgiving service which the Empress had ordered to be held at the Kazan Church. There had been much singing, candles and incense, bowing and kissing of ... Cathcart could not see what but it was all too much for his religious taste. In May, there had been more public rejoicing. The Russian forces had defeated a 30,000 strong Turkish army.

"She is not the least perturbed about the war," Count Solms continued as he paced. "She is busy buying up all the art in Europe. Most countries sell pictures and statues in the midst of peace but the Russian Empress buys them in the midst of war. But luckily it is mostly debt-ridden France that she plunders through her sycophantic philosophers there."

Lord Cathcart did not have much appreciation for art unless military battles were portrayed, but Jane had reported breathless with wonder that the Russian Empress had recently bought a collection of some 600 paintings, which included works by Rembrandt, Rubens, Hals, Watteau ... It was a long list and Cathcart recognised few of them but Jane had been very impressed. "It must have cost a fortune," she said.

"I wonder," Cathcart said to Solms, more to stop his restless pacing than for any real desire for an answer, "that funds are available for art when a major war is being fought. It takes considerable expense if wars are to be won."

"Oh, she has borrowed heavily from the Amsterdam finance markets. And you have seen the new paper money. Not worth the paper it's printed on." Solms waved his hand in the air.

"And yet Russia has been able to send 50,000 men to deal with the Turks," Cathcart observed, feeling more confident on military terrain.

"The Empress says those very troops go into battle against the Turks as if they were going to a wedding," Solms said.

That is not how Cathcart would have described the mood of the recruits he had seen on the streets. They had been marched along in chains.

"Well, let us hope that Russia continues to be successful in the field. An unsuccessful foreign war, as every power knows, tends to impair the authority of all despots. And this is the first foreign war the Empress has ever waged, is it not?"

"I would be careful of using the term 'despot', Lord Cathcart," Solms said. "Absolute sovereign is the epithet she prefers. But yes, she should have stuck to Poland. Instead, she supports the Orthodox insurgents there against the Catholic majority, the insurgents flee across the border to Turkey to avoid repression, Cossack troops in Russian pay pursue them and sack the nearest town, slaughtering all the Jews. What a mess. Where is the *casus belli* in all that, I ask you? Where is the justification?"

"A religious war, even if justly undertaken, is always of the most odious nature and of all wars of the most doubtful success," Lord Cathcart said. He felt a little uncomfortable with his own opinion. After all, he himself had been one of the Protestant English forces which had relentlessly massacred the Catholic Jacobites. "And will breed resentment and resistance which will last for centuries," he added.

Before Count Solms could comment, the doors to the Empress's chambers at the other end of the corridor opened and Count Panin emerged. He began walking towards them with his usual mincing gait but at a faster tempo.

Solms looked at the doors to the Grand Duke's chambers behind them in confusion. "But I thought – I expected – oh, never mind! Come, we must get to him before the corridor is used up," he hissed.

Cathcart, pleased to have some action, strode with military energy towards Panin. Solms hurried beside him.

"Ah, gentlemen," Panin said as they stood before him.

Block his way, Cathcart thought. Good ploy.

"The Empress has called a meeting of her advisors," Panin said as he tried to sidestep Cathcart and Solms. "I am just on my way to arrange it. I cannot be delayed. You will receive the news in good time."

"What news?" Solms asked. "Of the war?"

"The Empress is furious," Panin whispered. "General Golitsyn has retreated back across the Dniester, relinquishing all our gains. I pleaded with Her Majesty to give command to my brother to start with. He would never have retreated. Now she would replace Golitsyn with General Rumyantsev only because Orlov wishes it. It is not a military decision – Forgive me, gentlemen. I have said too much. I am overwrought."

Panin looked gaunt and near to tears. The loss of his betrothed had indeed affected him severely, Cathcart thought.

"Yes," Solms said, "it is always better to have a King to lead the troops into battle. Like our own King Frederick. This is one thing an Empress cannot do."

Panin frowned but then turned to Cathcart. "Ah Lord Cathcart," he said more briskly, "the Empress would summon you to discuss naval matters. We must take the battle to the seas, as England does."

Cathcart was just about to object that he was a military man and knew little of naval matters. Besides, England would never help a foreign fleet to rival her own, if that was possible, which Cathcart doubted, but he suddenly thought – although not a gambling man – at last he had a chip he could play with.

He bowed and said, "Of course, we are at Her Majesty's service."

Count Solms scowled as Panin made his way along the corridor. "You are aware, Lord Cathcart, that neither of our sovereigns would wish to take up war against the Ottoman Empire. Think of your trade routes. Think of France's enmity. Think of Austria. Would we drive them to help Turkey? Would we drag our countries into another European war?"

Fortunately, Solms gave Cathcart no time to answer his questions for Cathcart had no answers.

"No, we must maintain some sensible balance," Solms continued. "No one country must dominate. The Empress of Russia cannot be supported in her territorial ambitions."

Lord Cathcart sighed. He would seek advice from London.

Chapter Twenty-Six

Remembering the dawn risings of her youth when she had sneaked off in men's clothing to shoot ducks, Catherine rose earlier than usual one morning to ride out alone in the grounds of Tsarskoye Selo. As Empress of All Russia, she had limitless power but little freedom.

The palace at Tsarskoye Selo had been given by Peter the Great to his wife Catherine I. Bartolomeo Rastrelli had redesigned it for their daughter Elizabeth when she became Empress and its sumptuous and flamboyant style reminded Catherine of the Empress Elizabeth's whims and caprices. Catherine was wont to describe Rastrelli's style as a rich dessert topped with *crème fouettée*, but she had to acknowledge the harmony and symmetry of his buildings. She herself preferred straighter, more classical lines – except in nature. She abhorred the strict geometry of the French garden style, the unnatural cascades of water, the boringly straight *alleés*. She had ordered the gardens at Tsarskoye Selo to be re-landscaped in the English style. She had never been to England to view such gardens but Grigory Orlov's youngest brother Vladimir was one of the many who returned from their travels with enthusiastic reports of the natural setting of English gardens. "There is more work involved in the attempt to imitate nature and at the same time conceal the work," Vladimir Orlov explained as he showed her engravings of meandering paths, lakes, streams, slopes and groves. She had sent her head gardener to England to view the most famous gardens. His attempts at Tsarskoye Selo were yielding results now that he understood that she wanted to feel as if she were walking through nature. Unexpected vistas were opening up as paths were allowed to wander and there were even a few swells in the landscape.

The sun was rising as Catherine reached the lake. Yes, the column would be perfect in the middle of the water.

Chesme had been a naval battle. One of the greatest in history. It was Russia's first naval victory in 900 years and the Ottoman Empire's first naval defeat in over two hundred years. What glory she had led her country to! The column of white-and-pink marble from Siberia, of a quality even the Italians would envy, would be decorated with the bows of ships. It would be crowned by a bronze figure of an eagle symbolising Russia trampling the crescent of Turkey.

Much of the victory had been due to Alexey Orlov. Recovered from the illness which had kept him bedridden for months, he had been convalescing in Livorno in Italy when war with the Turks broke out. It had been his idea to send a Russian fleet to the Mediterranean to distract Ottoman attention from the meagre Russian fleet at the Black Sea.

The strategy had worked. A hundred enemy ships had been destroyed at Chesme on the Turkish coast, some twenty thousand Muslims said to have perished. Reports described how the earth and sea had trembled with the huge number of exploding ships, the tremors felt twelve leagues away. Alexey Orlov wrote to her that the waters of the port of Chesme had churned red with blood. Catherine had commissioned two large paintings to commemorate the battle based on drawings sent from Chesme. After the battle, Alexey had blown up one of his own ships to give artists an accurate impression of the devastation inflicted on the Turks. She had bestowed the title of Chesmensky on Alexey. Dear Alexey! If only she could love him and not his faithless brother. They had comforted each other from time to time, she for Grigory's faithlessness, he for always being made to feel less than his brother. He was a competent lover but there was affection rather than passion. "All I have suffered in this great battle," he wrote, "was the loss of the ring with your portrait. But it is only a loss if I have lost the regard of she who gave it to me."

Catherine immediately sent him another, set in ample diamonds.

Just weeks after the victory at Chesme, General Rumyantsev won two more major battles against the Turks on land, one of them when 150,000 Turkish troops vastly outnumbered his own 25,000. Catherine had joked in a letter to Voltaire, "If this war continues, my garden at Tsarskoye Selo will resemble a game of skittles, for after each noteworthy victory, I put up some new monument there."

As she now gazed across the lake, she thought of having a temple of remembrance built with a triumphal arch. All the great events of the war would be engraved on medallions. She would have Rinaldi draw up plans for it immediately. She would also arrange a firework display of the battles when the monument was finished. And she must not forget to order more silver medals for the troops. Twenty thousand had already been dispatched.

But in truth, she thought as she reined her horse in at the water's edge, I am weary of two years of war. I would have peace. Austria and Prussia, alarmed at Russia's gains, had offered to mediate. But she would dictate her own terms, if at all. Grigory Orlov, who remained in St Petersburg to coordinate Russia's military plans, favoured further gains. He fretted at not being in the field. "But I need you here to advise me. I have no other military genius at hand," she said peremptorily. But she knew in her heart that the reason she kept him close was that she did not want to lose him on a blood-stained battlefield.

He still did not come to her bed as often as she wanted him to. She felt resentful that she worked so hard with little recompense in her personal life, resentful that fate seemed to begrudge her love. She often wondered if things would have turned out differently if she had married Orlov. She doubted it. He was a man in the full bloom of his manhood, several years younger than herself. It was unjust that nature allowed a woman's bloom to last no more than a few decades while a man received several more. If she had married Orlov, she would have lost the throne and then him. At least as Empress she was able to shower him with gifts of wealth and privilege.

Although Orlov was always respectful to her and gentle in his ways, she knew in her heart that he did not love her. She was in thrall to his easy smile and his long relaxed limbs, but she knew she must learn to stop loving him. His carefree optimism which had once attracted her now weighed her down. "Let tomorrow take care of itself," he would whisper, if she pointed to the late hour, "whilst we take care of this hour given to us." The problem was that the late hour was now not always spent with her.

Catherine spurred her horse to a canter round the lake. The Chinese summer house was almost completed. She would organise a Chinese masquerade. She would have Chinese food served and Chinese music played. Everyone would come in Chinese costume. She would look through her books of drawings for inspiration for her own dress. It must be of rich silk with intricate embroidery and she would have a diamond necklace reset in a Chinese symbol. She would choose the most pleasing: power, love, victory. It would be a fine diversion.

Much cheered, she galloped towards the palace stables. Before breakfast she would look at some of her newly acquired paintings. Most of them were to be hung in the galleries at the Winter Palace, which were already overfull, but she had brought a few to Tsarskoye Selo with her. Among the 500 paintings she had secured for 460,000 livres from a Paris financier's family was a wonderful portrait of Danaë by Titian. The mythological princess lay in naked abandon, her flesh glowing warmly, as Zeus' gold rained down on her. She had the painting brought to her chambers and after having had herself bathed and plied with sweet oils, she had arranged herself exactly as in the painting, for Orlov. He had been impressed, had stayed all night and had loved her with his old zeal.

"My voluptuous Danaë," he had whispered.

"And you, dear Grigory, are my shower of gold."

She had thought of giving him the painting so that he would be reminded of his desire for her whenever his eyes lighted on it.

She had also arranged to meet Falconet later in the morning. He had been persistent in his attempts to see her but she was tired of his artistic petulance. She had done enough, had discussed his plans, had allowed her magnificent horse Brilliant to be trotted up and down endlessly on a wooden ramp for Falconet's sketches. She had repeatedly told the artist not to seek her opinion for she could not even draw. She had even sat for his young pupil Marie-Anne Collot, which had nothing to do with the monument. But she was curious about the attractive young girl. Was she really Falconet's apprentice? Or was it just another case of older men renewing their vigour through the acquisition of young flesh? Catherine could not imagine the pedantic Falconet in bed with anyone. He would show more interest in whether the folds of the covers met his artistic standards of aesthetic proportions. And perhaps he would have to measure the girl first.

He spoiled her enjoyment of art, repeatedly chastising her for placing statues of great artistic value in the hanging gardens, where, he said, the droppings of the songbirds left indelible marks on the marble. Or for hanging her favourite paintings where the sun would not only illuminate them as she wished but fade them into blandness. She would not discuss the monument with him any more. He had spoiled that for her too. Did she need to know that the serpent being trampled under the horse's hooves was not so much a symbol of Russia's power over its enemies but a necessary disguised support without which the bronze horse could not rear?

The only thing about the monument which still fired her enthusiasm was the plinth. The Thunder Stone excited her as few projects had done. It had been a feat of engineering genius to move the huge granite boulder weighing three million pounds from Lakhta in Karelia to St Petersburg. It had taken five months, progressing at about a verst a month on tracks which had to be dismantled and reassembled every 100 metres before it reached the Neva to be floated for the remainder of its journey on a specially built barge, supported on either side by two warships. Catherine had visited it often on its long, slow journey and had never failed to be impressed by man's ingenuity as she watched the four hundred men wrestle with the mammoth. In some ways, she saw it as her own struggle, moving Russia towards a better future.

And with that thought, her spirits fell again. What was the use of a beautiful English garden, of a luxurious palace, great works of art, monuments and celebrations when she was destined to be lonely. She had once told Voltaire that she was a busy bee. Now she felt like a lonely Queen Bee, on whom everyone depended. And they would throw her out when she had served her purpose. Or when there was another Queen Bee.

Catherine dismounted from her horse Caprice. Brilliant, her favourite, was still trotting ramps for Falconet in St Petersburg. The lightness she had felt earlier as she cantered through the parkland with the rising sun had given way to dark thoughts. She looked up at the sky, expecting to see clouds. But there were none. She had a sudden urge to remount her horse and gallop to she knew not where.

Chapter Twenty-Seven

Count Panin entered Catherine's study with some trepidation. It was unusual for the Empress to summon her son to Tsarskoye Selo. "Prepare for a longer visit," she had written to Panin. "I would spend some time with the Grand Duke." This was even more unusual. The Empress hardly knew her son. It was Panin he was closest to, Panin who sat at his bedside at night as he fought fever and fears, Panin who had sheltered him from the court's intrigues, Panin who had bought him a parrot to cheer him up.

"Ah, Count Panin," Catherine said, "pray be seated and take your ease. I would discuss an important matter with you. The Grand Duke is well? And happy to be with us?"

Panin answered carefully. "The Grand Duke is always happy to be near his mother. His health is stable and he looks forward to the fresh air and some hunting."

It was true. Paul was rarely allowed out in the city. At first, Catherine had cited fear of smallpox but since his successful inoculation, she now cited possible plots against his person. Paul was Catherine's only legitimate blood link to the throne. His death would remove her legitimacy. But Paul's legitimacy also made him the Empress's most dangerous rival to the throne. It was not so much assassins she wished to protect him from as those who would put him on the throne in her stead.

"We will celebrate his sixteenth birthday here," Catherine said cheerfully. "We will ask him what entertainments he would wish."

"He is very fond of French comedies, Your Majesty," Panin said.

"Yes, remember how he laughed in the theatre when he was but a boy and how it upset him if anyone applauded before him!" Catherine said. Almost fondly, Panin thought.

"But his childhood is gone and we must look to his future," the Empress continued more briskly. "He will come of age in three years and we must prepare him."

"Prepare him, Your Majesty?" Panin asked trying to keep the surprise from his voice. Did the Empress intend to groom her son as her successor after all? He himself had been preparing the Grand Duke for his future ever since he had taken charge of him ten years ago. His future as rightful Emperor of Russia. Panin kept this from Catherine, sure she would have him banished for treason. But he often reminded Paul that he was called by God to rule Russia one day.

The child would reply calmly, " I do not wish to. My mother can do it."

Panin would then say gently, "But after your mother. Only it is better not to mention it to the Empress because it will only make her sad to think that she must one day die like all God's creatures."

"Oh yes, it will make her very angry to die," Paul said fearfully. "We do not wish her to be angry."

Panin pitied the child. He was pale and delicate, often sick but always affable in manner. He learned quickly even if he did not delight in all subjects. Catherine had prescribed his curriculum. It was so full that the child rarely had a free hour to himself. The best professors in Russia taught him French, German and Russian, history and geography, mathematics and drawing, dancing and fencing, physics and astronomy, and religion. The Empress had recently added diplomacy and finance but had ordered Panin to steer clear of war and military matters. But Paul loved soldiers and weaponry and uniforms. Just like his father. Whatever was said behind closed doors, Panin was convinced that Paul was Peter's son. The physical resemblance was unmistakable, the squashed nose and deep set eyes. But his nature was a kinder one than his father's had been, which had suffered from a haphazard and sadistic upbringing. Panin's self-given task was to bring Paul up to be Emperor. He had much to eradicate from the influence of the capricious Empress Elizabeth who had had charge of him for the first five or six years of his life.

"Count Panin, it is time to discuss a suitable bride for the Grand Duke," Catherine now said. "It is of the utmost importance. Russia's future may depend on our choice."

The Grand Duke was in love. When he turned fourteen, the Empress had arranged for a young widow of good birth and background to instruct Paul in matters of the bedchamber. "A man," she had said to Panin, "must not go unprepared to his bride. I suffered nine years at the hands of an incompetent husband and nearly lost my life through his failure. My son will not inflict such shame." Unexpectedly, Paul had fallen in love with the kind widow-tutor Sophia Chartoryzhkaya, some ten years his senior. "I will marry her and no other," he declared to Panin.

"You may love her," Panin told him, "but you may not marry her." He instructed Sophia to be kind to the Grand Duke. "As long as you know your duty and your place," he said, "you will have a place here at court. But if you encourage the Grand Duke in any disobedience you will find yourself in colder climes."

Sophia conducted herself modestly at court and even the Empress tolerated the relationship of her son and Sophia. "She has a good influence on him," she observed, "he is calmer, less prone to rushing headlong here and there." And he is ill much less, Panin thought. Sophia had accompanied them to Tsarskoye Selo.

Panin limited his reply to a cautious "Indeed, Your Majesty." It was his experience that it was more politic to say nothing until one had heard more.

Catherine continued, "Such a bride must be compliant and obedient —"

Someone with no designs on the throne of Russia, Panin thought.

"Protestant and German —"

Which meant no Russian was to be considered. A

Russian bride would bring families and ambitions with her.

" – but of a minor house with no commitments to Prussia or Austria. For example, Sophia Dorothea of Württemberg. She is reported as robust in health and pleasing in looks and manner."

"She is but eleven years old, Your Majesty," Panin pointed out. "The Orthodox church forbids marriage for those under fourteen years of age."

"But in three years when the Grand Duke reaches his Russian age of maturity, she will be fourteen," Catherine countered him briskly. "The Princess of Nassau will not do – she is Catholic. Perhaps Princess Louise of Saxe-Gotha. Her grandmother was first cousin to my father."

Catherine stopped to consult what Panin presumed was a list of bridal candidates.

"But let us keep this all between ourselves for the moment," she resumed after a short pause. "I merely want to warn you that we must choose our bride in the next year or two and that I have begun the process since it may take time. There is no need to mention it to the Grand Duke. As you know, we expect a visit from Prussia this month. King Frederick sends us his brother Prince Heinrich, whom I knew in my youth before I came to Russia. I look forward to seeing him. He comes no doubt to recommend marriage candidates. There must be a long list of German princesses desperate to marry the heir to the Russian throne."

Panin was startled. Never had the Empress referred to her son as her heir before.

"But, we will have no Queen Bees, "she said laughingly, "will we, Count Panin? We must choose carefully."

Panin was puzzled. Bees?

"Tell the Grand Duke that I look forward to dine with him," the Empress said, rising from her chair to indicate that their talk was at an end. "He may bring his Sophia. She is a good girl and will keep him amenable and amiable."

Chapter Twenty-Eight

As he waited for the carriage – it would of course be a sleigh, he corrected himself – which was to take him to Moscow, Prince Heinrich looked out onto the frozen Neva. What a city of contradictions carved out of snow and ice only decades ago! Its Winter Palace rivalled anything in Europe, and fine mansions and palaces graced the banks of the river. There was no meander of medieval streets but rather wide avenues, spacious squares, and straight canals. But it was more a city still in the making. Even in winter the hammers of craftsmen rang out. There were myriads of tumbledown wooden houses, their ornately carved exteriors battered by the elements. Catherine had told him these were all to be replaced. "I found Petersburg almost entirely made of wood," she told him, "and will leave it made of stone and marble."

And what an opulent court! What extravagance! Prince Heinrich himself was fond of luxury and pursued pleasure with an easy conscience but he wondered how the Russians had the time or money to wage war. And wage it most successfully. They had defeated his very own forces at Kunersdorf just ten years ago, he who had never lost a battle till then. By some miracle, the Russian forces had not pressed on to take Berlin, instead retreating to Saxony. Was that arrogance or fear or mercy? Later King Frederick did say the money he had spent on cultivating connections at the Russian court might have paid off after all.

And now the Russians were winning victory after victory over the Ottomans. King Frederick was alarmed. "A monster is in the making and must be stopped," he had said as he instructed his brother to travel to Russia to persuade the Empress to settle for peace. Ostensibly, Prince Heinrich was there to advise on the choice of a German bride for the Empress's son. And to see the sights. And these he had certainly seen.

He had been afforded a most lavish welcome. Three ships had been sent to meet him at Reval and a very well appointed palace with an excellent wine cellar and chef was put at his disposal "until such times as he felt recovered from his journey", Catherine wrote in a note of welcome. On reaching St Petersburg a few days later he knew his mission of peace would fail. He was invited to attend a thanksgiving service at a great and cold cathedral for yet another victory over the Turks and was proudly shown the many Turkish standards captured in other battles. Catherine flaunted war. Peace would bring no glory.

Catherine had taken him to Tsarskoye Selo, a palace of great beauty with vast grounds of forests and lakes, and had proudly shown him her collection of monuments, illuminated at night with cleverly concealed flares in the snowy landscape. Peasants danced in national costumes and hunters blew their horns. The journey there had been by sleigh, equipped with mirrors so that he could see what Catherine called "the infinity of Russia in winter". It had been breathtakingly beautiful, Prince Heinrich had to admit. But only to himself. He remained careful and distant. He kept in his mind the images of his cavalry officers on bloody battlefields, slain by Russian swords.

Catherine herself surprised him. He remembered her as Sophie, the lively child of his Brunswick summers. She and his younger brother Ferdinand had been fond of mischief. He also remembered being considered as a possible husband for her before Frederick had arranged the match in Russia. What would have happened if she had stayed in Prussia to marry him? Where would Russia be now? And where would he be? He shuddered to think. Catherine, now forty, was a formidable woman, a full head taller than himself. And much too ... buxom for his taste. In any case, his taste did not run to women and certainly not to women who would be men, as Catherine seemed to. He had married as he must. But his wife Princess Wilhelmina was delicate of figure and aesthetically pleasing. They had no children. Both had been averse to the congress with each other necessary to produce them. Wilhelmina now lived in Berlin, enjoying her literary salons and congress with others while he was free to enjoy his own pleasures at his palace outside the capital. Such pleasures did not seem to be readily available in Russia, he thought morosely, although there was no dearth of handsome men. The Empress's favourite, Count Orlov, was certainly a man possessed of easy charm.

Prince Heinrich had tried to engage Catherine's interest in Frederick's recommendation for peace. She remained polite but adamant. "Ah, they foolishly wakened the sleeping cat," she had said. "And now the cat chases the mice and they are surprised. But the cat will only go back to sleep when it has had its fill or when there are no more mice to disturb it."

Prince Heinrich did not care for armies to be compared with cats.

"But, my dear Catherine, it is often a wiser strategy to recognise when to stop. You are victorious now but would you stretch your armies into defeat? Is it not better to consolidate your gains?"

"Oh, we will not be defeated, never fear, my dear Prince," Catherine replied cheerfully. "If Sultan Mustafa chooses to lead his country into losses, then he must answer for it. We have Azov, the Crimea will soon be ours as will Bessarabia, we have overrun the Turks in Moldavia and Bulgaria. We will soon take Constantinople if he is not careful. No, my dear Prince, it is Mustafa who must beg us for peace."

"But meanwhile your country must suffer the burden of the cost of war," the Prince persisted. "Surely your people would have peace? And enough to eat?"

"Oh, do not be concerned on their account, my dear Heinrich. Taxes are so modest that every peasant in Russia can afford a chicken in his pot every week."

"Not Henry IV's old chestnut again," Prince Heinrich thought. Catherine, he noted, often quoted the Good King Henry but this was the 18th century not the 16th. And Russia was not France.

"In fact, in some of our provinces which I have visited, the peasants prefer turkey," she added, rather airily, he thought. "It is true that we have to regulate grain but the peasants are producing more and more, and trade is good. And our population has increased in the last seven years by a tenth."

This was a major complaint of Frederick's. He had worked hard to rebuild Prussia after the devastation of war. Subsidies had been given to restore agriculture and rebuild towns and villages. Public stores of grain had been established for times of famine. He had issued laws and reforms for the good of his people. If anyone had a right to quote Good King Henry, it was Frederick not Catherine. But still the Prussian population did not increase at any appreciable rate. Decimated by war and plague, by loss of territories ... and by the loss of emigrants to Russia.

Catherine had not finished. "We may be at war, my dear Prince, but you will have observed that we emerge from each war flourishing more than when we began."

There was little Prince Heinrich could undertake against such intransigency. She had an imperial authority which her courtesy did not undermine. He had been instructed by Frederick that in the case of the failure of peace talks, Heinrich was to have Catherine concede to Frederick's wish for Polish territory, just "some little parcels of land" to make up for Catherine's Black Sea conquests. "Some ointment for the burns," Frederick had said. When Heinrich broached the subject, diplomatically but clearly, Catherine had shrugged her shoulders, "Why shouldn't we all take something?" she asked. Heinrich could not judge whether she spoke in earnest or whether the subject bored her.

If war – or rather an end to war – did not capture the Empress's attention, brides did. She required Prince Heinrich to give detailed descriptions of all the Prussian or German princesses he knew. Here, he could at least promote those candidates favoured by his brother the King. He had disillusioned her about her favoured candidate, whom Frederick did not approve of.

"Princess Louise of Saxa-Gotha, whom you favour for her family connections, is plump," Prince Heinrich said as neutrally as he could. "Very plump. And her mother, a woman strong in her convictions, would never allow her daughter to convert to Orthodoxy. Or perhaps not even to come to Russia."

King Frederick wished to further the suit of the house of Hesse-Darmstadt. "Such an alliance would suit posterity, theirs and ours. There are three daughters, one of them must suit. See that they are all invited," he had instructed Heinrich.

In this at least, Prince Heinrich had been successful. Catherine promised to invite the three princesses and their mother to Russia once she could give the matter proper attention. Meanwhile, she asked Heinrich to make sure the daughters met her criteria. "My future daughter-in-law, perhaps the future Empress of Russia, must evidence goodness of heart, liveliness in manner and fearlessness in travel. But if the princesses should demur, you may cite my own example. My mother came here under the pretext of thanking the late Empress in the name of her family for the various benefits which she had given them. The worst that can happen is that none of the daughters suits us but what have they to lose? Their expenses will be reimbursed and I will give them all dowries. And if they travel incognito, as my mother and I did, no-one will be any the wiser and their chances of a future marriage will not be ruined."

Prince Heinrich was not unwilling to play matchmaker.

While Grand Duke Paul was far from handsome and lacked stature, he seemed a pleasant enough youth. And there was certainly luxury to be enjoyed at the court of Russia, such as the Lutheran princesses from Darmstadt could not even dream of. Catherine had held a masquerade in his honour a few days previously. Such opulence, decadence, hedonism – wrapped in bows of so-called culture. Nearly four thousand guests had filled the apartments of the Winter Palace. Some of the costumes were very fanciful but there were many black silk dominos, flowing mysteriously round their masked wearers. Occasionally, a cloak would swirl open to reveal a flash of red silk or a bare leg. Prince Heinrich had chosen to wear a white domino. Catherine had appeared in a Grecian dress, white folds clinging to the roundness of her figure. There were Chinese and Persians, and Turks were popular among the men. A few ladies – or perhaps young men, Heinrich thought happily – had appeared in gauzy harem trousers. Trumpets sounded to announce the start of the formal entertainment and a very muscular Apollo ushered in the four seasons, played by boys from the Cadet Corps (Heinrich was taken with the beauty of Spring in particular) and the twelve months depicted by young women from the Smolny Institute, Catherine's educational project. Their elaborate dresses were of some transparent material that emphasized rather than covered their nubility.

An intimate supper was served to an inner circle of 120 people in a large oval room. Prince Heinrich, used to estimating ranks of troops, quickly calculated that more than 2000 candles lit the space. On a large gallery above, four orchestras played to the masked revellers thronging below. There were Cossack dances, Chinese, Polish, Swedish and Tatar. The formal programme ended at midnight with a very spectacular firework display. Prince Heinrich was astonished at the variety of colours, especially the fresh verdant green of a tree of fire, which swayed gently for twenty minutes under a canopy of white fire representing the sky. Dancing carried on till about five o'clock in the morning. Dominos were discarded, partners were lost in the crowds, new ones were found. Flushed with wine and excitement, people embraced intimately, including Catherine, Heinrich noted, whom he thought he saw in the arms of a Turk but he was too far away to make out whether it was her favourite Grigory Orlov or not. Bacchanalian, he concluded. While the ball whirled round him, he thought longingly of his more private pleasures in the quiet of his palace.

But now he must go to Moscow. He peered impatiently at his fob watch. Punctuality was certainly a trait obviously valued more in Prussia than Russia. Had he known he would have to wait so long, he would have taken a short stroll along the river to view the one thing that had impressed him deeply during his visit. An enormous piece of Karelian granite had been transferred inch by inch to St Petersburg and erected on the banks of the Neva. It was to form the plinth of the monument being cast in bronze by the Frenchman Falconet. It was indeed a feat to be compared to the building of the pyramids or the Colossus of Rhodes. Catherine claimed it was the largest stone moved by man. Not even animals had been used in dragging it on its long journey. This was indeed 'daringly performed', the inscription Catherine had ordered on the commemorative medal. But would such a monolithic plinth not overpower any monument, no matter how grand or well-executed?

His thoughts were interrupted by the appearance of a servant. His sleigh and a small retinue were ready to depart. He was to travel incognito to avoid the delay which protocol would cause if it were known that the brother of King Frederick the Great was visiting Russia. What sights and wonders awaited him in Moscow? he wondered.

Chapter Twenty-Nine

Catherine was glad Prince Heinrich had left for Moscow. It had been a tiring visit. She had done her best to keep the Prince entertained with feasts and balls, concerts and operas, fireworks and theatre. She would not have him report that she, a princess of Prussia herself, had not brought civilisation to Russia. But he was as stiff as she remembered him from her youth when she and his younger brother Ferdinand used to run about while he sniffed at them disapprovingly. And surely his dress was not *à la mode* in Berlin? Red waistcoat and blue breeches? And his hair! Cut short and thick with a high toupée atop! And his only talk was of peace with the Ottomans or carving up Poland between Russia and Prussia. Frederick was evidently afraid of her power. What a heady feeling! To have great Prussia afraid of Russia, a Russia she had created! She would concede nothing unless it suited her and at present, it suited her to keep Russia free of all allies and commitments. She would decide what was best for Russia, and for Europe.

But meanwhile she would make sure that Prince Heinrich reported positively on her sovereign abilities on his return to Prussia. A good start would be to report flatteringly on him. His inbred politeness would dictate that he return the compliments ten-fold. She would praise their conformity of ideas, his cheerful disposition, his honest character, his elevated mind, his cultured sophistication. She would emphasize their deep friendship and respect for one another. Yes, she could feel a letter, perhaps to Voltaire, in the making. He would report to King Frederick, perhaps even send him a copy, and to many others.

But first she must peruse the latest communiqués from the battlefields. Turkish attempts to recapture Moldavia had been successfully repelled but there was rumour of

Austrian support for Turkey in the form of troops at the Moldavian border and loans of money to the Sultan. It was little wonder that Frederick of Prussia wished Russia to sue for peace if Austria was going to gain territory from the Ottomans. But first they must wrest it from the Russians and this Catherine would not allow.

But she had another enemy to contend with, an invisible one not so easily vanquished. Turkey was rife with the plague and it had no respect for borders. Her army doctors reported cases of "infectious pestilential distemper" in the ranks but were reluctant, or unable, to declare it plague. In autumn, however, hundreds of cases were reported in Kiev, which left little doubt. Catherine knew this posed a very serious threat to her empire. The city was the main supply centre for the Russian troops in the south and what passed through there would eventually arrive in Moscow, then St Petersburg. She still refused to allow the word "plague" to be used – she would not have the world know she was not in control nor the Ottomans that her forces were weakened by their disease nor her troops weakened by panic – but fear motivated her to order strict protective measures to be taken. Cordons were to be set up all round the Ukraine. She sent the head of the medical chancery, Dr Johann Lerche, to Kiev. He was a Prussian who had done much to advance medical practice during his forty years in Russia and Catherine trusted and respected his knowledge.

On arrival in Kiev, Dr Lerche had immediately ordered that all dispatches be handled only with tongs and then fumigated with vinegar, gunpowder and sulphur. Vitriol was to be added to the troops' drink rations although in his report to Catherine he expressed his doubt that such large supplies could be found at such short notice. Those who died of the plague, or "putrid fever with spots", were to be buried seven feet deep in their clothes. Anyone approaching the troops with obvious spots and fever was to be turned away or shot if they desisted. All communication with the local population was forbidden or strictly controlled. Dr Lerche noted in his report that since the female camp followers had been evicted and the men not allowed to leave the camp in search of female company, incidents of disease had decreased. They were still high among the local inhabitants, however, some hundred per day. Dr Lerche had reported the resistance to quarantine measures among the local populace, due to their "deep simplicity and stubbornness". To conceal the source of plague and the consequent threat of being evacuated from their houses and sent to quarantine camps, they left their dead to rot in the streets. It was not surprising, Catherine thought. Kiev, fought over by Russian, Poles, Turks and Cossacks for centuries, had always been a problem. The population had proved itself truculently defiant on more than one occasion. They were more Cossack than Russian.

Catherine scanned the description of the symptoms which Dr Lerche had sent, as he said, to forewarn his medical colleagues in Moscow in the very unlikely event of the pestilence reaching there. All reports from the south were transcribed for her on fresh paper. Even she did not trust fumigation. *The disease*, she read, *always begins with great pain in the head ... nausea but difficulty in vomiting ... The sick fall into a very great despondency and anxiety ... fever and delirium ... Buboes and carbuncles appear ... suppuration ... Skin takes on a blue tinge and darkens ... a proliferation of dark spots ... Death mostly follows especially if untreated.*

Catherine shivered and tried to remind herself that her terrible headache was a frequent rather than a new occurrence.

Dr Lerche pleaded for more medical staff. "We have lost fifteen army doctors and assistants to the disease. We need six more doctors, ten surgeons and twenty surgeon's assistants, or even barbers. I am particularly aware that our efforts to increase the number of medical experts in our realm is only in its infancy but I beg Your Most Gracious Majesty to send those who have even a little knowledge, perhaps even my own students."

His next paragraph caused her to gasp in alarm.

"Your Majesty will agree that this is of vital importance in light of my findings that the occurrence of the disease can be traced clearly from Khotyn, where Russian troops engaged in victorious battle, along our supply lines through Poland to Kiev and that Your Majesty would not wish me to have concealed these findings from her. We must pray for the speedy onset of a hard winter for the pestilence breeds in warm and wet weather, such as is prevalent here, even in autumn."

Catherine threw the letter down. Russia had not succumbed to the Turks and it would not succumb to their plague. She would –

Suddenly, the door flew open and Grigory Orlov rushed in, "Catherine, we have bad news."

Catherine had rarely seen Grigory with such serious mien. He tackled all difficulties with a confident smile.

"A defeat?" she asked.

"Worse," he said. "The plague has reached Moscow."

Chapter Thirty

Count Panin gave his full attention to the two ambassadors standing before him. He kept his expression pleasantly receptive, he thought, in the face of their barely concealed indignation and impatience. He liked Lord Cathcart and had played a game of billiards with him. The Empress had even joined in. Count Solms had not.

In his efforts to establish a Northern Alliance in Europe to counteract the Bourbon-Habsburg threat, Panin had built up close ties to both men. Prussia and Britain were the cornerstones of the alliance and the present crisis must not be allowed to destroy his careful work.

"Count Panin," Lord Cathcart began, "it is essential that we be kept informed of what is happening in Moscow. You know that my family is here. It is irresponsible to have exposed my children to this terrible danger. Had we been properly informed in December or even January when the disease first broke out, I would have sent them to safety in England."

"There was no plague in Moscow at that time," Panin answered evenly. "But if there had been, the worst thing you could have done, my dear Lord Cathcart, would have been to send your family on the road. Or sea. The vapours of the disease lurk amongst travellers. It is more advisable to keep your family in a safe place. As St Petersburg is. We have effective cordons in place on all approaches to the city."

Before Cathcart could answer, Count Solms said, "King Frederick is particularly incensed that his brother was allowed to go to Moscow, indeed sent by the Empress, when the authorities knew of plague incidents."

This was partly true, Panin thought. The Empress had indeed been informed of incidents of disease in the south and had ordered anti-plague cordons but the disease had crept ever nearer. In November she had been informed that streams of refugees fleeing the plague-ridden south effectively evaded the cordons as they made their way north. There were reports of victims just over 300 versts from Moscow. Catherine had known all this.

"Prince Heinrich was never in any danger," Panin said with emphatic indignation. "Why, it is proof of the safety of the city that the Empress arranged for his visit. She has a high regard for the Prince, both in respect for Prussia and in her personal affection. She would never knowingly endanger his life."

Catherine, however, had indeed considered cancelling the Prince's visit to Moscow.

"But on what grounds?" she had asked. "What reason shall I give? That the plague *might* reach Moscow? And we are not even sure that it is the plague. My troops have been written off as defeated by the pestilence and yet, there they stand, healthy, resurrected. No, we shall not spread rumour and panic. Especially in Moscow. It is much like Kiev, steeped in superstitions. They cling to their dark bearded past instead of embracing the clear light of reason. Who knows what chaos would ensue."

Count Solms brought up the point Panin knew he would. "But there was news of an outbreak of pestilence in Moscow while the Prince was there, in fact, just as he arrived. And he had to leave the city forthwith."

"Oh, but that was a small outbreak of some minor fever at the Infantry Hospital," Panin said reassuringly. "Which is on the outskirts of the city. There were only twenty deaths in four weeks, a fairly normal number for most illnesses. But still, all precautions were taken: isolating the area, fumigation – "

Lord Cathcart interrupted, "But they have not had any effect. The pestilence has flared again just two months later."

Another difficult point to deny, Panin thought. And one which had incensed the Empress.

"I can defeat the Turks but not their plague!" she had raged. "What use are my medical experts? Let us find out. Call a meeting of all members of the Medical College. I will have answers!"

Panin turned his attention back to the ambassadors.

"Not unexpectedly," Count Solms said.

Panin tried to think what he was referring to but only succeeded in looking puzzled.

"That the pestilence has flared up again," Solms said impatiently. "The vapours are kept frozen when it is cold enough but a thaw releases them. As one must know. And expect. And be prepared for."

"I have heard reports of hundreds dead in a woollen manufactory in Moscow," Lord Cathcart said in a rush. "Is this correct?"

The woollen factory could not be explained away so easily. It was situated in the centre of the haphazard city, in a crowded area where houses huddled together with barely enough room for a carriage to pass in the thoroughfares between them. More than 2500 worked in the factory. The disease had lurked there for several weeks before it was reported. The city physician had himself been ill and unable to attend to his duties. He had recently died of a "gangrenous ulcer on his leg". Catherine, who had avoided the word plague, was now sure it was plague.

"The disease," she declared, "has been brought to the factory in the wool which Greek merchants have transported from the Ottoman Empire. It is not inconceivable that it is a deliberate plot. Unable to defeat our forces honourably in the field of battle, the Turks have resorted to cowardly subterfuge!" Catherine had ordered the factory closed, its workers quarantined outside the city and all textile imports from or through Poland forbidden.

Panin now attempted to allay the fears of the ambassadors. "The Empress has replaced the Governor General in Moscow, has sent her best medical and other experts to identify and contain the disease. She has even halted the foundation work on the new Kremlin Place for fear of releasing noxious underground vapours. And these measures have proved efficacious. There have been few more deaths. So either the disease was not plague, as we tend to believe, or it has been defeated."

"Or it is dormant due to the unseasonal drop in temperatures," Solms said. "By summer, the disease will rear its ugly and dangerous head again, mark my words!"

"I say, Solms – " Cathcart began in protest.

"Gallons of vinegar seems to be the answer," Solms continued. "Better get some in while stocks last. I am having mine sent from Prussia. Make sure your English ships bring you enough of your apple cider variety, Cathcart, now that the seas are free of ice. "

"Gentlemen, gentlemen, there is no plague in Moscow!" Panin fought to keep his voice even. "It has been vanquished. Or never was. We must not spread panic. The Empress herself is planning to visit the city soon to oversee the restoration of the Kremlin Palace. What more proof of safety would you need?"

Panin spoke with a calm ease he did not feel. It was not only the noxious fumes of the plague that seemed to swirl in the corridors of the Winter Palace. An ill wind seemed to be blowing through the Court. Even the Empress was restless.

Chapter Thirty-One

The wooden houses were easy kindle to the fire as it leapt its hungry way through the city, lighting the night sky as it gathered strength. Catherine watched in mute horror, willing the flames to stop, begging God for a thunderstorm.

Orlov bundled her into a carriage, ordering the escort of Guards to ride at speed along the coast to Peterhof Palace.

"These conflagrations may have been started deliberately," he said. "Fires have sprung up simultaneously in many parts of the city. You must go and I will save what we can. As well as root out any plotters against you."

"Do not rest until every spark is extinguished," she commanded him. "Save my city!"

The carriage raced westwards, following the line of the coast. She could see fires on the islands, just a stone's throw across the Neva from the Winter Palace. As she looked back at the flames leaping across the dark hulks of buildings, tears filled her eyes. Was this how it was to end? Her beloved city in ashes?

But was this the way for an Empress to act? Weeping like a helpless woman? She would not be defeated, not by war or plague or fire. She would have the city rebuilt. No country could build as fast as the Russians. This way the wooden houses would be replaced with stone ones faster than she could have planned.

At Peterhof she paced restlessly up and down. She did not like the palace. It reminded her of her dead husband. Here he had led his decadent life. Here he had humiliated her. Here she had read out his abdication to him. And it was always damp from the sea air, winter or summer. Anxious for news, she could not sleep. Oh, that she were a man. She would mount her horse and wield her sword against all enemies. Rather like Falconet's drawings of the monument to Peter the Great. That was one reason she had chosen not to have a monument made of herself. A stately statue, a woman in decorous pose, holding perhaps a scroll of laws, would be fine for a hall in one of her palaces but would not capture the imagination of the people. She could not have herself, a woman, represented as a warrior on a rearing horse. She would not even be able to be portrayed sitting astride. And what warrior led a nation into battle side-saddle ? No, herself on a horse would not have done. Especially now that she had lost the attraction of youth. How had she aged so in these few years? In any case it might remind people of how she came to power – on a horse. It was better to put Peter the Great on the horse and her name beside his. She would be linked to his greatness and perceived as his legitimate heir.

Orlov's messenger eventually arrived in the middle of another sleepless night. St Petersburg was safe, every spark extinguished as she had ordered, Orlov wrote. But he urged her to wait a few more days before returning as the air in the city was thick with cinders and smoke. Catherine's first feelings of relief quickly gave way to misgivings. Could she trust Orlov? Perhaps he and his brothers were architects of the catastrophe. A deliberate bid to be celebrated as heroes by the people. Crowds and Guards had put more than one ruler on Russia's throne, as she well knew. Orlov could have himself declared their king, borne on a wave of gratitude and admiration. Oh, how the world loved a hero, especially one as handsome as Grigory riding about on his horse. Heroines had to find other means to gain and hold power – and most of them depended on men, she thought bitterly.

She tried to calm her fear and anger. In a few hours it would be daybreak. She would ride back to the city. She knew now she should never have left. She rummaged through the chest of clothes, looking for her riding habit. She would return to the city on horseback, not in a carriage. She would ride like a man, astride.

She was startled as another messenger was ushered in with a parchment bearing Panin's seal. Was this the confirmation of her worst fears? Had Orlov and his brothers betrayed her trust?

Dismissing the messenger, she tore open the letter and scanned the words quickly.

The news is bad, Panin wrote. *Our forces have suffered major defeat ... hold over the Crimea weakened... another ship lost in sea battle. ... emergency meeting of the College of War*

Catherine sank to her chair in relief. It was bad news indeed, but not the worst. The course of war could always be turned but a throne lost could not be regained.

Chapter Thirty-Two

John Rogerson, proud medical graduate of the University of Edinburgh, made his way slowly to the chambers of the Empress. He had been the court doctor for some two years and was privy to many secrets, both intimate and political. He had gained the position through his uncle, Dr Mounsey, personal physician to the Empress Elizabeth in the last years of her life and then to Peter III, Catherine's husband. "There is money to be made in the Russian court," his uncle had told him as he boarded ship at the port of Leith for St Petersburg. "They shower you with gold and land and serfs in gratitude for their health. But it is also a dangerous place. You must be cautious in diagnosis until you are sure. Above all, no-one must die in your care. If you are held responsible, you may find yourself doctoring in the Siberian wasteland."

Mounsey had left Russia when Catherine took the throne, returning to his native Scotland a very rich man. Rogerson thought enviously of his uncle living in comfort in his luxurious mansion while he had to navigate the bad health and hazards of the Russian court. Still, a court appointment was certainly better than the army, where he had served a short and gruelling stint. His friend Matthew Halliday, who had grown up on the farm next to his in Scotland, had been sent to deal with the plague in Moscow. Matthew, not having studied medicine, was limited to the skills of a surgeon which were not much called for at court. Another colleague, also a graduate of Edinburgh, had perhaps the most pleasant position at court. He was physician to the Empress's ladies in waiting, a position his grey hair rather than his credentials qualified him for. Rogerson hoped to have gained more than that by the time his hair turned grey. He conceded he had done well for his thirty years but he was impatient to better his position in society. If wealth were not to come his way, then he would court fame. He could deliver a paper to the Royal Society, write a treatise, find a cure. None of these, however, seemed possible being nursemaid to the members of court. Syphilitic ailments, prevention of pregnancy, secret pregnancies, vapours and indeterminate fevers, digestive colics due to gluttony and too much alcohol, sleeping draughts ... such were the cases he had to deal with daily. He approached each case diligently, no matter how trivial, and his reputation for successful cures had brought him to the Empress's attention. She had assigned to him the care of her son the Grand Duke Paul. His new position certainly put him a few rungs up the ladder but it could equally mean his downfall if the Grand Duke did not improve. At the moment, he feared the latter.

Ten days ago, just as the air in the city was clearing from the fires, the Grand Duke had suddenly taken ill with a very high fever and a drastic flux. Rogerson first suspected it was the plague which had flared up in Moscow. But he was at a loss to say how the disease had reached the sheltered prince. No-one in his retinue was ill. Rogerson had personally examined the Duke's servants. Although the dreaded symptoms of plague had not developed, the Grand Duke was very ill. If the fever did not break soon, Rogerson was not sure the boy would survive. He was not of sturdy constitution no matter what Dr Dimsdale had opined before the smallpox inoculation. The fever and constant diarrhoea would sap his life's strength.

Rogerson, however, was not prepared to alarm the Empress. The less said the better. Dr Mounsey was right. One must sit on the cusp of a diagnosis, ready to spring on whichever side developed.

He was ushered into the Empress's chambers. She was pacing up and down. Her complexion was pale, her eyes, normally bright, were dull. She was dressed in what she called her working robe, a lose kaftan of dark material. She wore no jewellery.

"I trust you have good news for me, Dr Rogerson?" she said without preamble. Rogerson thought he detected a note of fear in her voice. But perhaps it was more the fear he himself felt.

"Your Majesty, the Grand Duke's state of health does not worsen," he answered carefully.

"But nor does it improve!" the Empress retorted quickly.

"It is ... unchanged," Dr Rogerson said rather weakly.

"I do not wish to hear euphemisms," the Empress snapped. "I do not wish to be misled. I wish to know the truth. Is my son afflicted by the plague?"

"Your Majesty," Rogerson now said, rallying, "I detect no symptoms of plague in the Grand Duke. He would seem to be suffering from a fever, which we can call influenza."

Influenza was a suitably vague diagnosis. It could refer to an ague, to catarrh or coughs, to indeterminate fever. The term had been created by a doctor at Edinburgh University just fifty years ago to classify catarrhal fevers. Originally thought to be due to the influence of the stars, it was now thought to be more an *influenza del freddo*. Outbreaks of this type of fever were more prevalent when the winds or seasons changed. It had also been noted that an epidemic of influenza was heralded by an outbreak of colds in horses. Rogerson remembered as a young boy the horses on his father's farm wheezing and braying like donkeys as their eyes and noses streamed. Rogerson himself had taken ill in that epidemic just before he went to university.

Although it was now summer in St Petersburg, it was unseasonably wet and drafts of chilly air seeped into the palace. He checked the stables himself, pretending to admire the horses. They were all glossy, healthy creatures, in better health than many at court.

Dr Rogerson had consulted his notes when the Grand Duke fell ill. Many of the symptoms of influenza were not present. The boy had a quick pulse and fever but no catarrh, he had severe head pains but no vertigo. Most puzzling was the persistent diarrhoea. None of his colleagues had noted this as a symptom of influenza. Still, Dr Rogerson was fairly sure it was not the plague. There were no buboes or carbuncles.

"And how do we treat this influenza?" the Empress asked him.

"Above all, we must keep him warm. There must be no drafts. And there must be no agitation. "

"Ah, yes, drafts again," she sighed. "But he will not be bled," she added in the tone of an order.

"No, we will dilute his blood and the virulence of the fever with thin liquids."

"Dr Rogerson, I expect amelioration in the next day or two," the Empress said with a hint of desperation in her voice. "We must have it. The nation is ... worried. We are worried."

Rogerson had heard the whispers when the Grand Duke had not been able to take part in the recent celebrations for his name day. Count Panin, who was genuinely fond of the boy, confided his fears to Rogerson. "If it is God's will to take the Grand Duke, the legitimate heir to the throne of Russia, I fear for his mother. The pro-Russian faction, especially in Moscow, will gain in strength. You must bring him back to health!"

Rogerson bowed to the Empress. "I too hope to bring you good news in the next few days."

As he returned along the corridor to the Grand Duke's chambers, Rogerson felt the burden of Russia's future on his shoulders. Melodramatic, perhaps, he thought wryly, but true, for such was Russia. As for himself, if the Grand Duke recovered, Rogerson's future was certain. He too would be able to buy an estate in Scotland. If the worst happened, he would either be sent home or to some remote part of the Empire. Perhaps that would not be such a bad thing in the end, he thought. There was probably bountiful material for scientific contribution in regions where few of his profession had travelled. After all, his uncle Dr Mounsey had made his name – and fortune – by bringing rhubarb from the East to the West.

Rogerson, fired with new purpose, determined to check his notes for further remedies. Perhaps some blistering would be beneficial.

Chapter Thirty-Three

Catherine regarded the heap of papers on her desk. She had lost interest in writing. She owed Voltaire a letter but what could she report? Misfortune heaped on misfortune. The Turks were gaining the upper hand again thanks to help from the devious Austrians; St Petersburg had been almost razed to the ground, perhaps deliberately; calumnious writings had been circulating in the salons of Paris describing Catherine as a usurper and the country she ruled as backward – she who had dedicated herself to bringing the light of reason to Russia. Her son Paul was dangerously ill – his death could mean her ruin. The supporters of the dead Ivan had not given up. His two brothers and sisters still lived, imprisoned near Archangel.

Is this what it had come to? The end of all her efforts? The reward for her sacrifices? She could not go on fighting alone. Her son would die, the war would be lost, plague would gain the upper hand ... Where was Orlov? she cried inwardly as she swept the papers violently to the floor. "Grigory!" she called out as her head sank to the desk.

PART FOUR
1771-1773

Chapter Thirty-Four

Count Panin removed the miniature of his fiancée, Countess Anna Sheremeteva, from his pocket to gaze at it, as he often did. How beautiful she was! And how immensely rich! If only she had lived, he would have had light in his life. He could have imagined a future after Paul. Without him, Panin knew he had no future. He was certain Anna's death had been the result of his enemies' plots. The powerful and rich Sheremetevs were sure the Orlov brothers were responsible for their daughter catching smallpox. They could have put smallpox in her snuff box, her father said. He had retired from Court, a broken man despite his immense wealth. Panin suspected the Orlovs had now turned their attention to the Grand Duke, Panin's last hope.

The Empress kept to her rooms for weeks while her son remained seriously ill. Panin was grateful to the young Scottish doctor. Under anyone else's care but his, the Grand Duke would have slipped away, a prospect Panin could not contemplate. He had dedicated his life to the future Emperor of Russia, the rightful heir to the throne, the son of a rightful Emperor who had been murdered in cold blood so that his wife could sit on his throne. Yes, Catherine was a usurper. But Panin would support and defend her to keep the throne safe for his charge. Without Paul, Panin was nothing. And neither was Catherine.

If Paul did not survive, Panin determined to leave Russia. Catherine must fend for herself. After all, she had her band of Orlov brothers. The thought of them, of Grigory Orlov on the throne, strengthened Panin's resolve to approach Lord Cathcart on the matter of a position at the court of England. Before he could do so, however, the

Grand Duke began to improve and within a few weeks, he was as healthy as he had ever been, which was much more than could be expected. The Empress showered Dr Rogerson with rewards of money and lands and appointed him her personal physician.

Paul had undergone a transformation during his illness. The affable boy was replaced by a gaunt and awkward youth – with a beard. Catherine, elated at the good news of her son's recovery, laughingly said at table one day, "It is said in Russia, is it not, that one must be ill before a beard can grow. So that's all it was? Five weeks of serious illness for a beard? Then his will be a luxuriant growth but fortunately we do not wear beards here and thus I need not be reminded of my anxiety."

The courtiers laughed but Panin thought the joke in extremely poor taste.

The Empress gave Panin strict orders to take care of the Grand Duke and to follow Dr Rogerson's instructions. "And we will renew our efforts to find him his bride. His 17th birthday approaches and on his 19th he will celebrate his Russian maturity."

Catherine took up her many projects with renewed energy, especially her writing. She was once more full of good cheer despite constant rumblings of war.

Even the news that Austria had signed a treaty with the Ottoman Empire supposedly offering support against Russia left Catherine unconcerned.

"Oh, the Habsburgs will never raise arms against us," she said. "Their threats are those of a spoiled child. Well, we will let them have something if they are worried about our power. We have enough. All may come to us with their requests. Frederick has asked for a slice of Poland. And he shall have it. I made war and now I shall make peace. That is the correct order."

Meanwhile, Catherine ordered her generals to concentrate their efforts on securing the Crimea. "The

Crimea," she told Panin, somewhat presumptuously he thought, "will be the pearl in my Crown." Panin knew that the Black Sea was indeed of crucial strategic importance just as the Baltic Sea was in the north. Trade routes to Persia would be open to Russian ships, caravan roads to China. But Catherine's territorial ambition seemed to know no bounds. "My Empire," she continued, "will stretch from sea to sea and beyond. Perhaps one day there will be a peaceful Greece under Russian rule. Voltaire has said that I am destined to rule Greece."

Those few weeks were carefree ones at Court. Catherine spent a lot of time at Tsarskoye Selo, scribbling for hours every day, tending her gardens and entertaining with music and dances. The interlude, however, was short-lived.

At the beginning of August, reports came from Moscow of a large outbreak of plague, with some 400 deaths every day. People were fleeing the city, spreading the plague in their wake. Chaos reigned as most of the nobility fled to their country estates leaving their serfs to fend for themselves. Even Governor General Saltykov deserted the city, citing weak health. By September the death toll had reached 800 a day, the streets blocked with abandoned corpses.

Catherine called her Council and raged. "We spent months putting measures into place! How was Moscow caught unawares? How dare a Governor General leave his post? Must I go there myself? If I must, I shall!"

Suddenly, Orlov's voice broke the stunned silence.

"I shall go," he said calmly. "I shall leave tomorrow. I shall quell the panic that threatens the city and I shall contain the plague. I welcome the opportunity to serve Your Majesty and my country."

"I saw him before he left," Lord Cathcart later told Panin. "Capital fellow. A real soldier. Said he had missed all the action in the south and was seizing this opportunity to prove his worth."

Panin knew that Catherine's affections had cooled towards Orlov. He was not sure why - his infidelities were long known and tolerated. Her lack of warmth seemed to date from the fires in the city in spring. Was Orlov's heroic offer now an attempt to regain favour with the Empress? Or an attempt to gain influence in pro-Russian Moscow? Surely he would not risk his life for a gain so uncertain?

Many turned out to see Orlov off. In a mere twenty-four hours, he had organised a large retinue of his own Guardsmen, city administrators, medical experts and regular troops. The sun was setting as the procession set off, Orlov at its head. Panin had to grudgingly admit that he made a very fine figure on his horse, his handsome face creased in smiles, his hair blowing in the wind. Many ladies apparently thought so too, blowing him kisses or weeping into their kerchiefs. If Russia needed a hero instead of an Empress, Orlov was the perfect answer.

***

Orlov had been gone only two days and was still on the road when terrible news of riots came from Moscow. A hundred people had been killed, nearly 300 arrested, many wounded. An archbishop had been murdered, torn to pieces by the angry mob. According to reports, the cause of the riots was an icon of the Mother of God on the Kremlin wall. It was said to have miraculous powers and those affected by plague gathered there to touch it in hope of a cure. "Mindful of Your Majesty's ban on the gathering of people in public places to avoid the spread of disease," one report said, "the archbishop endeavoured to disperse the crowds. In addition, crossroad clerics had taken advantage of the people's despair and persuaded them to donate what money they could spare to have a silver covering made for the icon. It is said that the Archbishop suspected the clerics of lining their own pockets. He ordered the box of donations, some 200 roubles, to be sealed and brought to his monastery. This angered the crowd, many of whom began to shout that the church was stealing the Blessed Mother's money."

On hearing the news of the archbishop's cruel murder, Catherine fell into a deep melancholy. She curtailed celebrations for the ninth anniversary of her coronation, inviting only the foreign ambassadors to pay their respects. "We cannot celebrate while my subjects are dying of disease," she said, "but in truth I am not sure whether I have the right to celebrate my sovereignty. It has been a very bad year. Our hopes lie with Count Orlov."

Count Panin was not sure how successful he wanted Orlov to be. The plague had to be stopped but would Orlov use success to further his own cause, whatever that might be, or for the greater glory of Catherine? Panin reminded himself that there was great support for the Grand Duke in Moscow and the Ivan party was still strong. But they had all fled the city. Would the rabble make Orlov their king?

Meanwhile, the Empress had secluded herself away in Tsarskoye Selo. The gates were kept permanently locked and guarded. Messengers had to deliver their missives at the outer entrances. Papers were then fumigated and read out to her. She would touch nothing from outside. No-one was allowed in without the Empress's express permission and even then had to be inspected by one of the physicians she kept at hand round the clock. She had ordered the Grand Duke to stay in St Petersburg, with Dr Rogerson in attendance. "It would not be good for my son's recovering health to travel by carriage at this time. Who knows where the plague lurks."

"I am unwell," she confided in Panin, one of the few granted access to the palace, on one of his visits to the Empress. "My whole left side aches."

"Drafts, perhaps, Your Majesty?" Panin ventured.

"Perhaps it is my heart. It carries many burdens. It grieves for my people and prays for Count Orlov's success and safety."

Count Panin noted the great change in Catherine. She left her hair unpowdered and it was streaked with grey. Her face was lined, her eyes dull. She wore her working robe most of the day and spent much time praying or writing. She would not venture out into the grounds and took her meals in her chambers. Three of her ladies-in-waiting had accompanied her to Tsarskoye Selo. Panin berated them.

"You must look after the Empress, rouse her interest, play music, read to her."

"Her Majesty has ordered us to spend our time in prayer," one of them answered. "She said she is too old and too tired for entertainment."

Panin agreed about the Empress being too old. She was over forty. Women lost their life's force after that. It was in the order of nature. They could not even bear children. In two years the Grand Duke Paul would come of age. A young man is what Russia needed, with a wise counsellor. If Count Orlov remained loyal and did not try to seize power for himself in pro-Russian Moscow, if the plague were vanquished, if a suitable bride were found for Paul and heirs secured, if – it was a treasonous thought but might the Empress not fall dangerously ill?

Chapter Thirty-Five

Grigory Orlov arrived in Moscow in late September to the aftermath of the riots which had killed the Archbishop. To appease the clergy, he ordered a splendid public funeral and made a generous donation in the Empress's name to his monastery. Four of the rioters were executed, two of them found guilty of murdering the archbishop. The other two had been chosen by lot since Orlov knew he could not execute nearly 300 rioters without inciting another riot. Some sixty were knouted, their nostrils torn by tongs, and then sent to hard labour in Siberia. Another ninety were lashed. Orlov released the remaining hundred and fifty, sure that the people would see that justice was thus fairly served.

The rioters had complained about the misery the anti-plague measures had brought to their lives. The public baths had been closed; all gatherings, even for church services were forbidden. Families affected by plague were torn from their homes, healthy or not, and abandoned in plague houses. Orphaned children ravaged in the streets like wild dogs. Wild dogs were being hunted down for food.

Count Grigory Orlov immediately created a Commission for the Prevention and Treatment of Pestilential Infectious Distemper, which met every morning under his leadership to coordinate tasks. In truth, he should have named it the Plague Commission but Orlov knew he must keep panic at bay in a battle where the enemy remained invisible and elusive. Members of the Commission included not only medical experts but also representatives from the city's civil servants, police officials, clergy and merchants. Orlov needed all the reins in his own hands if the plague were to be vanquished.

Orlov ordered the public baths reopened against the majority of the Commission who argued that proximity encouraged transference of infection, but Dr Lerche, who had much experience in fighting the plague, observed that cleanliness would be advantageous. "I have noted that the disease is most rampant amongst the less favoured levels of society. In the army, its incidence is lower due to regular nourishment and daily baths." It was true, Orlov thought. There had only been two cases amongst his troops and they had, against orders, visited the city's most famous pleasure house. He must enquire if they had survived.

Under Orlov's guidance, the Commission coordinated the distribution of food, clothes and money. Orphanages were opened. Orlov promised freedom to any serfs who volunteered to work in them as well as in hospitals and plague houses. Many factory serfs, abandoned by their owners, accepted the offer. Prisoners were released to act as gravediggers. No-one was allowed to be buried within the city walls no matter how hallowed the church grounds were.

Orlov was tired. Sometimes he felt he himself was falling ill with the plague. He had ridden through the worst affected areas, ordering the burning of wooden houses, the fumigation of more, the removal of the swollen and fly-ridden black corpses, around which large rats skulked. The rats made him uneasy. He would not have them feeding on the city's dead. He ordered fires to be built in each area and manned by police. Those of the population who delivered rats to the fire would receive a quarter kopek for each rat. The whole city stank of smoke and rank flesh. His own clothes reeked of vinegar.

"How many now?" he asked wearily at the Commission's latest session.

"We count 600 deaths a day," one of the civil servants answered.

Orlov sighed. He had been fighting for a month and they were no nearer the end.

"Courage, Count Orlov," Dr Lerche said. "The disease is being contained. The daily death toll was 800 before you arrived."

"What more can be done? Where is the outbreak most dense? Must we burn more houses?" Orlov asked.

"Most deaths are now in the pesthouses and the hospitals. We must maintain strict quarantine," Dr Lerche said.

Orlov thought of his estate at Gatchina. He had received many palaces and lands from Catherine but Gatchina was his favourite, or would be when Rinaldi's work on its architecture was finished. Catherine had bought the whole village for him and it lay picturesquely, like a painting, on the slopes of a crystal clear lake. In his mind, Orlov now breathed in the fresh country air. That was all he longed for. He was tired of luxury, tired of whipping his flagging appetites. He had taken on the plague to give his empty life meaning.

All he knew was soldiering but while his brother Alexey had been gathering victories and laurels in the war with the Turks, Orlov was forced to sit on Catherine's commissions, endlessly discussing the war with those who had no idea of what war meant. For them it was a theoretical map, not battlefields strewn with the severed limbs of the dead and the dying. And what did Catherine know of real life? He had fallen in love with the bookish princess, who rode and shot like a man, who knew how to have fun and whose sensual appetites matched his own. She knew nothing of war and plague, of beaten serfs and starving children. She knew how to write, how to pontificate, how to rule – alone. Orlov sighed. He knew what he wanted now. He knew his dream. A simple life. At Gatchina. With a wife and family. He could imagine them picnicking at the lake, white muslin and ribbons fluttering in the breeze.

Orlov, suddenly aware of the silence in the room, cleared his throat.

"Gentlemen," he said, "this disease shall not defeat us. I shall not leave this city until it is eradicated."

Chapter Thirty-Six

Count Panin ushered the Grand Duke into his mother's presence. Sophia Chartoryzhkaya followed several discreet paces behind. Catherine was resplendent in gold brocade. Her hair was dressed and diamonds glittered abundantly at her neck. She made no attempt to embrace her son as he bowed to her. Panin knew, as everyone did, that the Grand Duke reminded the Empress of her dead husband, of her years of misery with him. The likeness to Catherine's murdered husband was more pronounced after the Grand Duke's illness, the nose wider and flatter, the eyes more sunken. Paul kept a portrait of his father in his room and often remarked on the resemblance himself. He was certainly not a handsome youth, puny in figure and in stature not as tall as Catherine. Although he held himself straight and his gaze was direct, even Panin had to admit he lacked regal demeanour. Panin regarded the boy, for so he still thought of him, with a critical eye and wondered what more he could he do for his charge before his coming of age rendered Panin superfluous. He had had dancing lessons since he could walk and although he danced well, his calves remained straight as a child's, his silk stockings wrinkling where they should have bulged. He was fond of military exercises and diligent in their practice but his shoulders remained as narrow as a girl's. His natural appetites had been encouraged by giving him to the tutelage of the charming widow Sophia. Panin had questioned her. With downcast eyes, she had testified yes, the Grand Duke was certainly virile and, she added, "very enthusiastic". Perhaps he was expending too much of his strength there, his sap draining away instead of into his muscles, Panin thought He must talk to the Empress about allowing her son more freedom in riding out. Yes, that might do it. More riding.

"Count Orlov will return from Moscow!" the Empress

declared. "Our hero! Russia's hero!"

The plague in Moscow had abated but Panin knew the credit was due to the onset of winter rather than to Orlov's heroism. Still, it was a relief that he was returning. A hero in Moscow was a dangerous thing.

"Indeed, Your Majesty," Panin murmured.

"He shall be here soon! In some ten days! Oh, we must prepare a welcome for him!"

The Empress was almost girlish in her excitement, Panin thought.

"So soon, Your Majesty?" he asked. "Will there be no quarantine to observe? As we have recommended for all travellers?"

Anyone wishing to enter St Petersburg was obliged to spend thirty days outside its gates. Few had fallen ill with the disease but it would take only one to endanger the whole city.

"No, no. He has served his quarantine in Moscow. He is as strong as an ox. I will have him come straight to me. How we have missed him!" Catherine turned to Grand Duke Paul and extended her arm. "Come, Paul, you will walk me into dinner and sit by my side at table. Our foreign guests will hear us sing the praises of our Russian heroes, who have all but defeated the Turks and vanquished the plague. You will feel the justifiable pride in being heir to such a magnificent throne."

Count Panin, surprised by the Empress's almost affectionate acknowledgement of her son, remembered to offer his arm to the waiting Sophia Chartoryzhkaya as the Empress and the Grand Duke swept along the corridor.

***

Grigory Orlov luxuriated in the hot water. He looked out on to the frost-spangled grounds and anticipated with pleasure the hard ride he would enjoy before breakfast. The air would be fresh and he would take great gulps of it, purging the memory of charred houses, black corpses, weeping women and starving children. 55,000 lost in a battle where the thrust of a sword was useless.

Orlov thought with satisfaction of the hero's welcome Catherine had prepared for him. There had been a sumptuous banquet and ovations, musical compositions and military parades. The Empress had a gold medal struck with his image and a marble medallion designed. "And," she had said breathless with excitement, "I have commissioned your very own triumphal arch at Tsarskoye Selo. It shall be grander than all the Turkish victories together. It shall bear your name. 'Moscow saved from Disaster by Count Orlov.'"

Alexey, on leave from the Ottoman front, had commented in a low voice as he poured the wine, "Well, brother, quite the Emperor now. The time may be ripe to fulfil your dreams."

But those were not Orlov's dreams anymore. He had once been in love with Catherine but he was no longer and had not been for some time. He would always be loyal to her, always serve her but he did not want to be married to her. He wanted a wife who wanted to be a wife – and a mother. He wanted someone to protect, someone who would look up to him. He did not want to be a man kept by a strong woman, no matter how many riches it would bring him. But he knew that while Catherine would tolerate a lover, she would never condone him taking a wife.

On the first night of his return, Catherine had come to him with nothing under her silk robe but diamonds. He had pleaded exhaustion. "Let me lie in your arms and find rest," he had said. When he woke in the morning, she had already risen.

On the second and third nights, he satisfied her desires out of pity for what she had become. And it was only thoughts of his once lithesome princess, she who rode like a

Guardsman, hunted like a man and delighted in games in and out of the bedchamber, whose eyes outsparkled her diamonds, which enabled him to do so. But for how much longer? He was trapped in a dream he no longer wanted.

Chapter Thirty-Seven

Sir Robert Gunning, Britain's new ambassador to the Russian court, had a lot of catching up to do, but his predecessor Lord Cathcart was not there to brief him on his arrival, having already returned to England with his family. Gunning had been unexpectedly sent to Berlin first, to acquaint himself with King Frederick's plans, if any, to halt Russia's dominion in Europe. Britain was not involved militarily in the Ottoman War but, like Prussia, was keen to maintain a certain balance of power, and Frederick was a potential ally in this aim if in few others.

Gunning had then been instructed to proceed to St Petersburg, where he was to work closely with Count Solms while at the same time furthering Britain's agenda, which had more to do with its own empire than with the Ottoman Empire. Gunning was to reveal this agenda, however, to no-one but the Empress. The American colonies were restless, and King George must seek allies where he could. Gunning was instructed to find out what would entice Russia into supplying Britain with troops in case of colonial rebellion across the Atlantic.

It was certainly a diplomatic mission of some import and, if executed with success, would ensure Gunning's political future, but the Russian court seemed to demand skills he had not yet acquired. He did not even know what they were, he thought. He felt he was on a stage, or more correctly, as yet a spectator watching actors dress in elaborate but ill-fitting costumes, play enigmatic parts and then disappear backstage. The Winter Palace was magnificent and Gunning had walked through its many gilded, chandeliered and mirrored halls, impressed by works of art crowding the corridors. On his way to find a water closet or even a commode one evening, he had stumbled along dark passages of unworked wood and stone which led nowhere. A backstage. He had ended by relieving his increasingly urgent need in a corner outside, a solution used by many before him, judging by the evidence. Still, he must concentrate on the higher things in life. He must rise above the petty.

"The problem is," Solms was saying, "that if the peace talks fail, we will have war on every front. Austria is ready to join forces with the Ottoman Empire against Russia and has already moved troops into Moldavia and Wallachia."

"And Prussia's alliance with Russia would bind your King to fight with Russia against Austria," Gunning said, anxious to prove his political mettle. "And risk losing Silesia, so hard won," he added.

"King Frederick has no desire to lead Prussia into another war!" Solms seemed rather impatient. He had remarked to Gunning that the frequent change of British ambassadors did not facilitate his own work. He himself had held his post as Prussian ambassador at the Russian court for almost a decade now, surely a sign of his sovereign's trust and his own competence. "We are just recovering from the last," he added more patiently. "Our King would have peace in Europe."

"And his plan to achieve it is masterly," Gunning conceded. "Instead of everyone fighting over territory in the Ottoman Empire, he proposes compensation in Poland."

"A country so beset by civil strife that only stronger dominion will serve it," Count Solms said.

"It is already under the dominion of Russia," Gunning remarked.

"Precisely. That dominion will now be diluted to everyone's advantage. Prussia has asked for no more than a small sweep of the Baltic coast bordering on its own lands –"

"But a very strategic sweep, you will agree," Gunning interjected.

Solms ignored the remark. "It has been agreed that

Russia take Polish territories, bordering on its own lands in the east, which will bring it two million new subjects. And Austria will receive the lion's share of two and a half million new subjects in the south."

"The agreement has yet to be ratified," Gunning noted. "If there is no peace with the Ottoman Empire, the Polish project will fail. The Austrians will only accept the Polish compensation if Russia makes peace with the Turks."

"At least all parties, even the Turks, did agree to meet for formal talks. Count Orlov rode off to Moldavia with his usual retinue and fanfare. The hero of Moscow will now be the hero of Focşani."

"Focşani?" Gunning asked, puzzled.

"Where the peace talks are being held," Solms said patiently. "In Moldavia. Russian territory – for the moment. Russia plays host. And Orlov must extract the best terms he can."

"He is surely more of a soldier than a diplomat?" Gunning felt competent in political matters but the personalities at the Russian court perplexed him.

"Well, his brother Alexey won his laurels and many rich rewards in his battle against the Turks. But it was your own countryman, the Scottish admiral Samuel Greig, who was the real commander of the Russian fleet. Alexey Orlov was not much more than the figurehead. He would have achieved nothing on his own. Had hardly been on a boat let alone command a man o' war."

"But what has that to do with his brother at the peace talks? Does he also need a Scot to negotiate for him?" Gunning regretted his sarcasm but these Scots were everywhere. And they were certainly not his countrymen. One could take the notion of British too far. At least Catherine's favoured Governor of Livonia was a fellow Irishman.

"My guess is that Grigory Orlov insisted on going to get his own Turkish laurels," Solms said. "And not with peace talks."

Gunning was alarmed. "You do not mean he would seek more war?"

"If he does not seek it, he is going the right way to achieve it. My sources tell me he is insisting on total independence of the Crimean khanate in every respect. The Ottomans cannot accept this. They may be persuaded to give up their political hold but they will not give up spiritual suzerainty over their Moslem subjects. Orlov knows this but will not be moved on the issue."

***

Gunning decided to broach the subject of Britain's secret agenda as soon as possible with the Empress. If war continued in the Crimea, there would be no Russian troops to send to the American colonies. Fortunately, the Empress had singled him out at cards that very evening to play piquet with her, a rare and privileged opportunity for confidential exchange. Having made a few general observations on the nature of empire, he carefully moved on to his main point.

"Your own empire is vast, your Majesty. Many would benefit from your experience in ruling it. Your peoples are diverse and you recently called their representatives to an Assembly, a most admirable undertaking and one which has reaped justified praise throughout Europe."

"Yes, Sir Robert, it is a cause close to my heart to unite my subjects under one set of just laws, laws that they are happy to accept," Catherine said, examining the cards in her hand.

"Then they must set aside their own laws. Or what were their own laws. Or indeed any future laws." Gunning was floundering. "What does one do if such subjects do not accept the laws of the empire?" he added in a rush. "Obedience must surely be enforced?"

"Ah, I think you speak of your American colonies," the

Empress said as she picked up another card. "My dear Ambassador, I never base my hopes for success on any one mode of action. There are times when it is better not to be too precise." She laid her cards on the table. "There! I have won. And now, if you allow, I must look to my other guests."

Gunning stood and bowed. As her heavy skirts swept past him, he wondered again if he had the right skills for this court.

Chapter Thirty-Eight

Catherine regarded her ladies-in-waiting indulgently. This was her inner circle, educated by herself. They served as a disciplined example to the other two hundred or so women in the court, a web of wives and widows, sisters and daughters both legitimate and illegitimate, nieces and cousins ... She must have a list made of them all, with ranks and relationships. And she would compile a set of rules for all to follow. Perhaps she could have court dresses designed, uniform in style but coloured to show different ranks.

The new harpist played well. Catherine was soothed by the gentle ripples of music and by the whispers of silk as her ladies bent over their sewing. Only one of them, a niece of Grigory's and a recent addition at his request, was playing dreamily with a ring. Catherine was too content to chide her. She had come through the worst. Tired of war, conspiracies and plague, she had spent much of the spring working in the gardens at Tsarskoye Selo despite an unseasonable cool spell. Orlov had laughed at what he called her 'plantomania' but had given her full rein to do as she wished at his grounds in Gatchina while he was away. She would prepare some botanical surprise for him, something which would flower abundantly by the end of summer when he was due to return from the peace talks.

"You know, my dear ladies," Catherine said, "that by now our angels of peace will be facing the Turks. Count Orlov will charm them as he does everyone, does he not?"

Her ladies, immediately laying down their needles and silks to give her their attention, murmured their agreement. The harpist continued to play softly in the background.

"Is he not the most handsome man you have ever seen? The most upright, the most pleasant, the most loyal," Catherine continued, knowing she was enthusing too much but delighting in talking about the man she still loved.

Suddenly, there was a slight clatter on the marble floor and Catherine, startled, looked down to see a ring roll towards her. Orlov's young niece, Catherine Zinovyeva, jumped up, blushing. The ring rolled towards Catherine while the girl stood undecided, twisting her fingers agitatedly.

"How nervous you are, child," Catherine said lightly as she bent to pick up the recalcitrant piece. "Surely I am not such a taskmaster that you are terrified of me?"

Catherine was about to beckon the girl to her to return her jewellery with a gentle admonishment when something about the ring caught her attention. It was a heavy piece, much too big for a slim finger, but it was the bright emerald set in gold which caught Catherine's eye. It looks familiar, she thought, as she turned it over in her hand. Her eyes glanced over the inscription on the inside and ice clutched at her heart. *Catherine & Grigory*. Catherine fought for breath. She herself had given Grigory this ring. She looked up in confusion. The girl now stood with head bowed before her.

"Please leave us alone," Catherine managed to say to the other ladies-in-waiting.

When the doors closed on the last one, Catherine walked to the window, her back to the girl. She must remain calm. There would be a simple explanation. She was Grigory's niece, after all, and not yet fifteen.

"It is a fine ring, Catherine," she said. "How did you come by it?"

"My uncle, Count Orlov, gave it to me for safekeeping," the girl stuttered, her voice almost a whisper. Catherine would not turn round. This would be her undoing, to face a truth in the flesh too terrible to contemplate. She was pretty, the young Catherine, just on the cusp of the full bloom of womanhood but with enough of a young maid's innocence and freshness to attract the most jaded appetites.

"Safekeeping?" she asked evenly. "And what danger is it

in? Are the Count's belongings not safe here at my Court?"

"I am sorry, Your Majesty. I meant no wrong!" The girl still spoke in a whisper but a note of terror had crept into her voice.

"Wrong? What wrong could you possibly mean?" Catherine kept her own voice as neutral as she could although she could feel the panic rising in churning waves within her. She felt she might be sick.

The girl began to weep. "He said he loved me!"

Catherine had no need to ask who. She held the evidence in her hand. To seduce the child, to give her the very ring she had given him as a token of her own love, of their love – the panic had now reached the surface and screams threatened to replace the breaths she could not take.

The girl's sobs were louder now. "He said he wished to marry me. He gave me the ring as a token of his promise."

Marriage! Catherine managed to say "Leave me at once!" and wait the few agonising seconds till she heard the door close before falling into a heap on the floor.

***

Count Betskoy entered the Empress's chambers with a heavy heart. She had not been seen in public for over a week, which was just as well, he thought as he regarded Catherine's swollen face and unkempt hair.

"I have been betrayed most cruelly," she wept. "I have known of his other women and accepted that, even taking others to my own bed to keep his interest, but surely he is married to me in all but the formality? Was the ring given to him by me not a betrothal? He cannot marry another!"

Betskoy did not think it would help to remind her that she had often refused to marry Orlov when he most wanted it.

"He cannot marry his niece," he said calmly. "The laws of consanguinity will not allow it. The Church will forbid it."

"The reality is that he asked her, that he promised her!" Catherine sobbed.

"You do not know that. She is but a child, infatuated."

"And the ring? I know that! I have it here as proof." Catherine thrust her hand out. "That cannot be denied!"

"He perhaps gave it to her as one would give a plaything to a child."

Betskoy looked at Catherine with pity. Even if he was not her father, he had felt like a father to her all these years. But he was also her advisor. He must rouse her from her destructive self-pity. He must waken the Empress in her. He must kindle some anger in her, even hate, to replace the self-pity.

"Catherine, you have lost a lover and it is a harsh personal loss," he said softly. "But you must not jeopardise your throne. You must not lose that too. And you must especially not lose it to the lover you have lost."

Catherine looked at him, her eyes suddenly alert again.

"What do you mean? Does he have designs on my throne too? Is my broken heart not enough for him?"

"You know that he has much support from the more ... Russian amongst us. He has much power and wealth. You have raised him high in society and now he acts as if it is his due. He is not mindful of to whom he owes it all."

Catherine had stopped pacing. "Go on," she said tersely. Betskoy, breathing a light sigh of relief, continued.

"There have been reports that Count Orlov has been a dazzling presence at the peace talks. But it is not his words the Turks admire. It is his coat of diamonds. A coat of great brilliance which, I have it on good authority, cost a million roubles." Betskoy knew this was the sum which Catherine had allocated to Orlov to secure a peace treaty advantageous to Russia.

When Catherine remained silent, Betskoy continued. "You sent Count Orlov to speak for Russia, for your wishes for a just peace so that your Empire may thrive. He has, however, taken matters onto his own hands. He wishes to pursue war with the Turks, to take the Crimea completely from them. He has insulted General Rumyantsev, who follows your instructions not to take up arms, and has said he will lead your armies himself. These are not the actions of a loyal emissary but of one who acts as he will. He has even set up his own court at Jassy, some two hundred versts from where he is supposed to be at Focşani. He is said to entertain lavishly." Betskoy paused. "He may think of himself as Emperor," he added quietly.

His words at last had the desired effect. Catherine rose to her feet. "Emperor? I am Empress of Russia! There shall be no other! I will have him recalled and cast in chains – like all other would-be usurpers!"

"There is perhaps a better way, Your Majesty," Betskoy said. "You must show him that not only does he not rule Russia but that he does not rule your heart."

"I have no heart left to rule," Catherine replied. "But I do have an empire. And I shall not desert my people even if I have been deserted. I shall return to St Petersburg."

Chapter Thirty-Nine

Count Panin agreed to help with the plan, as Betskoy knew he would. He had little love for Orlov and had often tried to supplant him in the Empress's affections with young officers.

"I agree with you, Count Betskoy," Panin said in his slow manner. "Count Orlov is arrogantly certain of his hold over the Empress. Whatever displeasure she feels towards him for his many misdemeanours vanishes as soon as he is in her presence. And it will be the same again. He could reignite war with the Turks, marry his child cousin but still charm the Empress into forgiving him. I fail to comprehend it. She is in every other way a most intelligent woman."

Betskoy thought Panin exaggerated the Empress's gullibility but did not wish to hold up practical matters by arguing the point. Panin took his time in speaking but what he had to say was generally worth listening to.

"So do you have a candidate?" Betskoy asked directly, hoping to encourage Panin into the same manner. "He would be most successful while she is in this vulnerable state."

"Yes, I do have someone in mind," Panin would not be hurried. "He is young, not yet thirty, handsome enough and well educated. His gentle manners are the exact opposite of Orlov's."

"And his figure?" Betskoy asked. "You know the Empress is very particular about ... physical attributes."

"He is a lieutenant of the Horse Guards and as such has the bearing to match," Panin said. "The Empress has already noticed him. He has been in command of her guard detail at Tsarskoye Selo. When she left for St Petersburg, she thanked him personally for keeping such good order and gave him a golden snuff box."

"He must remain at her side wherever she goes,"

Betskoy said. "This will not seem unusual after the fears caused by the latest plot."

There had been a recent uprising in the Guards. Several young officers, bored with nothing to do, drunk and over-boisterous, had mapped out a revolution which would put Paul on the throne and the Empress in a convent. They had made lists of all courtiers divided into who would stay in the new court, who would be exiled or executed. Their main targets were the Orlov brothers. Betskoy viewed it as a naive game played on paper but when Catherine heard of it, she had ordered the culprits knouted and sent to Siberia. She had tripled the guards at all her palaces. It was impossible for anyone to come near her.

"Everyone knows that any discontent is with the Orlovs," Panin said, "not with the Empress. It is not her *person* which is in danger. I do not think she would be harmed. Her throne taken from her, yes, but not actually ... "

Betskoy did not want to consider what Panin left unsaid.

"Well, in any case," Panin continued, "once rid of the Orlovs, the Empress will be safer. And Lieutenant Vassilchikov will help us to unseat her favourite."

"Has this lieutenant been told of what is expected of him?" Betskoy asked with mounting impatience. "I mean not just guarding the Empress and never leaving her presence. Can he ... be more to her?"

"Oh, I don't think the bedchamber itself will be a problem," Panin said. "The real task is a more difficult one. He must become her Personal Chamberlain. He must take over not only Orlov's place in her bed, but also his chambers, his place beside her at table, his offices. And he has a brother, who must also be given a trusted position at court. Orlov must feel threatened. As he will be."

"Whatever happens," Betskoy concluded, "the Empress must not consent to see Orlov at any time. She will succumb if she sees him. She must break with him completely. And we must help her to do that."

***

"It is most puzzling," Sir Robert Gunning observed to Count Solms. "They are never apart. They behave towards each other with great affection. I would say, on occasion with happy intimacy." He did not express his disappointment that the Empress had less time for him. She had always received him warmly and they had enjoyed many conversations together. He had been sure she was becoming more open to friendship with Britain. And perhaps she had flirted with him. Her eyes had sparkled at him, she had teased him and once or twice laid her hand on his arm to emphasize a point. Gunning was careful to flatter her, pay her compliments and while he basked in her favour, the favour of an Empress after all, he had no wish to become intimate with her. Still, it rankled that she neglected him.

"I too am puzzled and none too happy about it," Count Solms remarked. "Vassilchikov is definitely Count Panin's man. They are often closeted together. The Orlov brothers rage. Alexey has again said while deep in his cups that it was he who put the Empress on the throne. Dangerous talk."

"The Empress seems unconcerned. She is in the best of moods, happy and content," Gunning said, adding with a touch of resentment, "And only interested in festivals and pleasure." And that young lieutenant, he thought, who was courteous but unremarkable. Why had she chosen him?

"Yes, yes," Solms concurred. "The matter of governing is being neglected. And now Orlov has left the peace talks with nothing decided. Just left with no warning. Once word reached him that Vassilchikov had been ensconced in the Winter Palace as the Empress's Personal Chamberlain, he jumped on his horse and made haste to reclaim his position."

"But I have heard that he has not been allowed to enter the capital," Gunning said, "that he is being detained at his estate in Gatchina?"

"Ostensibly quarantine for having come from the plague-ridden lands in the south." Solms gave particular emphasis to the first word. "But he apparently receives every courtesy and comfort. The Empress sent servants and provisions from the Court to welcome him."

"So he is not detained? She will welcome him back when the quarantine is over? Vassilchikov will be sent packing?" Gunning asked.

"It is an odd business, Gunning. One fears the resentment of the former favourite if one plumps too soon for the side of the new one, who will perhaps not have the good fortune to maintain the position, and one is apprehensive of displeasing the new one if one waits too long to show him deference," Solms said in his ponderous manner. "I have recommended to my King, as you should to yours, that we should wait before taking or forcing sides."

"My thoughts exactly," Gunning agreed. "One never knows what games are aplay, for they may indeed be no more than games."

"Games too have winners and losers," Solms observed dryly.

Chapter Forty

Grigory Orlov looked at his older brother in disbelief.
"Me? Unwell? Is that what she said?" he asked.

"Yes, she said you had attacks of illness and that you were to take a year's leave from Court to recover your health," Ivan said as he poured the wine. "Either here at Gatchina, or any of your other estates, or even abroad."

"But there is nothing wrong with me except anger at being treated so!" Grigory strode impatiently back and forth.

"Ah, perhaps that is what she means. But she has softened the blow, if blow it is, with a gift of 10,000 serfs in whichever region you please."

"More riches will not help. I have a surfeit of them," Grigory said morosely.

"Oh well, brother, I disagree. One can never have enough riches. "

"How could she supplant me in my absence? Is that why she sent me to Focşani? Was it all a ploy to get rid of me?"

"Well, it was you who wished to marry our cousin. Is she here with you, by the way?" Ivan asked looking around.

Grigory ignored the question. Of course, his cousin was here with him instead of at her father's estate as the Empress had ordered. Catherine's fury would be terrible if she found out. On the other hand, perhaps she should find out. After all, she had replaced him with some young officer. Perhaps it was time for an official separation. Orlov yearned for a family, a normal life, which he could never have with Catherine. He once thought he could. He thought they could be happily married and rule Russia together. But Catherine had changed after he and his brothers had put her on the throne. She did not want to share her power, only her bed. And now he had lost even that.

Grigory turned once more to his brother. At least, Catherine had not banned his family from Court and was happy to use Ivan as her emissary. And as soon as the peace talks had broken down, she had ordered Alexey to return to the Ottoman front to renew command of the Russian naval forces.

"So that is her latest offer. Now that I am not dead of the plague, I have another illness, which a year's absence and 10,000 serfs should cure?" Orlov could not keep the bitterness from his voice.

"Well, she did say she would hope to welcome you back to state service when the year is up. You have read her letter."

"Yes," Orlov said, picking up the paper. "She writes, 'I shall never forget how much I am obligated to all of your family and their many qualities which have been useful to our empire and will be again in the future.' She tries to keep us in favour. She knows our strength."

"Well, without us her husband would be on the throne with Vorontsova as Empress," Ivan said carelessly as he helped himself from a carafe of wine. "And she would be back in Prussia. Or worse."

"She says," Orlov said turning the paper, "that all she seeks is 'mutual tranquility'. Does she have that with this Vassilchikov? What kind of a man is he?"

"Oh, he is a nonentity. Presentable, biddable. Not much of a man really. Can't imagine him holding his drink or wielding a sabre," Ivan said scornfully.

"And the Empress? How does she seem?" Orlov asked with pretended nonchalance.

"The truth? In robust health. She looks well and is in brighter mood. She laughs a lot. She does not work as much. In fact, her council members complain and the diplomats wait every day in vain to see her. She seems to be having a rest from governing."

"This does not bode well for us, Ivan," Grigory said. "There are many who would plot against us. And influence the Empress against us."

"Yes, Count Panin seems very pleased although all he has been able to conjure up is an ingenuous young officer. Hardly a coup," Ivan said, passing the carafe to Orlov.

Orlov shook his head. "But a clever move that could shape the game."

"Look, Grigory, you wanted your freedom, now you have it," Ivan said impatiently. "Wait till the dust dies down and marry your little love and be happy ever after. You have enough land and palaces to do that. You and Alexey have been well rewarded."

"But she is Empress. She can take back what she gave. And she can send our cousin to a nunnery. No, Ivan, I will have to play this carefully. I must let her think that I still want her and yet hope that she does not want me."

"Ah, you do not like being cast off with a few trinkets like a courtesan who has lost her shine? You would do the casting off?" Ivan said with a laugh.

"That is the usual way of things but one cannot cast off an Empress. No, I would wish to be able to hold my head up in society. I would wish not to be shamed or disgraced. And I would wish to keep my offices."

"And your diamond coat, no doubt," Ivan said. "Well, give me your message. I will do my best for you."

"Thank the Empress her for her concern but tell her I am fit to return to Court to resume my duties at once. And will do so as soon as I have her permission."

"I doubt she will allow that, Grigory. She does not speak ill of you but it is clear what she is asking. That you do not come to Court. For a year."

"And what will happen at the end of that year? We do not know what the future holds. We must act now. I will rely on her sense of duty and any affection she still has for me not to force the issue. Her conscience seems to prick her, judging by the generosity of her gifts. Assure her of my affection for her. Tell her my only wish is to see her again and to serve her loyally."

"As you wish, Grigory. But I am not sure your message will be favourably heard." Ivan suddenly leapt to his feet. "Come, I am famished. Let us eat!"

As he followed his brother to the door, Grigory's thoughts lingered on his problem. He was sure Catherine would allow him to come to St Petersburg. But did he really want to? He turned to look out of the window to see his young cousin walking by the lakeside with a few companions, their dresses fluttering in the light breeze.

Chapter Forty-One

"Oh, it drags on and on," Catherine said wearily. "I cannot work, I cry when I am alone. Why couldn't he go away for a year, as I asked? I have seen to his every comfort. I have shown respect."

Betskoy, like most of the court, was puzzled by Catherine's attitude. On the one hand, she seemed happy and carefree with the young Vassilchikov, on the other she mourned Orlov but would not see him. Fortunately, there was general agreement that if Catherine were to see Orlov, she would fall back into his faithless arms, such was his hold over her. Orlov's behaviour was also puzzling. No one knew why he insisted on coming to court. It was well known that he was in love with his cousin, whom he hoped to marry. This should rule out any ambition to be reinstated as the Empress's favourite. Not knowing Orlov's motives, however, Betskoy deemed it prudent to steer Catherine clear of him.

"Precisely, Catherine," he said briskly. "It is Count Orlov who shows a lack of respect in not following his Empress's wishes. And we cannot forget that he endangered the Russian Empire by leaving the peace talks and angering the Turks into further aggression. This is not the behaviour of a loyal subject."

"But such a grand gesture! " Catherine said, her face suddenly animated. "The behaviour of a man in love!"

Or a man desperate not to lose his position or wealth, Betskoy thought.

Aloud, he said carefully, "But Your Majesty is content with Alexander Vassilchikov. He is all you would wish for. Young in vigour, faithful and discreet in comportment, and very fond of Your Majesty?"

"Ah yes, Count Betskoy. He is all that Count Orlov was not. He is biddable, respectful, always at my beck and call – perhaps that is the problem."

"Problem? Is there a problem?" Betskoy kept his voice calm but he felt some alarm at the use of the word. Would the Orlovs return after all to rule the Court and the Empress with their arrogant, easy ways?

"There is a lack of ... excitement, of passion, of tension. It is too easy," Catherine said. "I thrive on challenges. And Orlov was a challenge. And still is."

Count Orlov was indeed proving a challenge. He was insistent, through his brother Ivan Orlov, on not relinquishing his offices and on coming to the capital to see the Empress. The more he insisted, the more favours she threw at him. On the other hand, she had initiated a formal separation, the conditions of which would now be stated in a decree for public consumption and given to the Senate. Most details, however, would be kept confidential. There would be an outcry at the continuation of Orlov's annual pension of 150,000 roubles, at the marble palace being built for him by Rinaldi on the banks of the Neva with 100,000 roubles for its furnishings, at the 10,000 serfs, at two silver dinner services, one specially made for him in France, at the many palaces at his disposal with countless carriages and servants. And he was not to be held to account for leaving the peace talks. The subject was not to be mentioned.

Catherine's voice broke into his thoughts.

"There is one more thing I would like to settle," she said. "You will remember that when I became Empress, I obtained for Count Orlov the title of Prince of the Holy Roman Empire."

Betskoy remembered. Orlov had wanted a royal title at the time because he was hopeful of marrying the Empress. He thought being a Prince would make him more acceptable. The title had been granted but he had never been allowed to use it after it was clear that such privilege would enrage his opponents. Besides, a foreign title would make him a foreigner, which would alienate the Guards.

"The Count," Catherine continued, "has requested permission to use this title now. I will grant his request."

Betskoy thought quickly. Would it matter? Prince or Count? Perhaps it would detract from his Russian hero image. This would be a good thing. He must consult with Panin. Meanwhile, he chose a diplomatic response.

"Well, if he is going abroad in any case, it may be of some help to him."

"And I have decided to grant his main request," Catherine said with a note of defiance.

"Which is?" Betskoy was too alarmed to be anything other than direct.

"That he may come and make his farewells here at court. And to me."

A disaster, Betskoy thought. He will exert his hold over her. It must be prevented. He must inform Panin at once.

As if reading his thoughts, Catherine said,

"I have discussed this with Count Panin. Like you, he would not advise it, and you will both try to dissuade me. But you must not, for it will be of no use. My mind is made up. I am not a weak and foolish girl. He will come and I will see him and then send him away again."

Betskoy made to speak but Catherine held her hand up. "No, dear Count. You know as I do that Count Orlov will not give up until he has seen me. It is a challenge. He thinks I will fall into his arms. I will accept his challenge and much as my heart weeps, I will win this round."

Chapter Forty-Two

"It is an impenetrable chaos," Count Panin said with exasperation. "One can understand nothing. Old Bestuzhev may have been right. He said women do not belong on the throne. They murky the clear light of reason with feelings men do no suffer from."

The outburst from the usually reserved Panin surprised Betskoy. Orlov's return had certainly unsettled him. "Come, my dear Count, let us not descend into treasonous thoughts," he said cheerfully. "The Empress has behaved impeccably. She has not met with Orlov alone at any time. She showers Vassilchikov with fond attention. She is polite to Orlov in public."

Panin was not to be appeased. "Yes, yes but what are we to think of it? She wants him, she doesn't want him. The wheels of government grind to a halt in her indecision. The Turks are flexing their muscles, determined to win back what we fought so hard for. And the very person responsible for the break-down of the peace talks is swaggering around the city as if he owns it. Orlov is back to his old self, flirting with all the women, drinking with the Guards. Why, he has even charmed the hapless Vassilchikov. Has the Empress not ordered him to leave? What holds him back? Are they meeting in secret?"

Panin had watched the return of Grigory Orlov with dismay. He had arrived unexpectedly one snowy night in December and the Empress had received him the next morning. Betskoy had been present at the audience but refused to divulge any details of their first meeting. Panin now tried again to find out more, frustrated that he had not been invited to the meeting with Orlov.

"You were present when they met, Betskoy. What was said? How did the Empress act? What did Orlov demand? What promises were made?" Panin, normally the source for others, was not used to seeking information but was unable to curb his torrent of questions.

"There was nothing of that nature, as I have said before," Betskoy said evenly. "Orlov knelt before her Majesty most gracefully and declared himself her most loyal subject. And his delight at being back in her presence." Betskoy paused. "Perhaps he was dressed less flamboyantly than usual," he added, a little lamely. "At least, he had the sense not to wear the infamous coat of diamonds."

Panin knew Betskoy would not stray from his script. He would go on to say that the Empress had welcomed Orlov back but was concerned about his health and recommended a rest from his duties. She had enquired after his comforts at Gatchina and if he had everything he needed.

But was it all true? Panin was sure there were things going on behind his back. The Empress planned to reinstate Orlov. Why else would he be enjoying such freedom, moving about court as he wished, attending the Empress's card parties, friendly and relaxed with everyone. With Orlov gone, the Court had been more peaceful, the Empress happier. Panin's main fear was that Orlov's return would endanger the Grand Duke's future. If Catherine were to marry her ex-lover – that is, if he was indeed her ex-lover and not her current one, the Orlovs would rule Russia for decades to come.

The Grand Duke Paul had more right to the throne than his mother and must rule Russia after – well, when she no longer did. Catherine, however, did not treat her son as a Crown Prince. A few months ago Paul had turned eighteen, the age of maturity for German princes. The Court, and Paul himself, had expected Catherine to order a special celebration, to bestow honours in his name, perhaps allow him to set up his own court, but the day had passed almost unmarked. The Empress had called Paul and Count Panin to one of the smaller audience chambers and had delivered a short speech on the duty of a sovereign to rule justly. She then declared that Paul was now formally responsible for the administration of his hereditary estates in Holstein, part of his father's domains – but that she would continue to manage them for him. Count Panin knew that she had quietly negotiated a treaty of exchange with Denmark: Holstein for Oldenburg and Delmenhorst. Would she give away his birthright, his only refuge in danger? She could have the treaty ratified any time she pleased now that the boy had come of age. Catherine had concluded the birthday audience with her son by saying, "Of course, you are a Russian prince, and as such your maturity will be celebrated at your next birthday with all due festivity. Until then Count Panin will continue as your personal governor."

Betskoy's voice broke into his thoughts. "You are pensive, dear Count. All will be well. The Empress is in control."

"I do not like it, Betskoy. It seems that parts are being played, that there is dissimulation. The future of the Grand Duke, of Russia, even of the Empress is put at risk by these ... these ... love games!"

Panin moved to his desk and picked up a scroll of paper.

"I have here," he said more calmly, "a report from my brother the General on the latest pretender to the throne. Perhaps it will persuade the Empress into ... some seriousness?"

"Not another resurrected Peter?" Betskoy asked. "We have had at least ten since he died."

"You may scoff," Panin answered, "but this one is a Cossack deserter by the name of – " Panin paused to glance at the paper in his hand, "– Emelyan Pugachev. He has turned up in Yaitsk –"

"Yaitsk?"

"The city the Cossacks call their capital, " Panin said

impatiently. "This deserter has gathered much support. The Cossacks are a wild, discontent bunch and half of them are not Cossacks but brigands and thieves, runaway serfs and other fugitives. Our troops suppressed an uprising against conscription there this past summer. It is a lawless place. But they are falling at the feet of this saviour-tsar, as Pugachev is calling himself. He promises to free them from German tyranny."

"It is absurd. It cannot be taken seriously. He cannot be taken seriously. The Cossacks cannot be taken seriously – they know nothing but stealing and riding horses," Betskoy said authoritatively if repetitively.

"It is true," Panin conceded, "that most of them are illiterate, as Pugachev himself is, and therein lies the danger. They live thousands of versts from here, far from civilisation. They are discontent and volatile. They will march behind this pretender and gather more discontents as they do. And while our Empress is playing one lover against the other, the hordes will be tearing down the gates of the Kremlin!"

"A dramatic scenario, dear Count, but I think the point you make is that our Empress needs to cast an eye beyond her inner chambers to her Empire? And perhaps you are right. I will do what I can to expedite Orlov's departure, which may free the Empress's attentions for matters of state."

After Betskoy's departure, Count Panin poured himself a glass of wine despondently. If he had not taken an oath to protect the Grand Duke in recompense for his father's murder, in which he had no part but in which he did not feel completely blameless, he would have packed up and left Russia without delay.

Chapter Forty-Three

"The point," said the Prussian ambassador, "is that there is a certain balance at Court once more. One can at least gain an audience with the Empress. It is not the time to be distracted by affairs of the bedchamber. The territorial divisions in Poland are not ratified. The Turks have taken up arms again. And that Cossack deserter that the Empress sent to Siberia a few months ago has escaped yet again and is fomenting unrest. Much too near the Turkish front. He persuades the Cossacks not to fight."

Sir Robert Gunning said, "Poland is not our affair. My government has pursued a policy of non-intervention although the Poles have begged our help. More we cannot do, Solms. And as for Turkey, if Count Orlov had not upset the peace talks, the Ottomans may have been more conciliatory. Instead, Orlov is reinstated in all his offices and the Empress has forbidden his name to be mentioned in connection with the failure of peace."

Gunning had become more accustomed to the ways of the Russian court. Without compromising his principles or the instructions from his own government, he had learned to flow with the moods of the Empress, whose favour he enjoyed. He was often invited to dinner, concerts or card evenings and it was then that the best moments were to be seized. He had watched as Orlov charmed his way back into the inner circle, making friends with the Empress's favourite Vassilchikov and being affectionately but respectfully pleasant to the Empress herself. Catherine, as far as Gunning could observe, was meticulously correct in her behaviour towards her ex-lover. Solms, he was sure, would not mention King Frederick's *bon mot* on the subject. The Prussian King had apparently quipped that Orlov had been reinstated in all his previous offices by the Empress except that of copulation. Only he had used a more vulgar term. Gunning frowned in disapproval and turned his attention to Solms, who was in the throes of a tirade against Orlov.

"Count Panin," he was saying, "is enraged at his return to grace. It is still a conundrum, the whole matter. Orlov is forbidden to come to the capital but he comes. He is told to leave but takes his time doing so and returns two months later although the Empress had stipulated a year. He has lost no standing in society but enjoys the freedom from the restraints of Court life. He is happy, surrounded by women as always. Do you know what his favourite topic of conversation is?"

The question surprised Gunning. "I'm afraid I am not privy to –"

"Money!" Solms spat out. "He boasts of how much money he has to spend. And all from state coffers. I do not understand the Empress. A woman in love is unpredictable – and dangerous."

"But is she in love?" Gunning asked. "With Orlov? I don't think so. He has set up house with his young niece, and everyone, including the Empress, turns a blind eye. With young Vassilchikov? No, I don't see that he has held her interest. She tolerates him, almost maternally."

"But her mood is too ... heightened not to be caught in some affair of the heart," Solms said. "Or body," he added. "You are often in her presence. Have you noticed ... anyone?"

Gunning suddenly remembered Catherine laughing in delight.

"Now that you mention it," he said slowly, "that officer she recently promoted to Lieutenant General was present at dinner a few times after Orlov had left. The one with the damaged eye."

"Grigory Potemkin? Ah yes, I have seen him prowling around Court when he has been on leave from the front. He is an old protégé of the Empress. She was once very fond of him and then the Orlovs warned him off with a billiard cue in his eye. Do you think he is sharing her bed?"

Gunning, not caring to discuss the Empress's bedchamber activities, said curtly, "I doubt it. He has returned to the Turkish front. But let us take up the more serious considerations which bring me to you today, Solms. My government is willing to support the Empress in Poland but we find it difficult to countenance the reported acts of violence there. The Russian ambassador has threatened the destruction of Warsaw should their parliament not ratify the partitions. I have heard that some senators who oppose the territorial divisions have been sent to Siberia, others have had their lands confiscated, and some have even been threatened with execution. Does your King support these methods of coercion?"

"I think the reports are vastly exaggerated," Solms said carefully. "Warsaw is occupied not only by Russian forces but by our own Prussian troops and those of Austria too. The Polish parliament has no alternative but to comply. We have no need to apply force. Our combined presence is sufficient."

"Well, you must ensure that your allies do not resort to violence. Our government will not support coercion. The vote for ratification must be seen to be ... voluntary." Gunning knew that no parliament would vote freely for the carving up of its country. He also knew Catherine could not be stopped on a chosen course of action, especially if there were troops involved. Still, he must complain even if it was no more than a formality. But he did not relish the prospect of expressing his government's concerns to the Empress.

Solms interrupted his thoughts. "Has there been any news from the Turkish front? It is some time since we have attended a *Te Deum* in the Cathedral. Last year, they were regular occurrences."

"I believe the lines are still being fought over the Crimea," Gunning said. Indeed they were, and British trade routes again under threat. "A perennial problem. But the Ottomans will be anxious for an acceptable peace. They have Egypt and Syria to contend with. It would be a good time for the Empress to re-open negotiations. Peace would benefit all." Especially his own government, Gunning thought. Britain did not like the idea of Russia expanding further into its own sphere of influence in the Near East. At the moment, however, it was busy with its American colonies, where resistance to British rule was increasing.

It was Gunning's task to persuade the Empress to make peace with the Turks and ensure that Britain would benefit from any concessions, particularly access to the Black Sea. He relied on Count Solms to lend this cause support.

"I fear the Empress will be distracted by more domestic affairs," Solms said.

Gunning looked at him sharply.

"No, no, not affairs of the bedchamber, at least not Her Majesty's. The charming princesses of Hesse-Darmstadt arrive with their mother this very month. One of the three will marry the Grand Duke and become future Empress of Russia. Yet another bond between our countries."

Gunning reflected that the last German princess to come to the Russian court had been Catherine herself. Not only was there no trace of her Prussian roots but she had also failed to become Frederick's ally, except when it suited her own needs. But perhaps it was in the nature of foreign sovereigns to become less ... foreign. Their own King George belonged to the House of Hanover but had never been there and spoke only English.

"Why three?" he asked.

Solms looked puzzled. "Why three what?"

"Princesses. You said three princesses. Surely they are not summoned for the Grand Duke to choose from? How ... ," Gunning stumbled. He did not know what he thought. Barbaric? Medieval? Russian? He settled for a lame "unsubtle".

"Not at all, Gunning. You have such an English sensitivity. Yes, yes – " Solms held up his hand to halt Gunning's objection, " – I know you are Irish or British but not English. My apologies. Such national sensitivity. The princesses, I may say, merely accompany that sister who has been chosen. Or will be."

"Then we can look forward to a time of festivities," Gunning said, forcing a cheer he did not feel. There would be weeks of betrothal and nuptial celebrations, he thought. No-one would care about Turkey or Poland. Or pretenders to the throne. Most importantly, he fretted, he would rarely see his own hearth in the surfeit of banquets and entertainments to welcome the German princesses.

Bidding Solms a speedy farewell, Gunning determined to return home for dinner with his family while he had the chance. Sanity and peace could still be found there, at least.

Chapter Forty-Four

Catherine paced up and down the polished parquet restlessly. She had arrived at Gatchina that morning and had taken an eager walk through the gardens. She was pleased with the results of her English landscaping. A beautiful park was developing along the shores of the lake. If only people could be cultivated like plants, she thought.

There was still much work to be done to complete Rinaldi's 600 rooms, an ambitious project which had been inspired by his travels in England. There were to be elements of stately homes, castles and hunting lodges. Catherine liked the simplicity of the weathered limestone and the clarity of line, so different from the frothy baroque of Peterhof or Tsarskoye Selo. It was a palace that suited a man, she thought, or a woman who had more power than a man. She made a mental note to enquire if Orlov needed any special furnishings for the newly finished left wing. She must keep him happy – and loyal to her. With the Guards behind them, he and his brothers could unseat her from the throne and place anyone they liked on it. They had done it for her, with ease.

It was not only political calculation that made her generous to Orlov. She was fond of him, but she had learned that she could live well without him. Gone were the days of anxiety and tension, wondering whether he was coming, agonising over who he may have been with. They were not worth the few hours of pleasure which came ever more seldom. She felt liberated and had fewer headaches. But she could not live without love. Vassilchikov was a safe comfort. She liked to hold him in her arms much as she would have held her favourite doll as a child. She would, however, have preferred someone to make her heart leap, as Orlov had once done.

The door opened and Orlov strode into the room.

"Well, they are here," he said cheerfully without

preamble. "What a retinue! At least forty attendants and servants. Perhaps they imagined us uncivilised! But they will be surprised, will they not?"

"As are most of our visitors from Europe, Grigory," Catherine said dryly. "But tell me," she added impatiently, "what impression do they make? Are they presentable? Will they please me?"

"Oh, assuredly. The Landgravine is elegant and affable, her daughters, the princesses, a bevy of beauty. It is hard to tell them apart since I have only seen them together but their manners are such as you would wish."

"And they do not suspect that I am here?" Catherine asked. "You have dropped no hints?"

"On my honour, no. They know only that they will dine with some ladies of the court. And you are a lady of the court, are you not, Catherine?" he said playfully.

Since they had formally separated, Orlov was much more at ease with her. He was said to be living in domestic happiness with his niece, that he planned to marry her. The Church would be against it, and Orlov would seek Catherine's help. It helped her to know he needed her. She might still need him.

"And have they been well attended to?" Catherine asked. "I know what it is like to arrive in a faraway land. Comfort helps ease the pangs of separation. I remember the sable furs the Empress Elizabeth sent to us as we reached the borders. And a luxurious sled to transport us. The journey had been so cold and uncomfortable till then."

"Thanks to you, the princesses and their mother have had a surfeit of attention since they left Lübeck. They are well rested, in good humour and a little excited."

"Oh, I cannot wait to meet them," Catherine said with unfeigned enthusiasm. "I do hope one of them is suitable for the Grand Duke. By all accounts I have received, I think the middle one, the Princess Wilhelmina, may please us best. But I will reserve judgement."

"It was a thoughtful gesture of yours to meet them privately here before their formal arrival in St Petersburg," Orlov said.

"And it was good of you to help me in my little ruse with the hospitality of your palace," Catherine returned the compliment. "I know I can count on your loyalty and discretion. I must be assured that our hopes are not in vain. If they do not please us, there will be no formal arrival. They will return to their home, none the worse for the journey and with compensation for their troubles." Catherine's tone was serious but then she added gaily, "But I am determined to like them. Or at least one of them! You may show them in now, Grigory, and we will all dine together."

***

"It has all gone exceedingly well, Betskoy! I am pleased," Catherine sighed.

Only three days after the arrival of the princesses and their mother in St Petersburg, the betrothal of the middle daughter Wilhelmina to the Grand Duke Paul had been agreed on.

"The Grand Duke has made the right choice in Princess Wilhelmina," Betskoy commented. "She is charming and intelligent." Betskoy knew that the choice had not been the Grand Duke's but the Empress's. The Grand Duke had complied willingly – it was not difficult to be pleased by the lively Wilhelmina. The new couple sat happily together at all formal occasions. Sophia Chartoryzhkaya, Paul's mentor, was appointed Wilhelmina's lady-in-waiting.

"Yes," Catherine commented, "she combines most fortunately those characteristics which her sisters possess singly. Amélie is charming but not too intelligent and the young Louise is too intelligent with little charm."

"And perhaps Princess Louise at fifteen is a little

young?"

"Ah, Betskoy, you forget that when I came to Russia to be married, I was barely the same age!" Catherine exclaimed. "But you are right," she continued more calmly, "I was very young. And was given little guidance. But that shall not happen to Princess Wilhelmina. Or Grand Duchess Natalya, as we must now call her. Didn't she pronounce her baptismal vows well in Russian? Not as clearly as I think I did, but well enough."

"We hope she follows your example in other things too, Catherine," Betskoy said. "That she too will one day make a fine Empress."

"Let us not talk of future sovereigns while I still reign, Betskoy," Catherine said sharply. "It is most thoughtless."

"I do beg Your Majesty's pardon. It was a well meant compliment but clumsily expressed. Your Majesty was saying about guidance?"

"I have written everything out for the new Grand Duchess. Here, you may look." Catherine handed him a scroll.

Betskoy took out his magnifying glass. Catherine had a fine hand but his eyes were failing.

"Brief maxims for a princess who will have the happiness to become the daughter-in-law of Her Imperial Majesty the Empress of Russia and the wife of His Imperial Majesty the Grand Duke," he read aloud. Catherine was very fond of maxims, he reflected, but they were seldom brief and judging by the thickness of the paper bundle in his hand, the new Grand Duchess would have much to read.

"You need not read it all," Catherine said. "A cursory glance will reveal my main points. She must conform to the customs of her new country. As I did. We cannot have foreign influence. She must become Russian in all ways. As I did."

"Indeed, Your Majesty," Betskoy murmured.

"The unity of the imperial family is of paramount importance. She must have a tender attachment to her mother-in-law, the Empress, and to her husband. Read the third page," she instructed, "I have stated it clearly there."

Betskoy raised his magnifying glass once more and began reading aloud. "She is under obligation to disclose to the Empress and the Grand Duke those who have been indiscreet, dishonest or audacious in their attempts to rouse sentiments in her contrary to the attachment she must feel for the Empress and the Grand Duke. To help protect her from such harmful influences, she must trust only those whom the Empress has chosen for her. She must avoid all closeness with persons who have not been approved for her by the Empress."

"Perfect!" Catherine said in praise of her own words. "It is clearly said. I know the dangers of the Court and I will protect her from them."

"Are the young people to have their own Court after the marriage?" Betskoy asked.

"No, I do not consider it wise. They will be left open to all sorts of influences and insinuations. The ministers of foreign courts would be specially active. No, the Grand Duchess Natalya will have enough to do learning Russian. And I have compiled a reading list for her edification and education. She may have dancing lessons so that she appears graceful at balls. I have allotted her an annual allowance of 50,000 roubles. I received 30,000 as Grand Duchess and it was not enough. But she must live modestly and not fall into debt. Above all, she must not involve herself in political matters. And soon, she will produce a child and I will allow her to keep it with her to occupy her. She will be assured of a most happy future," Catherine concluded contentedly.

The path Catherine had mapped out for her daughter-in-law was a narrow one and not one which Catherine herself had taken, Betskoy thought. Yes, she had read and danced but she had not loved her husband or trusted the Empress Elizabeth and had failed to produce an heir for nine years. She had sought political power as a way to personal freedom and had ruthlessly rid herself of her husband after snatching his throne. Little wonder that Catherine did not wish the pattern repeated. But the beginnings were the same: a German princess, betrothed to a pro-Prussian Grand Duke, disenchanted and resentful of an all powerful Russian Empress. And there were many birds of prey circling, both Russian and foreign, waiting for a chance to pounce on any morsel of influence.

Betskoy changed the subject. "Will there by any special celebrations for the Grand Duke's Russian majority in September?"

"We will have a ball but I think we will combine all celebrations in the wedding, which will take place on the 29th September, just nine days after the Grand Duke's birthday. Preparations are already well under way. But you remind me, I must speak with Count Panin. He has served us well as the Grand Duke's governor but it is now time for Paul to assume his role as the head of his own family. He will need no tutor."

Betskoy had always been fond of Catherine, ready to believe she was indeed his natural daughter, at times even wishing it. But recently he had been disquieted by her behaviour. There was the confusion over Orlov and Vassilchikov, her reluctance to treat her son as her heir, her refusal to take the Cossack rebellion seriously, her belief that she could defeat the Ottomans again. And now she would get rid of Count Panin, probably because Orlov wished it. She could keep Panin at court, he could still head the foreign ministry. In a court rife with suspicion and intrigue, Panin was respected among the foreign ambassadors. He was devoted to the Grand Duke, a relationship like father and son. But for some reason,

Catherine was very wary of Count Panin. Orlov still frightened her with stories of plots in Paul's name with Panin's backing. If Catherine, however, openly acknowledged Paul as her heir and enhanced his standing at court with appropriate offices, there would be no plots. His supporters would bide their time.

"Do not look so morose, Betskoy," Catherine said, "I will make sure Count Panin is generously recompensed for the services he has rendered the Grand Duke. I have made a list."

She shuffled through papers on her desk. "Yes, here it is. An estate with 10,000 serfs and an income of 30,000 roubles – from our new Polish territories. They have proved a valuable source of rewards for our loyal friends."

And a means of making sure they became Russian, Betskoy thought. Poor Panin! He would now benefit from the partition of Poland, which he had strenuously opposed.

The Empress continued reading from her list. "A dwelling of his choice in St Petersburg – for there is no need for him now to reside at Court, and I will give him 100,000 roubles to furnish it and for a wine cellar – he has such fine taste, and for carriages of his own. He shall have a silver service. And I shall make him a field marshal with a pension of 30,000 roubles a year. There! Will he not be content?"

"Undoubtedly, Your Majesty. Very generous, indeed." Betskoy knew Panin would not be content to lose his influence at court no matter how well he may live outside it.

"But now I must go to the princesses," Catherine said. "Our wedding robes are being prepared and I must supervise the choice of materials. Their own taste is a little ... serious. I shall lend the bride some jewels. We must sparkle and dazzle. The people expect it. And our guests from Europe must find us magnificent."

As Catherine swept out, Betskoy sighed. The state

coffers would be emptied. Ten days of extravagant celebrations, of dresses and jewels, banquets and balls, free wine for the populace. The Russian officers at the Turkish front would have very limited supplies in the near future. They must curtail their territorial aims if they were not to suffer defeat. The state coffers could not supply both weddings and wars.

Chapter Forty-Five

Count Panin had invited Sir Robert Gunning and Count Solms to dinner 'for old times' sake'. They both knew that Panin, no longer part of the inner circle at Court, sought information. But they both agreed that they liked the Count and there would be no harm in spending an evening with him. He was still *persona grata* after all.

Count Panin kept an excellent table and this evening had been no exception. Much as he opposed French policy, Panin's chef was French, as were his wines. The men dined well.

"The Empress says the Grand Duke's wedding brought her a daughter-in-law and two friends, one old and one new," Panin said with a slight interrogative tone once the servants had cleared the table.

"But it is balanced, my dear Count. One friend is German and one is French," Solms said, rather jovially, Gunning thought. The Prussian ambassador had drunk quite a quantity of the robust red wine.

"But the German one lives in Paris and is a close acquaintance of the French one," Gunning offered, wishing to add accuracy.

"Gentlemen, gentlemen, "Panin said a little peevishly. "We are not playing guessing games."

"But there is nothing to guess, dear Count," Solms said cheerfully. "You know it all already. Baron Friedrich Melchior Grimm was a member of the retinue escorting the bride's eldest brother. He publishes that fortnightly newsletter about literature and so on –"

"*Correspondance littéraire, philosophique et critique*," Panin interrupted in his very precise French. "Written exclusively for crowned heads of state. By hand. And circulated through the embassies to avoid the over-enthusiastic French censorship. Our Empress is a loyal subscriber. As your emperors too, surely?"

"We may have an empire, and a very large one at that, but our sovereign is a king," Gunning said indignantly, "not an emperor."

"Ours too," Solms said, "I mean neither is ours. An emperor that is. Although he is in fact but not in name. You see it's a question of – "

"Yes, yes, my dear Count Solms," Panin interrupted. "But let us rather return to Baron Grimm. He spends a large amount of time with the Empress. Closeted away with her for hours, I hear?"

"The Empress presses the Baron to stay on in Russia in her service," Solms said. "The Baron, however, feels he is too old at fifty to make such an extreme change but he does not wish to insult the Empress by declining outright. And so she calls him to her and tries to persuade him and they remain in conversation for hours."

"The last session lasted for seven hours, I heard," Panin said bitterly. "Can one talk for seven hours?"

His question hung in the air. None of the three men wished to give voice to the suspicions implicit in it. The Court was enjoying a calm phase. Orlov was leading a quiet life, Vassilchikov continued as obedient chamberlain, the newlyweds were happy. And the Empress was almost serene. Was Grimm the cause? Gunning found the German affected. He wore white powder on his face and a rather outdated but intricate wig and his dress was perfectly tailored from expensive materials. He was a colourful and intelligent person, his wit as sharp as his longish nose. And at fifty, he was old.

"Well, I can say with authority," Solms said, clearing his throat, "that the Baron plays cards and chess with elegant skill. And he is possessed of much of that information in high society which might be called gossip. No doubt the Empress is entertained."

"He has indeed been the cause of much gossip himself," Panin said. "Ran off with that Madame d'Epinay, who considers herself a *philosophe* and spends her time with all those men. She was Rousseau's friend and Grimm snatched her from under his nose. Now Rousseau is his sworn enemy."

"Yes, how very ... French," Solms said. "Grimm has obviously been influenced by French ... culture?"

"My question is," Panin said energetically, "what do these philosophers want with the Empress? Or she with them?"

Gunning found the questions justified. The day before the wedding Denis Diderot had arrived from Paris, wan and exhausted from the exertions of the journey. He had taken to his bed following the festivities and was not seen for several weeks. Now he too was ensconced daily with the Empress. While Grimm was in the Empress's company at all hours of the day and late evening, Diderot was called to her after dinner, the Mystery Hour, usually reserved for her lovers. His nose was even more pointed than Grimm's and he was one decade older. He wore his hair short and unpowdered and never wore a wig, which made him look very thin on top. With his rather worn plain black suit, he looked somewhat like a bedraggled bird. There were too many of these Frenchmen at court, Gunning thought. Falconet, the sculptor, was one of them. He had been working on the monument of Peter the Great for years but the statue had not even been cast. Gunning reflected with satisfaction that his fellow countrymen did not linger in court, talking all day. They were out on the battlefields, or on the high seas leading the Russian navy against the Turks, or governing provinces. Or they were something useful, like doctors. The French were more ... parasitic.

Gunning cleared his throat. "Might these philosophers not be considered a dangerous influence? They are, after all, atheists."

"Ah," said Solms, "they will not cut off the hand that feeds them. That is why they seek the Empress's favours.

She showers them with money to buy libraries and art, to represent her in Europe, to spread word of her ... enlightenedness. It's a fair exchange really."

"You are right, Solms," Panin said. "The Empress toys with them. They are her playthings. She will not give up an iota's worth of her power for them. She is bored and imagines she brings French *salon* life to Russia. She cannot visit a *salon*, so the *salon* must be brought to her. She amuses herself, she has a lively mind that needs nourishment." Panin seemed to be addressing himself, trying out his own words to see if he was convinced by them.

"Never fear," Solms said cheerfully, "Grimm will not stay. Neither will Diderot. Once they have got what they want. The only danger I imagine they pose is to the Empress's treasury. There is a constant flow of Russian money into France."

"And both Grimm and Diderot are to be inaugurated into the Russian Academy of Sciences next week. It is all a farce," Panin said.

Yes, Gunning thought, a French farce indeed.

Chapter Forty-Six

"You know I did not wish to come," Diderot complained. "It was a dreadful journey. So long and so cold and such juddering and shaking of carriages. I felt my bones had all come apart. And now I am here and the water makes me ill. My digestion does not function as it should."

"But," Grimm said, offering Diderot a glass of spiced warmed wine, "you did come and you will benefit."

"I hope so. Unlike you, I have no money or patron. The Empress rescued me by buying my library and paying me to keep it. She can take it away again. It belongs to her. So I had to accept her invitation. Or command, as it was."

"And your conversations with her? She is pleased? Diverted? Inspired?" Grimm asked, hovering round Diderot with the carafe. "She summons you every day, which is a sign of favour."

"Oh, I write essays daily on subjects she chooses and then we discuss them. I can say anything I like. We are most informal. Sometimes I say wise things when I'm feeling stupid and perhaps also silly things when I'm feeling wise. But the Empress is tolerant as well as inspiring. Our conversations are wide-ranging and never flag." Diderot's voice had changed from the self-pitying invalid to the supercilious didact.

"Then you have no reason to complain," Grimm said curtly. He was rather fed up with his friend's ailments and in truth a little jealous of his success with the Empress.

"No, but I cannot stay here," Diderot stated flatly. "Even if the Empress has the soul of a Caesar and the temptations of a Cleopatra," he added more dramatically, suddenly reaching for a quill.

Grimm sighed in exasperation. Diderot thought all his epigrams worth noting. "Why? Has the Empress asked you to?"

"No, but she may. Then again, she may not. We do not agree on matters of importance. She is resistant to the sharing of political power. She does not see that all arbitrary government is bad even that which is firm and enlightened. I have told her so. I have told her that if the English had had three sovereigns in a row like Elizabeth, they would have been led to a state of servitude. And there has already been a surfeit of arbitrary heads of Russia this century, most of them women, which adds a further element of unpredictability. The country is indeed in a state of servitude."

"And you say all this to her?" Grimm asked.

"Oh yes, she is happy to debate with me. In fact, she seems to encourage it. She believes that only a sovereign such as she – enlightened, caring – can give her people what they need. She says they are as yet too uneducated to know what is best for them. And constantly asks me for a plan of education."

"Well, that is easy enough," Grimm said dismissively. "Take it from the *Enyclopédie*."

"Ah, but that is Rousseau's system. And you have successfully poisoned the Empress against him. No, I thought we would broach practical matters, such as economy, as a new course of possible agreement. I asked her, for example, in which provinces there are woollen manufactories. And do you know what she answered?"

"No, but I cannot think the question very ... inspired," Grimm said.

"She answered, 'Why, Monsieur Diderot, where else but in every province where there are sheep.'"

Grimm laughed.

***

Catherine was restless. The days were now short and the nights long. Her head ached from the candlelight and if too many candles were lit, her head ached from the smoke, no matter how pure the beeswax was. She imagined breathing in the freshness of the forest in spring but was overcome by a fit of coughing. Oh, that winter would end. But it had scarcely begun.

"You Majesty, let me pour you some wine," Baron Grimm said, with concern.

The philosophers had provided distraction. She had spent many hours with them, flattered by their attentions and flushed with her success in parrying with them. Yes, she could hold her own with the best minds that Europe had to offer. She could outwit them although they, especially Diderot, did not hold back in their open criticism of her. He was often so enthusiastic about his own opinions that he would slap her thigh or shoulder in triumphant emphasis. She had seen fit to curtail, however, what she perceived as his intellectual condescension. She turned to Baron Grimm, with whom she enjoyed a different *rapport*. Perhaps it was because they were both still German at heart. After sipping from the goblet of wine he proffered, she said,

"Monsieur Diderot thinks that I am his pupil and he the master, does he not?"

"On the contrary, Your Majesty," Grimm said, "Monsieur Diderot is filled with your praise. He is grateful that you deign to spend time with him. He lauds your intelligence, your perspicacity, your – "

"Ah, let us not exaggerate, my dear Baron," Catherine said briskly. "I like the little philosopher, who pecks about like a bird, when I throw him morsels to provoke him. But he is very critical of our rule. If I followed his advice, I would have to turn my Empire upside down – legislation, finance, administration, agriculture ... I do not think he would leave a stone in my kingdom unturned. What chaos would ensue!"

Catherine had indeed given Diderot his rein and was astonished at how far he went in his criticisms. Many had been sent to Siberia for much less. She would send him back to France. Let him criticise his own king. She had allowed Diderot to vent his political rage on her but Louis XV would have had him cast in irons.

"Well, I think that there must be some balance between ideas and practice – " Grimm began carefully.

"Indeed. Monsieur Diderot could write a book but would fail at governing a country. And that is the difference. He works on paper, which is uniform and supple and presents no obstacles to one's imagination or pen. But I am an Empress and must write on human parchment, which is sensitive and irritable."

Catherine was pleased with her analogy.

"And the sovereigns of France, of Prussia, of Austria?" Catherine continued. "Do they follow such ideas? No. They do not give up their power because they know that only a firm hand can govern. We sovereigns do as the French Louis XIV preached. In fact, we have no choice."

Grimm looked puzzled.

"Listen to the people, seek advice from your Council, but decide alone," Catherine cited. "And I do listen. To you and Diderot. To my own counsellors. I read and read. I ponder and ponder. But in the end, it is I who must decide, and I alone. Such is my divine right."

And at times, a burden, she thought. She was always alone. Orlov had gone, Vassilchikov was more of a child than a man. When she invited Grimm and Diderot to come to Russia, she had perhaps hoped that they would provide more than intellectual stimulation. But Diderot was too old and too slight in stature. And although Grimm had a fine figure and was gallant in flirting, she felt no physical attraction to him. She had drawn him out on his mistress Louise d'Epinay, who, by all accounts, was charming, intelligent, wrote books, argued with Rousseau and had all the *philosophe*s at her feet. Well, Catherine thought bitterly, Madame d'Epinay did not have an empire to govern. Grimm, Catherine knew, was anxious to return to Paris, to his work and his mistress and Catherine was grateful that he did not to press the point. She would allow him to leave, with her blessing.

"But Monsieur Diderot will leave us, I hear?" she said more briskly.

"His health, as you know, is far from robust," Grimm said. "He has often been ill and now that the winter cold has come, his frailty is more marked."

"And you too, my dear friend, have often been confined to bed with fever. It seems our climate does not agree with you either. You would leave us too?"

"Reluctantly," Grimm said. "I am honoured by your offer to stay here in your service. But you know I can serve you well in Europe. I can be your unofficial envoy there. I can look out for art."

Once he left, Catherine reflected, she would be alone again. Who would help her to fill the long, empty hours?

***

At the banquet that night Catherine kept her composure but her heart beat uncomfortably fast and her head pounded. Her son Paul and his new wife sat near her with their heads close together making no attempt to join the general conversation. Where was the head that should be close to hers? Catherine asked herself angrily. Surely she too deserved love. When the winter ice and snow yielded to the spring thaw, she would add another year to her life. Forty-five years! Was she too old to be swept away by passion? Or to attract it? She was tired of using her head, tired of ruling, of reading and writing. She wanted someone to love her, as Grigory Orlov once had. She cast a glance around the room but amongst the ambassadors, aristocrats and counsellors, she detected no more than possible dalliances and temporary distractions which would only serve to make her more aware of what she did not have. Suddenly, she rose from the table, startling her guests. She bid a curt good night and swept from the room, her maids following in a disorganized shuffle behind her. She knew what she wanted. Or rather whom. She would write immediately, summoning him back to St Petersburg. She was the Empress and she could do as she wished. No, she *would* do as she wished.

Chapter Forty-Seven

General Potemkin warmed his hands in front of the meagre fire. Cold seeped in all around. Despite the exhaustion felt deep in his bones, he could not sleep. It was not the freezing temperatures which kept him awake, nor the scurrying of rats looking for warmth amongst the half frozen bodies. It was his anger. They could have taken the fortress but Field Marshal Rumyantsev had called the retreat. Some officers were too fine for hand-to-hand combat, Potemkin thought scornfully. They did not like to get their impressive uniforms dirty or lose their wigs, preferring their chessboard plans – move these five thousand here and that ten thousand there. Battle, Potemkin thought, was about passion and blood and if uniforms did not get dirtied, then the fight had not been fought well.

Potemkin knew how to rally his men. In the summer heat, his troops weakened by mosquito-plague and dysentery, they had crossed the swell of the Danube under fire, a distance of some three versts. They had stormed the enemy strongholds, beating the Turks back in flashes of guns and swords.

The Russian forces now numbered a mere 35,000 on this front, with no new reinforcements promised. Rumour had it that the Empress was too busy with weddings and banquets, with French philosophers and new lovers. Well, let her. She had written to him but he would not answer. He would rather die in fields of mud and blood than play some court puppet.

Despite being outnumbered, Potemkin's troops had managed to force the Turks further back. His men were battle-weary, plague-ridden, short of weapons and ammunition. He cajoled them, ridiculed them, threatened them ... but fought with them every step of the way. Many of the Russian officers, huddled over their battle plans on paper, were jealous of Potemkin's successes and of his popularity with the troops and scathing about his unkempt appearance, lack of etiquette, and failure to follow orders. "Fine manners and clean hands will not take Silistria!" he retorted. The Turkish hordes were unpredictable and therein lay their strength – and weakness. It had taken many battles for the Russian officers to realise that behind their frightening cries to Allah and their mad swirling, there was no discipline. With patience, they could be easily routed. The Turkish forces, comprised of many colourfully clad national elements, fought in pyramid form, the bravest at the front, often driven by opium frenzy, and spilled towards the enemy like a river bursting its banks. The Tatars were much feared – and admired – for their prowess on horse. They circled and wheeled like a swarm of wasps but the Russians had learned not to engage but rather wait in formation until their adversaries had tired. The attackers then either fled or fought hopelessly to the bitter and bloody end against the disciplined Russian troops. Potemkin often thought it was more of a slaughter than a battle and had sometimes broken ranks to lead his men to what he considered a fairer fight on the open field. He had been reprimanded many times for disobeying orders but Rumyantsev forgave him because his sallies contributed to Russian victories if only because they confused the enemy.

Potemkin could have taken the strategic fortress of Silistria if the Russian officers had not panicked. After weeks of pressing on, his forces at last breached the walls. The Russian troops flooded into the streets of the citadel but the Turkish were fierce in their defence. His own men, now weakened by cold and lack of proper food, did not know the layout of the narrow maze of streets and ran into ambush after ambush. The order to retreat sounded behind them. Potemkin would have chosen not to hear it, as he had done many times, but he knew that without troops behind them, his men would be slaughtered. In anger, he slashed out at two Turks coming at him. Both fell as Potemkin wheeled his horse round and called for his men to follow the retreat bugle.

Rumyantsev would not attempt another full scale attack. Winter was upon them, and they would have to make camp, which meant going back across the river. How the Turks would rejoice to see the Russians yield the territory they had fought so hard for over the past few months. There would be no victory for the Empress to celebrate in her warm palace where she enjoyed the comforts of good food and wine and a soft bed to lie in and someone to twine her limbs round, Potemkin thought bitterly.

There would be no hero's return for him. But, he reflected, as he gazed out at the shadow of the fortress looming large against the sky, even victory would not have secured him the Empress's affections. He had returned a hero the year before, heavily decorated for battles won against the Turks and with Rumyantsev's personal recommendation to the Empress. Potemkin had wintered in St Petersburg, often invited to the Empress's table. He had entertained her, made her laugh, complimented her, flattered her, flirted with her, even once dared to kiss her. Grigory Orlov was out of favour and Potemkin felt sure Catherine would choose him as her new personal adjutant. But when the winter ice had melted, Potemkin was ordered back to the front with a promotion to Lieutenant General. Potemkin knew it was less a promotion than a dismissal from Court. He had been usurped by a milksop, a boy who could not even hold a sword. Well, let her have her pet Vassilchikov! He would run after no woman, Empress or not. He would fight for Russian victory, even if he died in the attempt. He would stay in this God-forsaken place and take up the battle in spring.

A shadow suddenly darkened the opening of his tent

flap. His adjutant stood to attention.

"A letter, General," he said. "I thought you might like to receive it despite the late hour. It bears the imperial seal."

Potemkin took the letter and dismissed the adjutant. He was not sure he wanted to read it. There would be more empty words, meaningless in this world of battle and blood, where life could be severed in an instant by a flash of sword or a burst of gunpowder. Wearily, Potemkin held the parchment nearer the candle.

Lieutenant General and cavalier,

I expect your eyes are too trained on Silistria to have any time for reading letters;

Ah, how right she was! he thought.

and although I do not know whether your bombardment has been successful, I am nevertheless convinced that everything you undertake has as its sole motive your ardent zeal towards me personally as well as to the dear fatherland, whose service you love.

Of course, word would not yet have reached her of the failure to take Silistria but was she implying that even failure would be forgiven? The words "ardent zeal" leapt out at him, like a note in the wrong key.

But for my part, I very much wish to preserve zealous, brave, clever and talented people, and so I request that you should not needlessly expose yourself to danger.

He accepted her compliments. They were part of Court etiquette. He did not understand, however, how he was to fight without exposing himself to danger. Did she mean he was to return to Court? He quickly read the last lines.

On reading this letter, you may ask: why was it written? To this I answer: so that you should have confirmation of how I think about you: for towards you I am always well-disposed.

Potemkin let out a long sigh. Yes, she did mean he should return to Court. She had tired of her milksop. She had chosen Potemkin and now summoned him to her presence. As soon as the Russian troops had crossed the river, he would make haste to St Petersburg and be there early in the new year. A place at the Empress's side was a place of power and he would not jeopardise this chance. He lay down on his camp bed, pulling his greatcoat round him. He knew he would be able to sleep now.

Chapter Forty-Eight

"Look, Nikita, the situation is not good. You must speak to the Empress, try to impress on her that the danger is real."

Count Panin regarded his brother. They had eaten well but had not emptied the wine carafe.

"You know I have no influence anymore," he said, "if I ever had. She will listen to you. You are the General and it is after all, a military matter. Did she not send sufficient troops to deal with the problem?"

"Our troops were hardly one month there when they were routed by the rebels in November. Small wonder. There were no troops to spare from the Turkish front and the Cossacks had artillery and were apparently well organised. The Empress has sent General Bibikov, an able and experienced leader, but what can he do? Pugachev is now calling himself Peter III and people are rallying to him in their thousands. He shows what he calls the tsar's marks on his body, the stigmata of his divine right, he says. More likely to be scabs from scratched flea bites but you know how superstitious the people are down there. They believe him and fall on their knees to worship him."

"But what control do we have in the remote provinces if the military fail?" Nikita Panin asked. "Why, in Kazan alone there about two and a half million people and only some eighty Russian administrators to manage them."

"The rebels will take Kazan. They already have Samara and Orenburg. They can only be stopped by decisive military intervention. The rebels rule by terror. Those who do not swear loyalty to the false Peter are hanged, the men upside down, the women raped first. Hundreds of them. Officers have been found headless, armless and legless ... some have been skinned alive. They are a savage bunch!" The General struck the table with his fist. "Before long, they will be at the gates of Moscow. Will the Empress then take notice?"

"When I last broached the subject with her, she said General Bibikov had the situation under control. She declared that the inhabitants of the province were restless and had always engaged in pillage but that once they encountered order and reason, they would give up their barbaric ways." Nikita Panin's tone was slightly ironic.

"Hah!" his brother scoffed. "Pugachev would laugh. Why, he himself is illiterate but he has 25,000 followers now. He has set up his own Court, a mirror image of this one. Why, there is even a Count Panin. And he has his own Empress, some Cossack woman he has taken after abandoning his own wife and children."

"And does Bibikov really not have control over the situation?" Count Panin asked, his impatience increasing. "Why can our forces not deal with these rebels?"

"He has had to resort to extreme measures and has hanged some captured upstarts," the General replied. "But he cannot report such things to the Empress. She orders him to fight the terror with her words of reason. She sends manifestos to be read out in every town exhorting the people to loyalty but words mean nothing. Pugachev promises something to everyone. The serfs shall have their freedom, the Old Believers their churches, the Tatars will be freed from military service and the poll tax, the Bashkir nomads guaranteed their way of life ... the list is endless. And all shall have grain and salt, land and no taxes. A perfect paradise. His success is in duping the dissatisfied and they are many. The Empress must see this. You must beg her to allow me to bring reinforcements to General Bibikov. We must stamp out this plague of terror!"

"The Empress seems distracted but by what I cannot say. I do no see her as often as I used to. But it would do well to persuade her to make peace, albeit temporarily over winter, on the Turkish front in order to deal with this Pugachev and his rebellion."

"The Empress would be well advised to heed us, her military officers," the General said, "But we do not have her ear. She is too ... preoccupied."

"Perhaps we can consult with the British and the Prussian ambassadors," Nikita Panin said thoughtfully. "They may be able to mediate a truce."

The General sighed.

"It is a sign of the times that we must rely on foreign envoys to save our country. I am reminded of Nero fiddling while Rome burned."

Chapter Forty-Nine

Catherine stood in front of the mirror in a new rose-coloured silk dress. It reminded her of when she had first come to the Court of Russia, a young girl of fifteen. She had worn rose silk then for her first presentation to the Empress Elizabeth. It had been a gown of artful simplicity, worn with no whalebone but allowed to drape her figure's natural shape. Regretfully, her natural contours could no longer be outlined in that way. Even when sharing her bed, she knew how to drape her nakedness to its advantage.

The new robe had been stiffened with corsets to narrow her waist and uplift her ample bosom, of which she was proud. The silk flowed abundantly over wide panniers, which had been measured exactly to ensure she would be able to go though the palace doorways without having to turn sideways. To make up for the lost sparkle of youth, hundreds of diamonds were stitched on to the bodice. She would not wear her usual Orders since it was to be an intimate dinner for twenty guests but rather a new diamond and sapphire set of necklace, earrings and brooch. She had been told sapphires reflected the blue of her eyes. She would have worn flowers in her hair but knew that trying to emulate youth would only emphasize her years. Instead her hair, intricately coiled, sparkled with more diamonds.

She viewed her reflection with satisfaction and hoped the General too would find pleasure in her appearance. He was ten years younger and, unlike Vassilchikov, had the vitality and virility of his age but with a decade or two of wisdom added. Not only was he a hero of the battlefields, leading her often outnumbered troops to victory against the Turkish hordes, but he was also a perfect courtier, always ready with a compliment of such exaggeration, delivered so passionately, that she could only laugh. And yes, he made her laugh.

General Potemkin had been her secret for several months, or perhaps longer. Years ago she had befriended him, attracted by his earnest love for books and his outrageous humour, by his youthful passion for her and his religious zeal. She had briefly considered taking her attraction further but after he had lost an eye to the Orlovs' jealousy – and she was sure it was the Orlovs – she had not wanted to endanger him further for at that time he would have been no more than a means to keep Grigory Orlov interested in her. She had still been in love with Orlov then. Had he not tired of her, she would have loved him always, she reflected sadly.

Now she was free to enjoy Potemkin's open admiration. She encouraged his flirtations, had even allowed him to kiss her briefly. He had such beautiful lips. And how she admired his strength! He was taller than Orlov, broader, with a lion's mane of chestnut hair. But his features were finely drawn and his half-closed eye added rather than detracted from his looks. She had often considered kissing the dimple on his strong chin but would make no advance until she was sure of his affection for her. Perhaps tonight would be different. Surely now that she had reinstated Orlov in all his offices and showered him with palaces, silver, serfs and a generous pension, her former lover would not grudge her the happiness of a new love. After all, she had turned a blind eye to his romantic attachment to his very young niece. As long as the object of Catherine's affections was the colourless Vassilchikov, Orlov would not object but in General Potemkin he would see a rival – not for her heart but for power. Well, it was her heart and her power and she would do as she wished – as long as Potemkin wished it too. But did he? In an agony of indecision, of longing for certainty in his kisses, of desire to be held by him, she gazed at her reflection, noting the high colour in her cheeks. "I cannot live without love," she thought, "and nor should I be expected to. I will make him mine."

***

General Potemkin raged like a caged animal. Catherine had welcomed him warmly but weeks had gone by and she had still not arranged for them to be alone together. His patience had run out. He knew she was attracted to him. He saw it in her eyes, in the flush of her cheeks. He could not bear it that Vassilchikov was still in her bed. He, Potemkin, had loved her for twelve years and had lost no opportunity to show her. The Empress, however, had taken other lovers and sent him off to the front. Well, he was tired of it all and was a fool to have come rushing from Silistria. He was determined to return to the battle front but not to the Turkish lines. Field Marshal Rumyantsev had made winter camp, and the troops would be limited to drills and maintenance and repair duties. Potemkin wanted action. Hearing that General Panin was leaving with troops to help General Bibikov quell the swelling insurrection in the Volga, he asked to join him. Panin had agreed but the Empress refused to let him go.

"I have just recalled you from danger and would not wish you to seek it again," she said at dinner one evening. "Besides, the rebels will be easily dealt with. You must stay and entertain us while you are recovering from the exertions of war." Potemkin could not argue in front of the other guests. The Empress had invited him to an 'intimate' dinner, raising Potemkin's hopes. He had paid particular attention to his appearance. Not only was he disappointed to find he shared the Empress's table with some twenty other guests but he was angered to find Vassilchikov in his place at her side. He vowed to attend no more dinners.

According to General Panin, the rebels would not be easily suppressed. More forces were needed. If Catherine did not act decisively, her empire would fragment into pieces. Panin and Potemkin were of the opinion that a man was needed to make such decisions. Catherine may be Empress but she knew nothing of battle. Well, if she would not have him in her bed and he was not allowed to fight, he knew what he would do.

***

Catherine looked at Betskoy in disbelief. "What do you mean, he has locked himself away in a monastery?"

"As far as my informers tell me, and I think it is part of the artifice that word does reach you, General Potemkin is now in the Alexander Nevsky monastery and devotes himself to theological reading, prayer, fasting and divine music," Betskoy said with some amusement in his voice. "Ah, and he has grown a beard," he added.

"You say 'artifice'. Do you think it is all a charade? And to what purpose?" Catherine asked in agitation.

"General Potemkin has always tended to ... drama, to extremes. You remember he has disappeared into a monastery before. After the ... eye incident."

"But why?" Catherine knew she was almost wailing. She was weak with disappointment. She had recalled Potemkin and favoured him with a warm welcome. She had waited for his advances but even the rose-coloured dress had not inspired him to ... indiscretions. He only had to say that he loved her. Oh, why had he not sought her out to say it?

"Why has he left our presence, and without our permission?" she asked.

"I think it is evident, Your Majesty. He is disappointed that he has not gained your affections – "

"Oh, but he has!" Catherine exclaimed. "But have I his? He did not say."

"How can he presume to approach an Empress, especially when the Empress's favour falls on another adjutant, who still shares her ... bed."

Catherine could not dismiss Vassilchikov and order Potemkin to occupy the chambers of her personal companion without knowing that he loved her with the passion she longed for. She had loved Grigory Orlov but, she reflected, he had probably never loved her. His aim, and that of his brothers, was to rule as sovereign at her side. Would he have spent time with her if she had had no power? And now he was ensconced with his child-niece in a love nest. That was the proof. Riches and power were no match for true love.

"But I must have proof that he loves me," she said, trying to keep her composure, "that he does not want me only because he would have my power or wish to share my throne. I cannot give my heart to endanger my empire. How can I know if he really loves me?"

"You can ask him," Betskoy said. "Or rather, send one of your ladies, perhaps the Countess Bruce, to find out."

Catherine was reluctant to send such an attractive messenger to Potemkin but she had little choice. There was no one else she trusted. The Countess had served her well and after the pox scare she was discreet in checking any man whom Catherine would have in her bedchamber. There had been very few of late, Catherine thought with concern. Had desire left her? She must have Potemkin back. She would send the Countess as her emissary but would instruct her that a close examination of the General would not be necessary.

***

"Ah, the poor monks went scurrying from the cloisters. Afraid of temptation, the poor things!" The Countess threw down her gloves. "I have come from there straight to you!"

"And to tell me what? Do not torture me, Praskovya!" Catherine said. "I will not beg!"

"Well, the news is good, or as you would wish it," the Countess said, settling herself in a chair with a swish of silk. Catherine often thought the Countess dressed too ostentatiously. Her costume today was more suitable for a

Court operetta than a visit to a monastery. There were even feathers in her hat.

Catherine would not give the Countess the satisfaction of asking again. Noticing this, Countess Bruce sighed and said, "You rob me of my fun, Catherine dear! But very well, I will narrate my experience. I was shown to his cell – yes really, he lives in a cell – but he was praying and kept me waiting. And you will never guess which icon he was prostrated in front of!" When Catherine did not comment but fixed a warning look on the Countess, she continued, "An icon of St Catherine! Ah, now you are pleased. I knew you would be and you will be even more pleased. But may I have a little wine? I am parched after the dusty ride."

Catherine poured a goblet and handed it to the Countess. She took a few sips and resumed.

"He kept me waiting quite some minutes and I was just about to interrupt his devotions when he turned and said, before I could even speak, 'You have come from the Empress. But it is hopeless. This is my destiny, to devote myself to God.'"

Catherine gave a sharp intake of breath. "I knew he did not love me, " she whispered.

"Ah, but wait. He has written you a song, an aria as in all great love stories. I cannot sing it, of course, but I begged the lyrics from him." The Countess rummaged in her reticule and pulled out a crumpled scroll, which she offered to the Empress.

"No, you read it to me," Catherine said.

The Countess looked pleased. She sat up straight, took a deep breath and began.

"*As soon as I beheld thee, I thought only of thee,*

But O Heavens, what torment to love one to whom I dare not declare!

One who can never be mine! Cruel gods! –"

"It neither rhymes nor scans," Catherine interrupted.

"The music is needed. It is to be sung," the Countess said. "But listen. Here comes the part you wish to hear."

*"Why have you given her such charms? And exalt her so high?
Why did you destine me to love her and her alone?"*

"There! He loves you!" the Countess declared triumphantly. "Are you not pleased?"

"If he loves me, what is he doing in a monastery when I have shown him such favour?" Catherine asked. "How could he abandon me?"

"Ah, but he is very sad. He says his violent passion, those were his very words, have reduced him to despair. He decided to flee the object of his torment – again his very own words – since seeing you only made his intolerable sufferings worse."

"He said all that? Or do you embellish, Praskovya?" Catherine asked sharply.

"No, no, I swear. The man is the picture of misery. He has grown a beard, you know, which does not become him. It is a darker shade than his hair, which he has shorn somewhat." Noticing Catherine's look of alarm, she quickly added, "But not overmuch. He says he was beginning to hate the world because of his love for you and he now seeks respite in God's presence."

"I understand his words. But not the meaning. I have never declared against him. On the contrary, I imagined the affability of my welcome must have given him to understand that his homage would not be displeasing," Catherine said somewhat imperiously.

"Oh Catherine, you are sometimes blind to what is obvious. You must think less ... tortuously. How could he declare his love when you are bound to another?"

"Another? Ah, you mean Vassilchikov. But he does not mean anything to me. He is no more than an undemanding and undangerous companion."

"But does Potemkin know that? If you wish to love this man, you must tell him so. And then remove Vassilchikov." The Countess looked at Catherine triumphantly.

"It is a risk," Catherine said.

"Isn't love always a risk?" the Countess asked.

***

General Potemkin whistled cheerfully as he shaved. Prayer had indeed been effective. There had not even been time to grow a proper beard. His uniform had been cleaned and pressed, his sword and boots polished. Countess Bruce had come to fetch him from the monastery in a luxurious carriage, which was to bring him directly to the Empress, "Your torment is at an end," the Countess said. "The Empress awaits you." She did not say in which manner. Eagerly? Impatiently? Shyly? It did not matter. She awaited him. He would attend to the how of the matter. And he would become the Empress's consort.

Chapter Fifty

They could scarcely see each other through the steam of the banya.

"Are you still there, mon cher ami, my little dove? I cannot see you," Catherine said. She rarely used the banya. It required too much time but it was more that she did not think an Empress should cavort naked, or even almost naked, amongst her subjects, even if they were her ladies-in-waiting. The banya was usually mixed and she recalled her horror when Grigory Orlov first took her there. She was young then, and not as aware of her body, or its faults, as she was now, but her Lutheran upbringing was shocked at the lack of modesty. She had glimpsed shapes merging through the mist of steam and did not want to surmise what their activities were. Later, she had enjoyed visits with Orlov to the small country banyas when they were away from Court, on hunting trips. She remembered the excitement of Orlov beating her lightly with the birch branches as her body heated, then the exhilaration of rolling in the snow. That was decades ago but perhaps her suggestion to conduct her trysts with Potemkin in the banya was an attempt to revive that excitement. When she became Empress, she had tried to curtail mixed bathing. Men were forbidden to enter areas reserved for women unless they were banya servants, artists or doctors who sought to improve their skills. Countess Bruce reported that there were always plenty of artists and doctors to be found in the banya.

But Catherine and Potemkin met late at night, when the Court was sleeping, and they could be alone. The banya offered them privacy. Her room was not safe since Vassilchikov had still not been removed and her ladies were always flitting in and out.

Now Potemkin's voice reached her through the steam. "I am here, my Empress. Always at your side. Can you not feel me?" Catherine felt Potemkin's lips on her toes. He caressed each one before his lips moved along the sole of her foot, sending shivers through her despite the heat. Slowly, he left a trail of kisses the length of her leg.

Later, she said languorously, "Come, my dearest, we must go to the cooling pool. We are melting."

"I melt more from love of you than from the heat of the banya," Potemkin said. "There is a Russian proverb. 'A couple that sweats together stays together.' You do wish us to be together, my sovereign, queen of my heart?"

"You have given me love and I cannot live without it anymore. You have ruined me for any other!" Catherine whispered close to his ear.

"Ah, there will be no other, not for you and not for me," Potemkin said loudly and cheerfully before plunging into the cold water. Catherine admired his strong and lithe body as he swam vigorously. Emerging, the water streaming from him, he said, "The temperature is conducive to discussing what you are going to do with your little *soupe à glace*. Is it not time he left your chambers?"

Catherine, tearing her eyes from Potemkin's muscular nakedness, slid into the water. "Vassilchikov is harmless, I would not hurt him," she said mildly. "It's unkind to call him a cold soup. He is like a son to me."

"But you have a son. You can shower *him* with affection," Potemkin said, rubbing himself dry with towel.

"Ah, but he has a wife to do that," Catherine said, gazing up at him from the water. "You know, I liked that girl at the beginning but now she is profligate. They are in debt to twice what they have and always ask for more. I have given them much. 500,000 roubles so far this year!"

Catherine stretched out her hand for Potemkin to help her out.

"You ask for nothing but I shall give you much," she said softly as he pulled her from the pool.

"Come, my Venus, let us think of other things. I cannot

concentrate on money when I have the greatest treasure before my eyes."

Later, clad in loose robes, they lay on silk-cushioned couches, sipping cooled wine. A few candles gave out a warm glow. Catherine, afraid of detection, would not light more.

"If only we could stay in this little paradise forever," Catherine sighed.

Potemkin moved to lay his head on her lap. "An Empress can make her own paradise on Earth," he said. "And I will be at your side to help you. Always." He moved his hand to part her robe. "I and no other," he added.

PART FIVE
1773-1775

Chapter Fifty-One

"Well, gentlemen," Nikita Panin began as he raised his glass, "to the new imperial favourite!"

Sir Robert Gunning and Count Solms nodded as they lifted their glasses.

"And what do you make of him? Is he not an improvement?" Panin asked cheerfully.

"Well, certainly, he has more ... presence than Vassilchikov," Gunning said. "And I think he will leave his mark."

"The Empress is enamoured of him and, unlike Count Orlov, he apparently never leaves her side," Panin said. "Or no further than just a few rooms away. I have it on good authority that they write notes to each other continually."

"It would be well," Solms said, "if she turned her pen to other matters. Like the Turkish front, where fighting must resume now that winter is past, or the Pretender's rebellion, which gathers in strength. Being in love will not run an Empire!"

"At least, Potemkin is a man of decision, a man with experience both at Court and on the battlefield. I am sure he will take things in hand," Panin said. "And his ambition is limitless. But it remains to be seen whether the Empress will allow his influence."

"You don't mean – " Gunning began.

"No, no," Panin continued. "She will not marry him. I am sure of that. And if that is his goal, he will be frustrated in it. As Count Orlov was."

"They are very different, Orlov and Potemkin, would you not say?" Gunning asked.

"Not so different," Solms said. "Both are soldiers and

both are ambitious."

"And both are much admired by women," Gunning said, with perhaps a hint of jealousy.

"I think General Potemkin keeps the Empress happy, and she will do anything to keep him happy," Panin said. "But I agree with you, Count Solms. There is an Empire to govern and it is time the honeymoon interlude gave way to more practical matters."

"Do you have news from your brother? Is it true that the rebels have been defeated at last?" Gunning asked.

"The situation is still grave," Panin answered. "Reports say Pugachev has chalked up victories the whole length of the Volga. He and his rebels have not only taken whole villages but have over forty foundries and mines in their control, which guarantees them a supply of guns and ammunition. They are now attacking the copper foundries in the Urals. The factory serfs join them in their hundreds. And Pugachev has started conscription, each household has to supply one recruit and declare loyalty to the rebel cause. The alternative is death and confiscation of property."

"Unwilling troops do not fight well," Solms observed. "The Russian troops should be able to defeat them."

"The tide is turning slightly, it is true," Panin said. "Our forces fight well although vastly outnumbered. They have succeeded in scattering Pugachev's troops and forcing him eastwards." Panin paused to consult a paper on the table. "His losses were considerable. Over a thousand killed to 140 on our side. Another thousand cut down in the pursuit. And 4000 taken prisoner." He put down the paper. "The prisoners are a problem," he added pensively.

"The Empress has informed the foreign envoys that the rebellion has been suppressed. She declares a victory," Gunning said.

"There is no victory as long as Pugachev is at large." Panin said decisively. "Our generals now have to give chase, all the way into Siberia if necessary."

"Well," Solms said briskly, "at least he is not making for Moscow."

"Not yet," Panin said. "But when he rallies more support, he may turn. We have to keep him on the other side of the Volga."

"And what of Orenburg? Has it been re-taken?" Solms asked. "The rebels have held it under siege for months."

"General Bibikov has freed the citadel. It couldn't have held out much longer. But neither could the impatient rebels. Apparently, many of them had already turned tail and ridden their horses into the mist, so to speak." Panin consulted his papers once more. "You know that General Bibikov succumbed to fever shortly after. A great blow to our troops. I don't know who will replace him." He paused. "My brother the General would be a good choice, I think."

"I hear the Empress is distraught. She liked General Bibikov," Solms said.

"Well, she has Potemkin to comfort her," Gunning observed dryly. "But why is he not there fighting to save her Empire? Surely a man such as he is not content to just ... linger at Court?"

"Oh, I would not wish him gone if I were you," Panin said hastily. "Russia will profit more from him than from Count Orlov or Lieutenant Vassilchikov. He has the political intelligence which they lacked."

"But not the manners," Gunning said. "Have you seen how he runs about? Why, I was at a meeting with the Empress recently – "

Solms glanced up sharply.

"Just some – " Gunning waved his hand vaguely. "Shipping business," he finished lamely. "Anyway, there we were when General Potemkin barged in. Yes, there is no other word for it. The door flew open and there he stood barefoot in some kind of oriental robe which neither covered his chest nor his legs. He had a rose-coloured kerchief wound round his head and was chewing on a what looked like a parsnip! He certainly did not look politically intelligent. More like the barbarians he should be off fighting!"

"Yes, he is somewhat Russian," Panin said calmly. "Muscovite, one might say."

"He is overfond of gambling " Solms said.

"And he bites his fingernails," Gunning said triumphantly. "Till they bleed."

***

When Catherine woke, she reached out for him, knowing he would not be there. If he came to her, he never stayed the night, slipping off to his card games, which lasted till the morning. By that time, Catherine was at her desk, trying to concentrate, her body tingling with expectation. Nights of passion left her craving more. Even Orlov had not roused in her such hunger. It was not just that Potemkin was the better lover, which he was she thought as she smiled to herself, it was that her body responded involuntarily to his. All that she had experienced before, even through Orlov's titillating stories and erotic objects, was no more than a sea of shallow waves. Potemkin released storms in her, depths of which she had not been aware. Perhaps this was what the tale of the sleeping princess meant. The prince kissed her into life, real life.

She rose and put the little burner on for her coffee. She would dress later when her ladies were up. She sneezed. Surely she had not caught a cold. They were staying in the palace at Tsarskoye Selo rather than in the Winter Palace in St Petersburg, where Potemkin said she was too accessible to what he called time-robbers. It was true that the palace, some twenty versts from the city, afforded more privacy. Besides which, Potemkin's new quarters in the Winter Palace were not finished. He had refused to sleep in chambers which had been occupied by any of her other lovers.

"You have had at least fifteen lovers," he accused her. She saw his jealousy as flattering, as a proof of his love, but sensed he must feel the only one she really loved.

"I will make you a sincere confession," she had whispered. "I have had four before you. I had to take the first to rescue my life since my husband could not father an heir. And the last, the hapless Vassilchikov, I took out of desperation and because he was safe. The two in between lightened the burden of loneliness. Had I had a husband whom I could have loved, or who even loved me, I would have been faithful to him forever."

Now she sneezed again. She had probably caught cold from her vigil outside his room. He had not come to her the previous night. She had written a note beforehand asking if she should come to him or he to her but there had been no answer. She had left her door open. Unlike Orlov, Potemkin preferred her body unadorned and she had lain naked under the covers. The silk was cold against her flesh but she had tossed and turned herself into a fever of anxiety. Where was he? Had he tired of her already? Would he be in another's arms?

Perhaps he had misunderstood the message and was waiting for her in his chambers. Of course, that was it! She had risen and, throwing a robe round her naked shoulders, she ran the length of the drafty corridor which connected their rooms. His door was locked. She knew he kept it locked when he was not in his rooms. Catherine huddled outside, willing him to come and take her in his arms. She regretted coming barefoot as the cold seeped up through the stone floors. She did not know how long she waited but eventually reason, or the cold which cooled her febrile state, persuaded her to return to her own chamber where she fell into an uneasy sleep.

She must stop acting like a foolish girl, she reprimanded

herself as she began work on the heap of papers on her desk. There was so much to see to. They should take advantage of the uncertainty following Sultan Mustafa's death, either a new offensive or a resumption of peace talks to Russia's advantage. A new commander must be appointed to deal with Pugachev and his mob of rebels. New tactics were needed. Or more troops. Yes, perhaps a peace with Turkey advantageous to Russia would free troops for the fight against the rebels. There were petitions from serfs, complaints against serfs, reports from every corner of the empire, from every commission, from, it seemed, every person at court. Except one from Potemkin, the only person who mattered to her now.

She decided to work for another two hours and then go and see if he was awake. No, that was probably too early and he would be like a bear with a sore head. She would send him a note. Yes, she would write to him and after that she could concentrate on her work. *My dearest darling*, she began. Her pen flew across the paper. " *I rose at 5a.m. and it is now 7. I want to fly to your arms but I know you sleep. And I must work. Oh, but I am bored without you, my golden tiger. My night was long and lonely. I have given strict orders to my whole body, down to the smallest hair, not to let you know that it loves you so. I have locked my love securely in my heart, under ten locks: but it suffocates there; it will explode. But you know where to find the keys. Come and free me. I long for you.*

She threw down her pen. What nonsense! What an absurd torrent of words. She, who was known to be one of the best heads in Europe had lost her reason, the victim of a mad passion. She was enslaved to Potemkin and would forfeit the fine words of Voltaire, Diderot, Grimm — all of them – for just one night with him.

She did not care. Philosophers could not give her love. She would send her mad letter. She would be true to her feelings. Picking up her quill, she added a last sentence.

Goodbye my darling lion of the jungle. I count the hours, no the minutes, the seconds, until I see you again.

Catherine had warned Potemkin to burn her notes as soon as he had read them but he carried them in a bundle 'next to his heart', he said. She had destroyed most of his but now regretted she did not have his past words to soothe her fevered frenzy.

No, she would not send the note. She would take it to him. She stacked the papers in front of her. The business of the empire could wait. Her torment could not.

Chapter Fifty-Two

Count Grigory Orlov took the stairs two at a time, oblivious to protocol. Catherine had at last granted him an audience. Since General Potemkin had taken up residence at Court some four months ago, the Empress had become inaccessible, especially to former favourites. It was the new favourite who had personally dismissed Vassilchikov, with a shabby pension, Orlov thought. A renovated villa, a few thousand roubles a year, a couple of small villages and the usual silver dinner service. The young man was harmless and on his own admission, no more than a kept plaything for Catherine, but surely he deserved more compensation for his compliance. Or imprisonment, which is what it really was. He had not been allowed to have friends or even to go out unaccompanied.

Catherine greeted Orlov gracefully. She seemed slimmer and her skin looked rosy. Perhaps she had not powdered her face or had used some of the rouge which the French had made so fashionable. Orlov thought of his niece whose youth needed no adornments. In her he had found the serenity he longed for. He never tired of observing her freshness and did all in his power not to spoil it. He would marry her. He needed Catherine to help him overcome the objections of the clerics. But that was not his mission today.

"Let us dispense with niceties," Orlov began, "we know each other too well for that."

"Yes, and I know you well enough, Grigory, to know that you are not in good humour," Catherine said brightly. "Indeed, you are in very bad humour and I trust I will soon learn the reason."

"I have always supported you, Catherine. I was always loyal to you if not always faithful. But have you been loyal to me?"

"But of course! I hold you and your brothers in high

esteem, I am mindful of the services you have rendered me and the affection you bear me," Catherine answered with a light almost questioning hesitancy.

"And yet you have wrested offices from us and cast us to the mercy of our enemy!"

"But who can you mean? Who is your enemy?" Catherine asked carefully.

"Let us not dissimulate! You know that General Potemkin seeks to destroy us!"

"That is untrue. I have given General Potemkin strict instructions that my affection for you and your brothers has earned you my favour and that he must treat you well, as I am sure he has done."

"But we would not wish to be treated by him at all! Is it not enough to have him in your bed? Why, you can even shower him with orders and ribbons as you have done. He sounds like a veritable zoological garden with his White Eagle from Poland, his Black Eagle from Prussia, a White Elephant from Denmark! Why, even France has given him one reserved only for Catholics. I don't know what you have promised all these ambassadors for their bits of shining metal! Potemkin's toys! And although it is a disgrace to bestow on him the highest Russian Order of St Andrew, it takes no power from anyone nor bestows any on its recipient. But there is a line and you have crossed it!"

"How dare you speak to me like this, Grigory!" Catherine said angrily.

"Oh, I can and I will. Someone must. Not content with making Potemkin a member of the State Council, you and he have succeeded in ousting Chernyshev from the War Cabinet so that Potemkin can be its president."

"But Chernyshev went of his own accord," Catherine protested.

Orlov paid no heed. "We even kept our peace when you made him Lieutenant Colonel of my brother Alexey's regiment. The very regiment that helped you to power!

And how much has my brother done for you and your empire? But we remained civil. We swallowed our pride and sat at your table with him out of loyalty to you."

Catherine made to speak but Orlov raised his hand.

"But we will not tolerate, *I* will not tolerate, Potemkin being commanding general of all our armed forces. I will not serve under him."

"Then you will not serve at all," Catherine said icily.

"Catherine," Orlov began more gently, "reflect on what you are doing. You are creating a dictator, you are throwing away your power. He will use it. And maybe even against you. I have heard that he wheedles his way into your son's favour through Count Panin."

"You cannot frighten me, Grigory. General Potemkin loves me and I him."

"Love! I loved you too but I took no power from you, nor would you have given it. I fought for you, I served you. I did not use you."

"It is no use, Grigory. You will not persuade me against him and I hope in time you will come to have affection for him. I would like nothing better than that we should all work together for the good of our empire."

"Whose empire? His? For that is what happening, Catherine. You do not see it. You are blinded by what you call love."

"My eyes were closed to love. I never knew it till now. Affection yes, desire yes, companionship yes – men gave me many things but only Potemkin has given me love."

"That is a poor testimony for our years together, Catherine," Grigory said reproachfully. "But it is as it is. I cannot serve in Potemkin's Russia nor do I wish to throw down the gauntlet since that would mean a blow against you. I ask leave to go abroad. And I will advise my brothers to do the same."

"Then so must it be, Grigory. I will be saddened to see you go but must accept that there can be no enmity with

General Potemkin. I would consider any attack on him as treason to my person and office."

Orlov bowed low. As he rose, Catherine stretched out her hand but Orlov turned quickly towards the door.

Descending the stairway, he gave more rein to his angry thoughts. Catherine would probably marry Potemkin. She had refused to marry Orlov until he gave up asking. What did the one-eyed Potemkin have that he did not? As if his thoughts had conjured him, Potemkin came leaping up the stairs biting at an apple.

"Ah, Count Orlov! A pleasure, as always! You come from the Empress. Anything new?" He asked cheerfully.

"Not especially. Except that you are on your way up and I am on the way –"

"Down?" Potemkin interrupted with a glance to the bottom of the staircase.

"No, out. But I will be back!"

***

Catherine raised her eyes from the papers on her desk and turned to gaze fondly at Potemkin lounging on the sofa nearby. He was still in his quilted morning coat and his thick hair was uncombed.

"Let us go over these peace conditions again, my love," she said.

"Oh, but we have done it all, Catherine," Potemkin replied impatiently, waving a piece of sausage he had been chewing on. "General Rumyantsev must get full power to negotiate in the broader sense. You must not burden him with details, which will serve only to hold up the whole process with couriers to-ing and fro-ing between the Crimea and St Petersburg, giving the Turks time to regroup." Potemkin dropped the sausage in his lap, held up his fingers and began counting off his points. "Tell General Rumyantsev we want the Crimea, we want access to the Black Sea, preferably at Azov but as many ports as feasible, we want the right to protect Christians in their lands, we want right of ship passage through the Dardanelles – and anything else we can get. Rumyantsev has to yield as little as he can get away with."

"Ah, my love! You are so wise, so decisive. I have written as you spoke."

"And then we can turn our attention to this scoundrel Pugachev, who still dares to make your empire unsafe," Potemkin said lazily.

"Perhaps we can do that in the banya?" Catherine said. "It is late and we will be undisturbed." Catherine rose and pulled Potemkin from his chair. "Come, my love. Let us see if you are as clever at loosening my ties as you are at untying military knots."

Chapter Fifty-Three

Count Betskoy made his way to the Empress's rooms through the back corridors, which reduced the way by some ten minutes. Distances were immense in the Winter Palace and he felt his seven decades as he climbed the narrow staircases. The back corridors were rarely lit, the servants scurrying along with their own candles, and Betskoy stumbled a few times. His eyesight was deteriorating. He was also lost in thought, or worry.

Catherine, whom he loved as if she were his own daughter, was standing at the edge of a precipice, her empire on the brink of collapse. The Pretender Pugachev, having supposedly been routed by the Russians, had risen from the ashes with over 25,000 troops and had taken the city of Kazan in an orgy of violence lasting from dawn till dusk. The city's streets turned into rivers of blood.

Kazan was under 800 versts from Moscow, a distance which could be covered in a matter of weeks, if not days. The insurrection was swelling daily by the hundreds. Serfs were rising up against their masters, plundering their lands and slaughtering whole families. Hordes of them were said to be marching behind Pugachev towards Moscow. Reinforcements were desperately needed but the Turks were still engaging in battle rather than negotiating for peace. And the Russian generals needed every man on the battlefield in order to force the Turks into peace.

The danger had been underestimated, especially by Catherine. She was not herself. She was ... absent, was the word Betskoy finally settled on. She went through the motions of working, rising early every day as always, while her lover slept on. But her mind was elsewhere. He did not recognise who she had become.

Betskoy knocked at the door but entered without waiting for a response. Catherine was expecting him. It was she who had summoned him.

He was surprised to see that she was dressed officially, her Orders pinned to her velvet dress.

"My dear Count," she began, "I am on my way to the State Council. The news of Kazan has shocked me. I will go to Moscow immediately to be with that city in its hour of fear. I will not desert my people."

"I think such a move would admit to fear or even give the Pretender the idea of attacking Moscow," Betskoy said carefully. "At the moment, we have only unreliable rumours to go on."

"Oh, he wants my throne," Catherine said. "Or his throne, as he calls it. He says he is the rightful emperor, claiming to be my dead husband Peter III. Although he is not dead. Having escaped what he calls my 'murderous clutches', he has apparently been wandering the world for the last decade. He calls me the devil's daughter. How can my people believe all this? I have devoted my life to their good and now they rise against me to follow some madman! Have I not served them well? Have I not been a good Empress?"

"Insurrections in the Volga needed a firm guiding hand, as do your generals at the Turkish front, Catherine. When the power is ... distracted, cracks and fissures appear which are filled as one sees fit, which is not always what is fit." Betskoy tried to speak calmly as if discussing a wall that had to be repaired against drafts.

"Ah, you reprimand me," Catherine said sadly. "You think I have not given my empire my full attention. Is this what others think?"

Betskoy struggled to find the right words. He wanted to warn Catherine of the growing discontent with Potemkin's amassment of power. Many thought he comported himself as if he were indeed the Emperor. Catherine never made a decision now without having Potemkin first confirm it. But while power and wealth were attractive to Potemkin, the practicalities of governing seemed to bore him. Papers piled up in his chambers while Catherine waited for his comments and approval. The business of the empire ground to a halt on the whim of a favourite.

"Perhaps General Potemkin –" he began but Catherine interrupted him.

"Potemkin is an able adviser," she said warningly. "He may not write reports but his counsel on all manner of matters when we are together is invaluable."

"Catherine," Betskoy said, as one would to a small child who has been recalcitrant.

"Oh, you are right!" she suddenly burst out, losing her composure. "I am enslaved to him! I cannot live without him. I am ill with love!" She seemed relieved to unburden herself.

"Perhaps ill rather from late nights?" Betskoy said gently.

"Yes, yes, I do not retire now till one in the morning when I used to at 10 in the evening. But I still rise at 5 a.m. I do not neglect my work. But I do not work well. I cannot concentrate. I am constantly in a fevered state. What shall I do?" Betskoy could not remember seeing Catherine so agitated. She paced hectically up and down, wringing her hands, her face flushed. "I cannot stay still."

"Perhaps this passion will pass," Betskoy said soothingly. "It has been some six months. Most passions settle into normal life by then."

"But Potemkin is not normal. He is a man of extreme passions, of extreme feelings. One minute he is weeping because I have neglected him and the next he is making us laugh until we are both exhausted. He knows no ... middle way. He needs so much attention, so much love."

Betskoy remained silent. The Potemkin he knew was brash and unmannered, ambitious and ruthless. He had become a law unto himself.

"Catherine, you are the Empress and your empire is in danger. You must take the reins firmly in your hands again. General Potemkin –"

Betskoy was interrupted by a loud hammering at the door.

"Your Majesty! It is I, Count Panin. We have news!"

Catherine looked startled but gestured to Betskoy to open the door.

Count Panin rushed in, waving papers agitatedly in his hand.

"We have just received news that –" Panin broke into a fit of coughing. Betskoy quickly poured him a glass of wine.

Regaining his breath, Panin said, "We have news from the Turkish front. General Rumyantsev has secured a peace treaty which is everything and more that Your Majesty desired."

Catherine all but snatched the paper from Panin's outstretched hand. She read it quickly, turning pages hurriedly.

"It is indeed an honourable and advantageous peace secured by the negotiating skills of our generals, their arguments strengthened by further victories against the Turks in the field. I will go to the State Council immediately. We shall now resolve how to crush the Pretender's rebellion once and for all. After the Council, I shall order a service of thanksgiving to the glory of God and Russia!"

Betskoy stepped aside as the Empress swept from the room. He sighed with relief. The old Catherine was back.

***

"But how can I call myself an enlightened monarch when atrocities are committed in my name?" Catherine complained.

"I did tell you to give complete command to my cousin rather than share it with General Panin," Potemkin said lazily. "He is known to be a tyrant of a general. And merciless against his enemies."

"I gave him strict instructions, or you did, my love, not to use violence as repression or revenge. The people must want to be loyal to me, not forced. And General Panin has littered the countryside with gallows, I hear."

"My cousin reports that he will not consult with him. That he has said – " Potemkin stopped to consult the paper in his hand. "He has said that the blood of all traitors must flow. The General has ordered that all murderers first have their hands and feet chopped off, then their heads and their bodies left at the side of the street – "

"But that is gruesome! He must be stopped!" Catherine all but shouted.

"Too late, my love. In those villages where Russian officials were murdered, every third man is to be hanged until the culprits are given up and if not then lots are to be cast and every hundredth man will be hanged by the ribs and all the others to be flogged – "

"What? By the ribs?"

"Ah yes, it is an old form of hanging. The victim is hanged by metal hooks through the ribs –"

"That is barbaric!" Catherine interrupted. "General Panin must be recalled immediately! How can I hold my head up in Europe?"

"The General is on his way to Moscow – in triumph," Potemkin said. "He has put Pugachev in an iron cage and parades him though all towns and villages on the way. The Muscovites await the execution impatiently. They look forward to a particularly sadistic one."

"No, I will not have it! We are a civilised nation. I have brought my people enlightenment." Catherine's voice was resolute.

"I fear if you are too enlightened," Potmekin said as he reached for the wine carafe, "you will have no empire to rule."

***

Sir Robert Gunning said, "I am glad we were not in

Moscow. We would have been forced to attend the rebel's execution, with all due ceremony and joy."

"Apparently there was not much joy from the crowds," Solms said. "My Prussian friends who attended said the crowd was mad with disappointment. They expected a quartering and then a hanging."

"How bloodthirsty!"

"Ah, but you English hang, draw and quarter. The victim is still alive when disembowelled, no? There is no drawing out of intestines here in Russia. Just chopping off of parts."

"I say, Solmes, must we?"

"Well, the executioner apparently raised his axe and chopped off the rebel's head when he was supposed to chop off each limb first. He was nearly lynched by the crowd. Evidently, the Empress had ordered the execution to be done so. To show her clemency and enlightenment."

"Her empire is saved from the Turks and the rebels. But I feel a certain unease in the atmosphere, a certain rippling below the surface," Gunning said, "although I cannot put my finger on it."

"Yes, the Empress will surely have to exert a firmer grip on things now. The serfs and other discontents have flexed their muscles. They have glimpsed the possibility of change."

"Yes, I am sure the Empress has come to her senses again. She seems more like her old self," Gunning said.

Chapter Fifty-Four

"You must go to Moscow, Catherine," Potemkin said lazily from the divan where he lay sprawled out in his dressing gown. "St Petersburg is not your Empire, it is but a new tassle in its fringe."

"How can you talk so, Grischka? This is *my* city." Catherine's voice was sharp. "I have no love for Tatar Moscow."

"Nor they for you," Potemkin retorted just as sharply. "And therein lies the problem. You must celebrate victory over the Turks in the heart of the Empire. It must be a celebration such as Russia has never seen." Potemkin's tone became enthusiastic. "You can let me arrange it all. I have some excellent ideas. At the end, the Muscovites will respect you if not love you. They will accept you as Empress."

Catherine raised her eyes from her papers. "And do they not already?"

"Pugachev has given people ideas," Potemkin said, biting into an apple.

"Ideas?" Catherine asked, not looking up.

Potemkin waited until his silence caught her attention. When she looked at him, he said, not without some relish, "That the throne can be taken with enough force."

"Grischka, that is treasonous talk! My people respond to reason. And I am reasonable with them." Catherine suddenly paused to dip her pen into the ink. She scribbled quickly. "Yes," she said thoughtfully, "reason prevents treason."

"No, no," Potemkin scoffed, "pomp and celebrations do. Wine and roast oxen do. Music and dancing do. The people want to see and feel your power. They want to be part of it. At the moment, they feel as if they are looked down upon from St Petersburg." He crunched into his apple again before adding, "And I know just how they feel."

"What can you mean? That I look down on you?" Catherine looked puzzled. "But I love you. I cannot live without you."

"But you can rule without me!" Potemkin suddenly stood up and threw his half-eaten apple across the room. "I am no more than an amusement for your bed. One of the many you have had over the years. Well, I have had enough! I shall return to my troops."

Potemkin made for the door, his dressing gown flapping open, but Catherine moved swiftly in front of him.

"No, you must not sulk," she said soothingly. "Of course, you are right. We will go to Moscow." Catherine took his hand and led him back to the divan. "Come, sit and tell me of your celebration plans. Let us not bicker like an old married couple."

"Which we obviously are not," Potemkin growled.

"Not what?" Catherine asked as she tried to smooth his thick uncombed hair.

"Married!" Potemkin said angrily.

"You are my husband in my heart," Catherine said, still stroking his hair.

"But not on your throne!" Potemkin pulled his head away from Catherine's caresses.

"But Grischka, you know that there can be only one ruler, one sovereign. A throne cannot be shared. You are my most trusted advisor. There is no paper which you do not see. I ask for your comments on everything. Do I not?"

Catherine took his hand in hers again. "Do I not, my love?"

"But it is not my fault you do not see them," she continued when he did not answer. "The papers pile up. You do not have time. You sleep too long. You drink too much." She spoke fondly as she caressed his hand.

"Ah, you are a scold as well as an Empress," Potemkin said, reaching for another apple.

"Yes, like a good wife," Catherine said cheerfully. "Now come and be useful. I have some ideas for the rebellious Cossack territories. Pugachev may be gone but his followers remain. I will have no more repressions. We must have peace, harmony and loyalty."

"At least you gave Moscow an execution," Potemkin said, "although they say he ended badly. He nearly died of shock before they could execute him."

"Yes, he lived a villain and died a coward. Snivelling at the end. He was no hero and must not become one. We will obliterate all memory of him. The Yaik river shall be renamed the Ural and the Cossack capital Yaitsk shall become Uralsk. Through a new geography, we will create a new history. What do you think?"

"Yes, it is good to remove past traces and start afresh. Is that not what we have done?"

"Do not change the subject, my love. Of course, you are my new beginning, the star that guides me. All else is gone."

"And Orlov too?"

"Ah Grischka, you know you must not reproach me for my affection for Grigory Orlov. I owe him much. But it is you whom I love. Only you. How many times must I tell you?"

"Then marry me. That is the proof of your love."

"Let us not quarrel. Orlov is gone to Italy. He plans to stay away for a year or two."

"Why not forever?" Potemkin grumbled.

Ignoring him, Catherine walked to her desk and picked up a paper.

"I have a surprise for you!" she said brightly.

Potemkin did not respond. He had finished his apple and was now gnawing at his fingernails.

"Don't you want to know what it is?" Catherine asked gently.

"Another title?" Potemkin asked sullenly. "I do not want ot be some Ural lord. I am more than that."

"The village where the traitor was born – I have forgotten its unpronouceable Cossack name but that is no matter for it is no longer of significance – will be razed to the ground. I will have it rebuilt – " she waved her hand vaguely, "– elsewhere. And it shall be named Potemkinskaya! There! Are you pleased?" Catherine turned to Potemkin with an expectant smile.

Potemkin rose and came to her. Embracing her, he said softly, "I should be more pleased if you were named Madame Potemkinskaya."

"Nothing would give me greater personal pleasure, my dearest true husband, but I am and shall remain the Empress of Russia."

THE END

Author's Note

The fictional representation of a historical character allows the writer's imagination to fill in the gaps in the archives, ideally without sacrificing accuracy or authenticity. I have taken small liberties with documented facts to ease the narrative along – some characters have been promoted in rank more speedily than when they lived; battles have been fought a month or two earlier or later than they actually were; lovers come and go to a slightly different timetable ... The same sleight of the author's pen is not applied to authenticity in period detail. Yes, people did eat turkey in Catherine's Russia and the Winter Palace was originally yellow ...

Most words spoken or written by my fictional characters are taken, often verbatim, from contemporary records – but not always from the same characters who delivered them in real life.

In my eighteenth century Russia, characters have simplified names. Each Russian name generally consists of three parts, used in different combinations depending on who is speaking or being spoken to. Thus one character may appear under three or four names. I have dispensed with this, as with the widespread use of diminutives, to facilitate identification. Full names are given in the Index of Names.

The very light smattering of French words serves as a reminder that French was indeed the preferred language of the Russian court, and most others, in the eighteenth century. The meaning of any French word is easily understood from the context.

I have kept a few Russian words in their acepted English forms. The silver *rouble* was introduced by Peter I in 1704. An army captain earned about 200 roubles a year. A *verst* (Russian *versta*) was roughly equivalent to 1.06 km or 0.66 miles. The *banya* was a traditional steam bath, often public and communal, still popular today for health and social aspects.

There is a wealth of contemporary sources on Catherine's Russia: her own memoirs and correspondences, the dispatches of ambassadors, treatises on the plague and other illnesses, military reports, government papers, diaries and memoirs of her contemporaries, the minutes of many societies, etc. I have used these where possible.

Much has been written about Catherine the Great. The following biographies, on which this fictional account has also drawn, can be recommended for further reading:

John T. Alexander, *Catherine the Great. Life and Legend* (Oxford University Press, 1989)

Simon Dixon, *Catherine the Great* (Profile Books, 2010)

Isabel de Madariaga, *Russia in the Age of Catherine the Great* (Yale University Press, 1981)

Virginia Rounding, *Catherine the Great: Love, Sex and Power* (Hutchison, 2007)

Simon Sebag Montefiore, *Catherine the Great and Potemkin: The Imperial Love Affair* (W&N 2011

Index of Names
by category

Main Characters

Count Betskoy (Ivan Ivanovich Betskoy) 1704-1795, Catherine's advisor on education and President of the Imperial Academy of Arts. Lover of Catherine's mother, Princess Johanna, and possibly Catherine's natural father

Count Bestuzhev (Alexey Petrovich Bestuzhev-Ryumin) 1693-1768, influential statesman who served under Peter I, Elizabeth I and Catherine II (as Grand Chancellor)

Catherine (Ekaterina Alexeevna) 1729-1796, born Princess Sophie Auguste Friederike von Anhalt-Zerbst; 1745 married second cousin, Peter of Holstein-Gottorp, heir to Russian throne; 1762-1796 Empress Catherine II of Russia

Grigory Orlov (Grigory Grigoryevich) 1734-1783, Guards officer who, along with his brothers, led the coup which placed Catherine on the throne; Catherine's lover 1760-1772
Orlov's brothers:
Ivan Grigoryevich Orlov (1733-1791
Alexey Grigoryevich Orlov (1737-1808)
Fyodor Grigoryevich Orlov(1741-1796)
Vladimir Grigoryevich Orlov (1743-1831)

Count Panin (Nikita Ivanovich Panin) 1718-1783, close counsellor to Catherine and governor to Grand Duke Paul

General Panin (Pyotr Ivanovich Panin) 1721- 1789, Count Panin's brother and successful military leader

Paul (Pavel Petrovich) 1754 -1801, Grand Duke and heir to throne, son of Catherine and Peter III although his natural father may have been Sergei Saltykov; 1773 married Wilhelmina Louise (Natalya Alexeevna), daughter of Ludwig IX, Landgrave of Hesse-Darmstadt

General Potemkin (Grigory Alexandrovich Potemkin-Tavrichesky) 1739-1791, courtier and military leader, became Catherine's lover in 1774

Emelyan Pugachev (Emelyan Ivanovich Pugachev) 1742-1775, pretender to the throne who led a Cossack rebellion against Catherine 1773-1774

Envoys
Baron de Breteuil, Louis Charles Auguste le Tonnelier, baron de Breteuil 1730-1807, French aristocrat and statesman, ambassador to Russia 1760-1769

Earl of Buckingham, John Hobart, 2nd Earl of Buckinghamshire 1723 - 1793, English nobleman and politician, Britain's ambassador to Russia 1762-1765

Lord Cathcart, Charles Schaw Cathcart, 9th Lord Cathcart 1721- 1776, British soldier, diplomat, chief of the Clan Cathcart, ambassador to Russia 1768-1772

Sir Robert Gunning 1st Baronet 1731-1816, British diplomat, ambassador to Russia 1772-1776

George Macartney, later 1st Earl Macartney, 1737-1806, British diplomat, ambassador to Russia 1764-1768

Count Mercy, Florimond Claude, Comte de Mercy-Argenteau 1727-1794, Austrian diplomat and ambassador in St Petersburg 1762-1763 (later a noteable influence on Marie Antoinette in Paris)

Count Solms, Victor Friedrich Graf von Solms-Sonnenwalde 1730-1783, Prussian diplomat, envoy in St Petersburg 1762-1779

Rulers
August III King of Poland 1734-1763; also Grand Duke of Lithuania and Elector of Saxony (as Frederick Augustus II)

Elizabeth I (Elizaveta Petrovna) 1709 -1762, seized the throne from the child emperor Ivan VI in 1741 and ruled Russia till her death

Frederick II (Frederick the Great) King of Prussia 1740-1786. Viewed as a great military strategist and enlightened monarch but also as an oppressor of Poland
Prince Heinrich (Friedrich Heinrich Ludwig) 1726-1802, Prussian prince, brother of Frederick the Great, military leader and diplomat

George III, George William Frederick of the House of Hanover, British king 1760-1820

Ivan VI (Ivan Antonovich) 1740-1764, overthrown as an infant by Empress Elizabeth and spent the rest of his life in prison before being killed by his guards during an attempt to free him

Louis XV, King of France 1715-1774

Maria Josepha of Austria, 1699-1757, born Archduchess of Austria, married August III of Poland in 1719. They had 14 children.

Mustafa III, Sultan of the Ottoman Empire 1757-1774, sought to modernize the army and state but was caught in war with Russia, which coveted the Crimea

Peter the Great (Pyotr Alexeevich)1672-1725, ruled as Peter I from 1682 to 1725. Attributed with the expansion, reform and Westernization of Russia

Peter III (Pyotr Fyodorovich) 1728-1762, born as Karl Peter Ulrich, son of Duke of Holstein-Gottorp and Anna Petrovna, a daughter of Peter I. Named heir to the Russia throne by his aunt, the Empress Elizabeth. Married his second cousin Catherine in 1745; said to have been assassinated by her in 1762 shortly after he became Emperor

Poniatovsky, Stanislav August 1732-1798, ruled as King Stanislav II of Poland 1764-1795. Catherine's lover before she became Empress

Philosophers
Jean d'Alembert (Jean-Baptiste le Rond d'Alembert) 1717-1783, French mathematician and philosopher, co-editor with Denis Diderot of the *Encylopédie*

Denis Diderot 1713-1784, French philosopher, influential editor and contributor to the *Encylopédie*

Baron Friedrich Melchior Grimm 1723-1807, German-born French writer, contributor to the *Encylopédie* and editor of *Correspondance littéraire, philosophique et critique*. Trusted correspondent of Catherine

Montesquieu (Charles-Louis de Secondat, Baron de la Brède et de Montesquieu) 1689-1755, French lawyer and political philosopher, advocated the separation of powers

Jean-Jacques Rousseau 1712-1778, Genevan philosopher and writer, whose ideas influenced the French Revolution as well as the development of modern political and educational thought.

Voltaire (François-Marie Arouet) 1694-1778, French philosopher and prolific writer and correspondent, famous for his wit and polemic satire against church and state. Corresponded regularly with Catherine from 1763.

Doctors
Dr Thomas Dimsdale 1712-1800, English, pioneer of smallpox inoculation

Dr Karl Kruse 1727- 1799, German, court physician under Empresses Elizabeth and Catherine. Lived in Russia from 1750 to his death

Dr Jacob Johann Lerche 1703-1780, Prussian, came to Russia in 1731, St Petersburg's city physician, authority on plague

Dr James Mounsey 1710-1773, Scottish, Empress Elizabeth's personal physician, left Russia when Catherine took power. Introduced rhubarb to Europe

Dr John Rogerson 1741-1823, Scottish, Catherine's personal physician, spent 50 years in Russia (1766-1816)

*At Cour**t***
Sophia Chartoryzhkaya, a young widow employed by Catherine to educate her son in matters of the bedchamber

Princess Johanna Elizabeth von Schleswig-Holstein-Gottorp 1712-1760, mother of Catherine, expelled from the Russian Court by Empress Elizabeth for intriguing

Grand Duchess Natalya (Natalya Alexeevna) 1755-1776, born Princess Wilhelmina Louisa of Hesse-Darmstadt, first wife of Catherine's son, Grand Duke Paul

Praskovya Alexandrovna Rumyantseva 1729-1786, sister of Field Marshal Rumyantsev and wife of General Bruce, of Scottish descent, Governor General of St Petersburg. Confidante of Catherine

Sergei Saltykov (Sergei Vasilievich Saltykov) 1726-1765, Russian officer, Catherine's first lover and perhaps the natural father of her son Paul

Anna Petrovna Sheremeteva ?-1768, member of the wealthy Sheremetev family; betrothed to Nikita Panin but died of smallpox before they could marry

Count Stroganov (Alexander Sergeevich Stroganov) 1733-1811, Senator, President of the Academy of Arts, Director of Public Library, immensely wealthy.

Countess Stroganova (born Anna Mikhailovna Vorontsova) 1743-1769. Her early death put an end to divorce proceedings initiated by her husband Count Stroganov

Teplov, Grigory Nikolayevich Teplov, 1717-1779, Senator and State-secretary, amateur musician and art collector, supporter of Catherine

Vorontsov, family of statesmen, supporters of Peter III against Catherine, whom they regarded as a usurper throughout her reign

Prince Vyazemsky (Alexander Alexeevich Vyazemsky) 1727-1796, Russian Minister of Justice, Acting Chancellor of the Exchequer

Catherine Zinovyeva (Ekaterina Nikolayevna Zinovyeva) 1758-1781, Grigory Orlov's young niece and lover

Military
General Bibikov (Alexander Ilyich Bibikov) 1729-1774, Russian statesman and general-in-chief; died of cholera while leading the campaign against the rebel Pugachev

Count Chernyshev (Zakhar Grigoryevich Chernyshev) 1722-1784, President of the War College, Imperial Field Marshal and Minister of War under Catherine

Samuel Greig (1735-1788), Scotsman in Russian Navy from 1763, Grand Admiral of the Russian fleet

Captain Fyodor Khitrovo, captain of the Guard who helped Catherine to gain the throne but opposed her marriage to Grigory Orlov

Captain Mirovich (Vasily Yakovlevich Mirovich) 1740-1764, executed for his attempt to free the deposed Ivan VI from prison

General Rumyantsev (Count Pyotr Alexandrovich Rumyantsev-Zadunaisky) 1725-1796, brilliant military leader, led the Russian forces to victory against the

Ottoman Empire (1768-1774), Catherine's Governor in Ukraine

Captain Vlassiev and Lieutenant Chekin, guards (and murderers) of the imprisoned Ivan VI

Arts
Giacomo Casanova 1725-1798, Italian adventurer, who in the course of his colourful itinerant life, spent 3 years travelling some 4500 miles in Europe in an attempt to persuade governments to buy his lottery scheme

Etienne Maurice Falconet 1716-1791, sculptor of Swiss origin employed by Catherine to create an equestrian statue of Peter the Great, the later famous Bronze Horseman, symbol of St Petersburg. Falconet arrived in the city in 1766 but the statue was not completed till 1782

Baldassare Galuppi 1706-1785, a highly-regarded Venetian composer contracted by Catherine 1765-1768

(Francesco) Bartolomeo Rastrelli 1700-1771, Italian architect at court of Empress Elizabeth, designed many sumptuous palaces such as the Winter Place, Tsarskoye Selo, Peterhof. Catherine favoured Rinaldi's less baroque style

Antonio Rinaldi 1709-1794, Italian architect favoured by Catherine; during the thirty years in her employ as court architect, he designed many late baroque buildings including palaces, triumphal gates and arches, churches and theatres

Josiah Wedgwood 1730-1795, English potter, grandfather of Charles Darwin; 1762 appointed potter to Queen Charlotte; became famous for his jasperware, inspired by excavated Etruscan designs; in 1773 Catherine commissioned the famous 944-piece Green Frog Service, depicting 1222 views from England, Scotland and Wales

Read on to sample the first chapter of the sequel *Love and Other Affairs in the Empire of Russia*, related by Potemkin's five young nieces, who come to Catherine's Court and are quickly embroiled in its politics, intrigues and passions.

August 1775

Dearest Anna,

How much we have to tell you! We have travelled only a few hundred versts from home but everything is so foreign here that it might be ten thousand!

Our uncle General Potemkin, who in his kindness has taken us under his wing, is as affectionate as you may remember him and has showered us with gifts of jewels and fine dresses. We must not let him down by appearing as the provincial gentry we are, for his position at Court is very elevated. You cannot imagine how everyone runs to do his bidding, even, it is rumoured, the Empress. The Empress Catherine has greeted us warmly and has already appointed me maid-of honour. Her bearing is most elegant, most regal, and I have told my sisters we must emulate it. The Empress has a high forehead, large blue eyes and a well-curved mouth but her nose is a little long and her chin a little round. She has brownish hair. She is plump, with a very high bosom. Her complexion is not smooth and she wears dark rouge, perhaps a little too much. She appears healthy and has all her teeth, which are very white. My sisters, and perhaps myself, outdo her in beauty but her manner is graceful and kind. And she is said to be very educated – she conducts correspondence with the greatest philosophers in Europe. We, dear Anna, can make no claim to a good education but we have other talents which should secure us a permanent position at the Russian Court – and, of course, very advantageous marriages.

The Court is still in Moscow for the peace celebrations. I have had Uncle explain to me the significance of the treaty with the Ottomans since it seems to be a war which no one has won. "On the contrary," Uncle said, "while the Ottomans have not ceded the Crimea to us, they have been forced to recognise it as an independent khanate. And it is under our influence. We will make another attempt to annex it completely but for now we are content with what we have gained. War goes hand in hand with diplomacy." You will note, dear Anna, that I am anxious to learn and understand our new world.

There have been parades and processions of great splendour. Uncle took us to the main festivities outside the city. There were two pavilions which, he said, represented the Black Sea and all Russia's conquests. There were roads which stood for the rivers Don and Dnieper, the theatres and dining halls were named after Black Sea ports and there were many Turkish minarets. The coachmen and servants were dressed as Turks and Albanians and Circassians and there were even some black men in crimson turbans. I have never encountered a black person before.

There was a huge firework display such as you have never seen. The sky was filled as high and as far as one could see with huge bursts of bright colour. The Empress had gifted wine and roasted oxen to the people – Uncle said as many as 60,000 feasted on her beneficence. Can you imagine such a number?

We are overwhelmed by the magnificence of our new surroundings and while there are a few things one could grumble about, like the badly maintained water closets, I will not, for we are grateful to our Uncle for this chance to rise in the world – and to what heights! And I will do all in my power to ensure that our younger sisters make good marriages. As the eldest in your place, Anna, and as a substitute for our dear dead mother, I will put my own needs in second place to those of my sisters. Little Tatiana, with her mere six years, will need my guidance for some time to come.

I shall make myself indispensable to our Uncle and to the Empress. I will observe and learn. I will acquire, we all shall, that sophisticated veneer that we lack. The beauty of our sisters has often been remarked upon, especially that of Varvara with her golden hair, and that shall be our capital. Our sister Nadezhda has not been gifted with natural charm – where did she get that red hair and swarthy complexion from? She is but sixteen and good looks may still emerge. Although Katerina is younger, she already exemplifies a very fine beauty.

Yes, we must use our looks to gain what we can. I must harness Varvara a little – she flirts with everyone outrageously, including Uncle. I do not think the Empress will take kindly to that. On the other hand, it is better his attention is centred on one of our own, which I can control, than on an outsider, who may have another family to replace us. Listen to me! I who have been here but weeks talk of outsiders as if I am an insider! But yes, we are insiders because we are Uncle's family, and as such, the family of the Empress. I intend to keep it that way, no matter what it takes.

But enough of my responsibilities. I have instructed the girls to pen some lines to include in this letter and they will deliver some lighter reading, I am sure. Varvara will no doubt write to you of fashions (very French! very low cut at the bosom!), Nadezhda of music and food (have you ever seen an artichoke?), Katerina of the many compliments she receives (I think she keeps a note of them all) and Tatiana will no doubt tell you about her visit to an elephant, a gift to the Empress from an exotic Shah. I did not go, considering it more an outing for children, but now I wish I had since all the child can say about it is, "So huge, so huge!" I have tasked her with a small essay of description and perhaps you will be the beneficiary of that. Uncle says he will employ tutors for her as soon as we go to St Petersburg, where the Empress normally resides. It is almost at the end of the earth and I am somewhat uneasy at the prospect but I am told it is of great magnificence and that we will be well settled in Uncle's own palace there. Perhaps I can be mistress of his household.

We embrace you! Uncle says that since we are all truly one family now, he will secure a more elevated commission for your husband, to whom we also send warm greetings.

With affection,

Your sister Alexandra

Printed in Poland
by Amazon Fulfillment
Poland Sp. z o.o., Wrocław